"Thanks for the coffee."

"Anytime, Paul. I mean it."

He placed his hands on her shoulders and leaned in as though he was going to kiss her forehead the way he had yesterday at the clinic. As he moved, she inexplicably tipped her head back and looked up at him. His lips made contact with hers. The kiss lasted a millisecond, brief but electrifying. They both pulled back, startled.

Paul was the first to find his voice. "I'm sorry."

"No, I'm sorry."

"I only meant to—"

"I shouldn't have—"

"I didn't mean for that to happen," he said.

Neither had she. Or maybe she had. That would certainly explain why right now she wanted to grab the front of his shirt, pull him close and kiss him again, for real. The mortifying thought made her face feel like it was on fire.

"It's not a big deal," she said. *Liar.*

Dear Reader,

Welcome back to Riverton, Wisconsin. This fictional small town, steeped in the culture of America's heartland, is home to the Finnegan sisters—Annie, Emily and CJ—and I am delighted to share the second book in The Finnegan Sisters trilogy.

His Best Friend's Wife is Annie's story. She's the eldest sister and hers is a story about honoring the past while moving on after the loss of a loved one. Although I consider myself to be a city gal through and through, I am fortunate to have grown up in a rural farming community and will always have an affinity for small towns and the simple life. And while I don't have any sisters, Annie and I do have something in common—our love to cook for family and friends. I hope you'll enjoy spending time in Annie's kitchen.

If you read the first book in this series— *To Catch a Wife*—you'll know the Finnegan sisters were raised by a single dad. In this book, their father discovers that while second chances may not happen often, they're well worth the wait.

I love to hear from readers, so I invite you to visit my website at leemckenzie.com, where you can send me an email, sign up for my (mostly) monthly newsletter and learn more about my other books, including upcoming books in this series. Happy reading!

Warmest,

Lee

HEARTWARMING

His Best Friend's Wife

—

Lee McKenzie

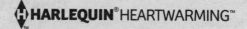
HARLEQUIN® HEARTWARMING™

Recycling programs for this product may not exist in your area.

ISBN-13: 978-0-373-36822-8

His Best Friend's Wife

Copyright © 2017 by Lee McKenzie McAnally

Printed in U.S.A.

From the time she was ten years old and read *Anne of Green Gables* and *Little Women*, **Lee McKenzie** knew she wanted to be a writer, just like Anne and Jo. In the intervening years, she has written everything from advertising copy to an honors thesis in paleontology, but becoming a four-time Golden Heart® Award finalist and a Harlequin author are among her proudest accomplishments. Lee and her artist/teacher husband live on an island along Canada's West Coast, and she loves to spend time with two of her best friends—her grown-up children.

Books by Lee McKenzie

Harlequin Heartwarming

The Parent Trap

The Finnegan Sisters

To Catch a Wife

Harlequin American Romance

The Man for Maggie
With This Ring
Firefighter Daddy
The Wedding Bargain
The Christmas Secret
The Daddy Project
Daddy, Unexpectedly

For Willa

CHAPTER ONE

THE RIVERTON HEALTH Center was one of Annie Finnegan Larsen's least favorite places in the world. A world that was admittedly small and familiar and filled with the people and places she loved. But this place was the exception. Bad things happened here. The only place she disliked more than here was the cemetery.

"I'll need to see your insurance card." The triage nurse had yet to look away from her keyboard.

Maintaining her outward composure, Annie plucked the card from her wallet and passed it across the counter. What were the odds that she would come to the clinic in a town where she knew everyone and encounter a nurse she'd never seen before? Anyone who knew her and her circumstances would be rushing to offer comfort and support, but not this young woman. She was fixated on her computer screen.

"Do you still live on River Road?" she asked.

Annie took a deep breath. "At Finnegan Farm, yes. I've never lived anywhere else. I'm here with my son," she said. "He fell off a horse this morning. He could have broken bones, a head injury. He needs to see a doctor. Could we please look after the paperwork later?" She wished she had it in her to be forceful, or at least impatient. Instead, she was polite. Too polite for her own good.

Still, something in the sound of her voice must have caught the woman's attention because she finally made eye contact and glanced around her computer monitor at Annie's seven-year-old son. Then she swung her gaze to Annie, brows arched, eyes brimming with judgment.

"Mom, where's Auntie CJ?" Isaac asked, ducking out from under the protective arm she had around his shoulders.

"She's parking the truck, honey. Keep still, okay? The doctor's going to see you right away."

Besides, CJ was more problem than solution. Annie had let her sister convince her that Isaac was ready for junior rodeo, and clearly he wasn't.

"I don't want to see the doctor. I want Auntie CJ to take us home."

"I'm right here, kiddo. How're you holding up?" CJ, still dressed in full riding habit, minus the helmet, breezed through the double glass doors.

"We're doing *paperwork*." Annie prided herself in always keeping her cool and having a tight rein on her emotions, no matter what the circumstances. Why couldn't she be assertive, more demanding? If she had those skills, then maybe she wouldn't have failed her husband. Eric would still be alive and Isaac would still have a father. She had tried to convince Eric that he needed to see a doctor, to find out why he was in so much pain. She should have insisted. No, *demanded*. Instead, she had taken a step back and let him do the typical guy thing and soldier through the pain.

CJ slung an arm around Annie's shoulder and led her and Isaac to the row of black leatherette chairs that lined two walls of the small waiting room. "Sit. I'll handle this. We'll have Isaac in to see the doc before you know it."

"He should be in there already. He could be—"

"Annie, I've got it. Sit, relax. Okay, I know

you're not going to relax, but at least try to chill for a couple of minutes. Isaac's fine. Look at him. He's fine."

Annie sat, guiding her son into the seat beside her, resisting the urge to pull her little boy onto her lap. Common sense told her that he was all right—he was walking and talking and insisting he wanted to carry on with his riding lesson—but what if he wasn't? He was her son, her only child, and he was so little and so special and he didn't have a father.

She tried to listen in as CJ spoke to the admitting clerk, then realized that her sister was deliberately keeping her voice low so Annie couldn't hear. She was probably telling the woman that Annie was the one who needed medical attention.

Annie focused on the double doors that led to the ER, willing them to open and a nurse, or better yet, a doctor, to appear. She hadn't set foot in this place in months, not since rushing her husband here with scarcely time to watch him take his last breath. Now she was here with her son, her precious boy and her only remaining link to Eric. Falling off a horse was not good. She should never have agreed to riding lessons, even though CJ was the teacher, and an excellent one at that. But Annie was his mother and it was her job to keep him safe. Given that this little daredevil was so much like his father, she had her work cut out for her.

CJ took the chair next to them, gently ruffled Isaac's already unruly blond curls. "It'll just be a few minutes. How do you feel?"

"I wanna go home and go back to the stable."

Annie met CJ's questioning gaze. "We'll talk about that later, after—"

Stacey McGregor emerged from an office behind the front desk. "Annie, Isaac. Hi."

Annie was instantly reassured by the familiar voice and the woman's brisk efficiency.

"What's this I hear about someone falling off a horse?"

"That was me!" Isaac said before Annie could respond, bouncing up from his chair. "I'm learning barrel racing 'cause I want to be in the junior rodeo."

"CJ's giving him lessons," Annie said, gently pulling her son back into the chair. She and Stacey had graduated from high school together. She was an excellent nurse and great with kids, having three of her own.

Stacey kneeled in front of Isaac and attempted to smooth his unruly curls. "Horseback riding? I'll bet you want to be a cowboy when you grow up."

"Yup. I'm gonna have a hat and a lasso and everything."

"I'll just bet you will." Stacey shifted her smile from Isaac to Annie. "A blue-eyed heartbreaker of a cowboy, that's what he's going to be."

Isaac giggled, and Stacey stood and took his hand. "Come with me. I'll take you and your mom in to see Dr. Woodward."

"Oh. He's still seeing patients?" Annie asked. She'd heard that Riverton's long-time family physician had recently been diagnosed with Alzheimer's. Heartbreaking news, but surely he wasn't still practicing medicine?

"Sorry, I guess you haven't heard. Not Doc Woodward Senior. His son."

"Paul? He's back in Riverton?" Annie followed Stacey into an examining room, simultaneously reassured to hear her husband's best friend was in town and here to look after Isaac, and a tiny bit disappointed he hadn't called to let her know he was home. She had always liked and admired Paul. It would have been good to hear from him. Keeping in touch with Eric's past made her feel more connected to him. Although Paul had been away from Riverton for years, he was an important part of that past. She wondered if he knew that Jack Evans, her husband's other best friend, was also in Riverton and about to marry Annie's other sister, Emily.

"He dropped in to the clinic yesterday, just briefly, on his way into town." Stacey tucked Isaac's chart into the plastic holder on the door. "Today is his first shift."

Okay, that explained why he hadn't called. He probably hadn't even unpacked.

"Can Auntie CJ come, too?" Isaac pleaded.

"Of course she can." Stacey beckoned her to follow. "How's everything out at Finnegan Farm?"

"Everything's great," CJ said. "Busy. My summer riding camp is winding down. We're boarding two new horses, and I just took in a rescue horse from a farm near Pepin. What about you?"

"Everything's good. I'm looking forward to having my kids in school next week. Even Ben's looking forward to getting back to teaching. I mean—" She cast a worried glance at Annie.

Annie was quick to brush aside the woman's concerns. "I know exactly what you mean. Eric used to get as excited about the start of a new school year as he looked forward to the end of the previous one. It's a thing with teachers. Please tell Ben I said hello."

"I will, for sure. Have a seat," she said to Annie and CJ. "Isaac, can you climb up here for me?"

He nodded, and scrambled up onto the examining table.

"My goodness, you're getting tall. What is your mom feeding you?"

Isaac giggled.

Annie watched from the edge of her seat, worried he could tumble off the high table if he didn't sit still. She felt her sister's hand curl over hers, silently reassuring.

"Are you looking forward to school next week?" Stacey asked.

Isaac nodded vigorously. "I'm gonna be in second grade."

"Are you? So is my daughter, Melissa." She held up a digital thermometer. "I'm going to slip this in your ear so I can take your temperature, okay?"

More nodding. "I know Melissa."

"I thought you might." The thermometer beeped. She looked at the digital display and then showed it to Isaac. "See those numbers, little man? Perfectly normal," she said, noting them on his chart.

This offered Annie no relief. Fever was not a symptom of a concussion or, heaven forbid, a brain hemorrhage. She knew because, even against her own better judgment, she had looked them up on her phone while CJ had driven them to the clinic.

"Would you like to stay up here?" Stacey asked Isaac, handing him a couple of small coloring books that came with a colorful assortment of animal stickers. "Or jump down and sit with your mom?"

"I'll stay up here." Isaac opened one of the books. "Do I get to keep these?"

"You sure do." Stacey turned to Annie. "Dr. Woodward's just finishing up with another patient and then he'll be right in to see you."

"Thanks," Annie said. She stood and moved to stand next to her son in case he started to feel light-headed, which *was* one of the symptoms they had to watch for.

Dr. Woodward. Paul. They had all known one another for most of their lives, although she and Eric hadn't seen much of Paul since he'd left for college and then went on to study medicine at one of the universities in Chicago. He had stayed there and had been practicing at a big-city hospital ever since.

Eric had always been a man of action, a little impulsive, even. By comparison, Paul studied the angles, thought things through. Eric's spontaneity had been tempered by his friend's careful consideration of everyone and everything around him. She was beyond relieved that Paul was here. If anyone would take extra-special care of Eric's son, it would be his best friend.

"See, Mom? This book's got dinosaurs. This one's *Diplodocus*. That's one of the plant eaters. Can I really take these books home with me?"

"Stacey said you could so, yes."

Isaac peeled the sticker off the sheet and stuck it to the matching shape on the coloring page. This was a good sign. His fine motor skills wouldn't be so precise if his vision was blurred, another of the worst-case-scenario symptoms. She smoothed his hair and listened to him chatter about each dinosaur as he applied stickers to the page. *Brontosaurus*, *Stegosaurus*, *Tyrannosaurus rex*. Then he opened the second book.

"Jungle animals," he said. "Is this a parrot?"

"I think that's a macaw. Parrots have smaller beaks."

"Maca-a-a-w," he said, peeling and attaching the sticker to the page. "Caw, caw, ca-a-a-w."

The door opened. "Someone told me there

was a little boy in here who's fallen off a horse. I wasn't expecting a crow."

Isaac giggled. "Uncle Paul!" He held up a hand and Paul high-fived it.

"Annie. How are you?" Paul asked.

Annie took one look at him and felt her spine soften. He opened his arms for her and she melted into them. She had forgotten how it felt to lean on someone, rest a cheek against a hard chest, breathe in a male scent with just a hint of woodsy aftershave. She pulled away. She should not be having inappropriate reactions to one of Eric's best friends.

He moved his hands to her shoulders, leaned in and kissed the cheek that had just sought comfort on a shoulder that was broader than she remembered.

"Oh, Paul. It's so good to see you. You have no idea." She looked into eyes that were not green, not brown. Hazel, she decided. She had never noticed the color before. Now she was sure would never forget them.

The tip of her nose turned pink—she could feel it. Her face didn't turn red the way a normal person's did. Only her nose. Anytime she was embarrassed or flustered, or whatever it was she was feeling at that moment, she ended up looking like Rudolph on a bender.

To cover it, she brought the fingertips of one hand to the bridge of her nose.

"Good to see you, too." He kissed her again, on the forehead this time, and turned to Isaac. "And who is this young man?"

"I'm Isaac."

"No way. Isaac Larsen's a little guy about this tall." Paul demonstrated by holding out his hand.

"Grandpa says I'm growing like a weed," Isaac offered, setting aside the sticker books.

"Your grandpa's right about that. Are you taking good care of your mom?" Paul asked, offering his hand to Isaac.

"Yup." Isaac accepted the handshake and gazed up at him. "I feed our dog and help bring in eggs from the chicken coop. Me and my dad used to do that, but he died."

Annie's breath caught in her throat.

"I know." Paul's tone was solemn. "I still miss him."

Listening to their exchange made Annie's chest tighten. Although they hadn't seen much of Paul in person, she had known he and Eric kept in touch, mostly by email and the occasional phone call. Of course Paul would miss him. After the funeral she should have done a better job of staying in touch.

"So, tell me about horseback riding." Paul

took a seat on a wheeled stool that brought him to eye level with her son.

"Auntie CJ's giving me riding lessons."

"That's pretty cool. English or western."

"Western." Isaac's enthusiasm was contagious. "I'm gonna be barrel racing at the junior rodeo and when I'm bigger I'm gonna be a real cowboy."

Paul laughed, then exchanged a quick smile with Annie before he turned his attention back to her son. "What's your horse's name?"

"Zephyr."

"Good name for a horse."

Annie forced herself to stop hovering and took the chair next to CJ, who was rolling her eyes.

What? Annie mouthed.

CJ placed a hand over her heart and pretended to swoon, and it was Annie's turn for an eye roll. *Behave!*

"Can you tell me what happened this morning when you were riding Zephyr?" Paul asked.

"I fell off."

"You did? Is Zephyr a bucking bronco?"

Isaac giggled again. "Nope. But I'm gonna ride one when I'm a grown-up cowboy."

Over my dead body, Annie thought.

"Were you wearing a helmet?" Paul asked.

Isaac nodded.

"Good." Paul pulled a small instrument out of his pocket. "This is a flashlight." He demonstrated by pressing on it and generating a beam of light. "I want you to look right at me so I can take a look at your eyes. Can you do that for me?"

"Yup."

"Good job," he said, slipping the penlight back in his pocket. "Pupils dilating just the way we like them to."

Annie knew his comments were more for her benefit than her son's. She appreciated his thoughtfulness even while she ignored CJ's I-told-you-so elbow jab.

Paul held out his hands, palms up. "Now I need to see if you're strong enough to be a cowboy. Can you press down on my hands as hard as you can?"

Isaac enthusiastically demonstrated his superhuman strength, repeating the test by pressing up, out and in against Paul's hands. He laughed when one foot and then the other swung involuntarily in response to a tap to the knee with a little rubber hammer.

"Dude, have you been working out? Lifting weights?" Paul asked. "Training for the Olympics?"

"Nope. I help my grandpa, though. He has

a wheelchair and he lets me push him around sometimes."

"How's your grandpa doing?" Paul looked to Annie for an answer as he ran both hands along her son's arms, then gently flexed them at the wrist, elbow and shoulder.

"He rides horses, too," Isaac said before she had a chance to answer.

Clearly surprised, Paul looked to Annie for confirmation.

"He's amazing," Annie said. "And yes, he rides. CJ runs a therapeutic riding program at the farm. Our dad was her test case and now he helps with the kids from time to time."

"Kids with disabilities often lead sheltered lives," CJ said, jumping into the conversation. "Seeing a man get from wheelchair to horseback and canter around the ring can be a real eye-opener for them. And for their parents, who can sometimes be *a little overprotective.*"

"No doubt," Paul said. "Good to know about your program, too. Do you take referrals?"

CJ grinned. "You bet I do."

Annie watched as Paul had Isaac lie back on the exam table and flex his legs while he talked to CJ. Apparently all checked out there as well.

"Can you sit up for me, champ? Good stuff. Now, do you remember how you landed when you fell?"

Isaac pointed to his left shoulder.

Paul turned to CJ. "Where was he riding? In a field, on a gravel road?"

"Oh, no. I give lessons in a covered arena. The floor has a thick layer of wood chips."

"So you had a pretty soft landing," he said to Isaac. "Can you peel off your T-shirt so I can take a look at that shoulder?"

Paul didn't offer assistance, and Annie had to resist the urge to jump up and help. Instead, he closely watched Isaac's movements as he bent and twisted and wriggled his way out of the shirt. Paul popped the earpieces of his stethoscope into his ears and held up the chest piece.

"Do you know what this is for?" he asked.

"Listening to hearts."

"That's right. I can hear what's going on inside your lungs, too." He reached behind Isaac, ran the tip of a finger along her son's shoulder blade as he did. "Can you take a big, deep breath and hold it for me?"

Isaac's narrow chest swelled.

"Good, that's it. Now breathe out."

Isaac let out a whoosh.

Paul moved the stethoscope. "Again."

After several repetitions, he draped the stethoscope around his neck and examined her son's shoulder more closely before he turned to Annie.

"You have a healthy little cowboy here. No sign of concussion, no broken bones. Even a hairline fracture would be causing some pain. He has the makings of a dandy bruise here on his shoulder, though."

Annie stood to take a look. Sure enough, a red-and-purple streak marred her son's pale skin. She lightly ran her fingers over it.

"Does that hurt?" she asked.

Isaac shook his head. "Can we go now? I'm hungry."

"Sure. We'll have lunch as soon as we get home." She felt silly for rushing here, assuming Isaac might have a head injury but not checking to see if he had any scrapes or bruises.

Paul caught her hand in his as she withdrew it from Isaac's shoulder, gave it a gentle squeeze and held on. "You did the right thing, bringing him in to be checked out. His shoulder might be a little stiff and sore for a few days. An ice pack will help with that if you can get him to sit still for a few minutes."

"Thank you. I was so worried."

"Perfectly understandable. Anytime you

have a concern, bring him in or give us a call. That's what we're here for."

She noticed he didn't say that's what *he* was here for. It was a silly thought. Why should he? He ran his thumb over the back of her hand, though, before he let go and helped Isaac put on his shirt. She wrapped her other hand around the one Paul had released, wanting to hold onto the warmth and reassurance of his touch.

"Now that you're back in town, you'll have to come to the farm for a visit. Coffee, maybe, or dinner."

He looked at her, his gaze a little intense and completely unreadable. "Coffee would be great. My shift here starts at ten so I could run out in the morning before I start work."

"Tomorrow?" Is that what he meant when he said in *the* morning, or had he meant *some* morning? She wished her question hadn't sounded so hopeful.

"Tomorrow works," he said without missing a beat. He held out a hand to steady Isaac as he jumped off the table, then ruffled his hair before opening the door of the examining room. "You let your mom put an ice pack on that shoulder, okay? Doctor's orders. CJ, good to see you again."

"Likewise." Not one to stand on ceremony,

CJ wrapped her arms around his neck. "Good to have you back in town."

"Good to be here." He turned to Annie. "See you in the morning." Then he was gone.

Her heart fluttered and the tip of her nose sizzled.

CJ looked her square in the eye.

"Don't you dare start with the I-told-you-so's," Annie said. "You heard what Paul said. Bringing him here was the right thing to do."

Her sister flashed an impish grin. "You were totally right. And hey, you even managed to land yourself a date."

"Shhh." She glanced at her son, but he was already out the door, sticker books tucked securely under his arm. "It's not a date. It's coffee with an old friend."

"It's a date," CJ said.

"It's coffee," Annie insisted. "At the house, in the kitchen, with all of you hanging around."

CJ slung an arm around her shoulders and they followed Isaac to the parking lot. For once, she seemed willing to let Annie have the last word. But as soon as they were in the truck, CJ was grinning again as she backed out of the parking space.

"I can't speak for you. But Paul? *He* thinks it's a date."

"What's a date?" Isaac asked.

"It's when two people go out to dinner and a movie," Annie said. "You know, like Auntie CJ does all the time."

"Auntie CJ never goes for dinner with anybody. She always has dinner at home, with us."

"Oh, that's right. She does, doesn't she?"

"Ouch. That was a low blow." For a few seconds CJ put on her well-rehearsed I'm-the-baby-in-the-family pouty face, then the evil little grin was back. "Riverton isn't exactly overrun with eligible men but you know, now that Paul Woodward's back...huh. Maybe I'll ask him to take *me* out for dinner and a movie."

When are you going to learn? Annie asked herself. CJ never settled for anything short of having the last word. But two things were certain—having coffee with Paul was not a date, and no one else in her family was going to date him, either.

CHAPTER TWO

PAUL SAT IN a cubicle behind the nursing station, added a final note to Isaac Larsen's chart and set it on the growing stack to be filed. He had grown accustomed to working with computerized medical records at Mercy Memorial in Chicago. After he settled in at Riverton Health Center, he would explore similar systems for this facility. *If* he decided to stay. Until his father's illness had progressed to the point he could no longer work or take care of himself, returning to his hometown to live and practice medicine was never an option.

Now, with his blood still simmering from Annie's casual embrace, he couldn't decide if coming back was a good idea or the biggest mistake he'd ever made. She was more beautiful than ever, more devoted to family than ever, more... More Annie than he remembered. The hug had given them both a little jolt—he'd felt her awareness collide with his—then she had quickly pulled away as though she had accidentally touched an exposed wire. He knew she would deny her reaction if asked, so he wouldn't. But he would take her up on the invitation to go for coffee tomorrow morning. Nothing would get in the way of that.

For now, though, he needed to make it through his first day.

Glancing at the roster, he saw he had one more patient to see before lunchtime. Mable Potter. Huh. She'd been his high school English teacher. Her daughter had made the appointment and was bringing her in to have her checked for memory loss. With her chart in hand, he sat a moment longer, trying to clear away thoughts of Annie, wishing he had the luxury to do nothing but dwell on them.

He had not been prepared to see her. Not like this. He'd had it all planned out. He would spend a few days settling in, then he would call her. In his head, he had rehearsed the conversation, steeled himself for the rush of emotion he would feel at the sound of her voice. He would act casual, off-hand, even though that wasn't his style. She would be happy to hear from him, invite him out to the farm.

He had considered dropping by unexpectedly, as his long-time friend Jack Evans would have done, but that wasn't his style, either. Too unpredictable. What if she wasn't home? Or, worse yet, what if someone was there with her? Not that she was seeing anyone. Jack had assured him she wasn't. It was too soon since Eric's death, and that definitely wasn't her style.

As these things tended to go, Paul's carefully thought-out plan to see Annie on his terms—after he had mentally prepared himself for their first encounter since her husband's funeral—had gone out the window. Instead, after a hectic morning of meeting the staff, seeing patients, figuring out the routine of a small but busy clinic, there she was. Tall and slender, wearing curve-hugging jeans and an orange-and-white, wide-striped sweater. Not a blond hair out of place. Troubled blue eyes.

Even now, the eyes haunted him.

The sadness, the lingering grief, was not a surprise. But the unexpected emotions that niggled his conscience, tugged at his heartstrings, were. Loneliness, a lack of purpose, fear. Her fear had troubled him the most. He had picked up on an almost obsessive conviction that her son had suffered a serious injury when, in fact, the kid hardly had a scratch and only minor bruises that would fade in a few days. Yes, an understandable reaction for someone whose young husband had died six months ago, but so unlike Annie. He had always seen her as the confident one, the person who fixed things, not the person who needed things fixed for her.

Still, if she was looking for a shoulder to lean on, he'd be happy to provide one, acknowledging that the idea was far from selfless. If he played his cards right, she might even be willing to lean on him more than a little. A guy could always hope.

Tomorrow, he reminded himself. Right now he had a patient to see, so he made his way to the examining room, tapped lightly on the door, let himself in.

"Good morning, Mrs. Potter. How are you doing today?"

"Do I know you?" The elderly woman's steady, blue-eyed gaze swept him back a couple of decades. The woman sitting next to her, probably in her late forties or early fifties, wasn't familiar.

"Twelfth-grade English. You were one of my favorite teachers at Riverton High. It's good to see you again."

Mable beamed at that. "I had a lot of students over the years," she said. "I wish I could remember all of them."

"No one would expect that," he said, extending his hand. "But they all remember you. I'm Dr. Woodward."

She didn't accept the handshake, shook her head instead. "No, you're not. Don't be making up stories, young man. I know Dr. Woodward, and you're not him."

The woman next to her placed a gentle hand on Mable's arm. "Mother, this is Dr. Woodward's son. He's a doctor, too."

"Are you?"

Paul nodded.

"Well, then. He must be proud."

Mable's daughter gave him a look that begged for understanding. "I'm Olivia Lawrence. I mean, Potter—I'm using my maiden name again. I'm Mable's daughter. Everyone calls me Libby."

"Nice to meet you, Libby." He accepted her perfunctory handshake and returned his attention to her mother. "My father is an excellent doctor. I only hope I can live up to his standards." The words were true enough. His father had been a great physician, just a lousy parent. "Now, how can I help you today, Mrs. Potter?"

"Well..." She glanced nervously at her daughter. "I don't remember."

Libby gently took her mother's hand. "It's okay, Mom. We all forget things from time to time. Right?" She looked to Paul for affirmation.

"We sure do." He sat on a wheeled stool. "The important thing to figure out is if you're more forgetful than usual. Do you live alone, Mrs. Potter?"

"I did after my husband passed on, but now I have my daughter home with me."

Libby smiled and nodded. "I've lived in St. Paul for many years—I'm a teacher like my mother—but I've had some recent, um, changes in my life and now I'm back in Riverton. I'll be living with my mother and teaching second grade at Riverton Elementary starting next week."

"Very good. You must be happy to have her with you."

The elderly woman brightened. "I am. Especially since that good-for-nothing reprobate of a husband of hers didn't come with her."

Libby sighed. Paul suppressed a chuckle, trying to recall the last time he'd heard the word *reprobate* used in a sentence. Probably not since twelfth-grade English. "I remember you always were one to speak your mind, Mrs. Potter. Now if it's okay with you, I'd like to ask you a few questions."

"You go right ahead," she said. "As long as they're not too personal."

Libby closed her eyes, shook her head.

After all these years, still not pulling any punches, Paul thought. The poor woman probably knew things weren't quite right and she was scared witless. Geriatrics weren't his strong suit, but for now he would go easy on her, he decided. Depending on what he learned, he might refer them to a specialist in the city.

"I'll tell you what," he said. "If you feel any of the questions are too personal, then you don't have to answer them."

"That seems fair." But she clung to her daughter's hand like a lifeline.

"How long have you lived in Riverton, Mrs. Potter?"

"All my life."

He looked to Libby, who confirmed the answer with a subtle nod.

"So you must know pretty well everyone in town."

"I suppose I do. I've taught a lot of them, too. And their children and their children's children."

"She even taught me," Libby added, her soft voice filled with affection.

"And you were a good student. A good girl, too. At least until you married that good-for-nothing…"

Reprobate. She seemed unable to recall the disparaging word that had come so quickly just moments ago, and since it didn't bear repeating, Paul pressed on.

"Where do you live?"

"On Cottonwood Street." He knew that was true, could even picture her cute little one-and-a-half-story home a few blocks from his father's place.

"Do you know what day it is?"

"Thursday. I know that because on Thursdays I go to the Clip 'n' Curl to have my hair done."

Close, but it was actually Friday.

"We did that yesterday, Mom," Libby gently reminded her.

"Humph. You don't say."

"Can you tell me what you had for breakfast this morning?" Paul asked.

"Why do you need to know that?" Mable asked. She looked confused and sounded defensive.

"I'm just checking to see if you remember."

"Well, if you must know, I had tea. And… porridge. I have that every day."

Again, Libby's almost imperceptible headshake indicated that this wasn't accurate. Since nothing would be gained by contradicting her, he continued with some casual conversation.

"When I was a boy," he told her, "I remember my grandmother telling me to eat my porridge because it would stick to my ribs."

Mable beamed, and most likely assumed she had answered the question correctly.

Libby patted her hand.

As he suspected, her long-term memory was intact. The short-term, not so much. Based on personal experience, these were symptoms he knew all too well.

"I'm going to refer you to a specialist in the city," he said to Libby. "I'll set that up today and call your home with the details."

"Thank you, Dr. Woodward. I—we—really appreciate it."

"I remember you," Mable said to him out of the blue. "You're old Doc Woodward's son."

"I am."

"You were in my English class, but that was a long time ago."

"So, you do remember me."

"Of course I do. You were friends with Jack Evans and that Larsen boy."

"That's right."

"You were a better student, as I recall. Homework always done on time, good grades. And now you're a doctor, too."

"I am."

"Well, your father must be proud. How is he, anyway?"

"He's doing well." There was no point in telling her that his father was a little lacking in the son-I'm-so-proud-of-you department, or that he was also seeing the Alzheimer's specialist in Madison.

"And those other boys?"

"A couple of months ago, Jack was appointed Riverton's new chief of police. He's living here now and engaged to Emily Finnegan. And Eric Larsen..." Paul had to pause, steady breath. "He passed away six months ago."

"He died so young?" Mable asked.

"Too young."

"Well, I'm sorry to hear that."

Libby stood and urged her mother out of her chair. "We should go, Mom. Thank you," she said to Paul.

"No problem. I'd like to see your mother again in two weeks. You can stop at the desk on your way out and have them set up the appointment."

"I will. I hope late afternoons will work because I'll be teaching during the daytime."

"That won't be a problem. I'll be taking

late appointments two days a week and for a few hours every other Saturday."

Paul let himself out of the room and returned to his desk. He updated Mable Potter's file, added it to the stack, then looked at his watch. He should run to his father's place, check on the old man, make sure he had eaten the lunch Paul had left out for him that morning. He hated himself for thinking it, but few things had less appeal.

Stacey stepped around the partition, another chart in hand. "Sorry, Dr. Woodward. Another patient just came in. Would you like me to tell her to come back after lunch?"

"What are her symptoms?"

"Sore throat, nasty cough, low-grade fever."

Paul reached for the folder. "I'll see her now, then I'll take a break." One thing about being in a small town, he could leave the clinic and be anyplace in five minutes.

"Thanks. I'll get her set up in an examining room."

He glanced at the file, recognized the name immediately.

Rose Daniels.

ANNIE WENT THROUGH the motions of preparing lunch without giving a lot of thought to what she was doing. Then again, why would she need to? She had made hundreds, no, more like thousands, of lunches. She had been making lunches for as long as she could remember. So while she put on a pot of freshly gathered eggs to boil and sliced thick slabs of home-baked wheat bread, her mind was elsewhere and her emotions were not in keeping with her role as maker of family lunches.

Her reaction to seeing Paul had been nothing short of inappropriate. He was her husband's best friend! She had been surprised to see him, and happy, of course, but not *that* kind of happy. It was easy enough to explain her reaction. She had been terrified that something might be terribly wrong with Isaac, angry with CJ for letting Isaac fall, impatient with the admissions clerk. Had her emotions been irrational? Of course they had. They had been out-of-character for her, and that meant all of her other actions and reactions had been equally over-the-top.

The timer buzzed. Annie removed the pot from the stove and transferred the eggs to a bowl of ice water. While they cooled, she finely diced a couple of celery stalks, minced several green onions and chopped a bunch of fresh parsley.

Paul wasn't just Eric's friend. He was her

friend, too. Of course she was happy to see him and relieved to know that he would be taking care of her son. She hadn't been able to rely on anyone but herself for a long time and it had been a relief to let someone else step in.

If she was being honest, she had at times resented Eric's carefree life. While he had gone off to college and earned a degree, Annie had stayed in Riverton and cared for her family. After they were married, she had stayed at home and baked bread while Eric had stayed after school and coached the senior boys' basketball team all the way to the state championship. While she washed, folded and put away a mountain of laundry, he took a group of students on a ski trip. In all fairness to her husband, he had never demanded any of those things of her. He only had to ask, and she was all over it. She had willingly taken on all of the responsibility. She always had.

And you probably always will.

One by one, she plucked the chilled eggs from the bowl of water, gave them a gentle smack against the cutting board and peeled the shells.

Annie had been only six years old when her mother left. Even in the early days before her mother walked out on them, Annie had vague recollections of being the caregiver, fetching her mother a glass of water from the kitchen and the bottle of pills from the bureau drawer because Mommy had a headache. Keeping her younger sisters entertained because Mommy needed to rest. Making lunch for her siblings because Mommy wasn't feeling well that day. Looking back, life had actually become a little easier after their mother abandoned them because there had been one less person to look after.

Her father had ended up in a wheelchair after a stint in Iraq. The details of that event had always been sketchy because he had sheltered his daughters from the horrific details. He had been the one person in her life who had truly needed looking after and yet she had very few memories of ever actually doing anything for him.

She dumped the peeled eggs into a crockery bowl and mashed them with her pastry blender, which was much more efficient than a fork, then tossed in the chopped vegetables, sprinkled on salt and pepper, scooped in some mayonnaise and stirred.

By the time she started high school, Annie had been everyone's go-to gal when it came to getting things done. She had organized bake sales and car washes, served on decorating committees, volunteered in the school library and served on student council. She had been a going concern and so had Eric. The difference had been that she created posters for the car wash to raise money for the boys' basketball team and made arrangements to hold it at Gabe's Gas 'n' Go, while Eric showed up in board shorts and dazzled all the girls by stripping off his T-shirt. And no one had been more dazzled than she. She always had to hand it to him, though. No matter how many girls flirted with him, he was always quick to point out that he was Annie's guy, strictly off-limits. She would have done anything for him, and he had never hesitated to ask.

Annie slathered butter onto slices of bread, spread them with scoops of egg salad, added leaves of fresh lettuce, cut the sandwiches in half and arranged them on a large white platter. There. Another day, another lunch. Time to call her father, Isaac and CJ. As she set out plates, glasses, napkins and a pitcher of milk, she found herself wondering what Paul was having for lunch. And then resisted the urge to pick up her phone and call him.

PAUL HAD HEARD an earful about Rose Daniels from his long-time friend, Jack Evans. She was from Chicago, twenty years old, the daughter of a street person who'd been murdered in the spring. Jack, still with the Chicago PD at the time, had been the lead investigator in the serial murders of three women, one of whom had been Rose's mother. In one of those bizarre, small-world coincidences, it turned out Rose's mother, Scarlett, a drug addict, was also Annie Finnegan's mother.

Scarlett had left her family in Riverton when her daughters were too young to remember. After Scarlett died, Rose had found out about her mother's abandoned family and had surreptitiously come to Riverton to check them out. Annie, being Annie, had taken the young woman under her wing and welcomed her into the Finnegan fold.

Jack had talked about the case at length because, being engaged to Annie's sister, Emily, he had a vested interest in it. Paul remembered him saying that, as a child, Rose had been in and out of foster homes. Now, with Annie's help, she had moved here and landed a waitressing job at the Riverton Bar & Grill. From what Jack had told him, Paul also knew the young woman had a serious drinking problem and the attitude that went along with it. Understandable for someone who'd grown up with none of the advantages, but his sympathy was overridden by his concern for Annie, who clearly had enough on her plate already. According to Jack, Emily had been devastated by the news of what had happened to their mother and still hadn't warmed up to her half sister, Rose. CJ wasn't a fan, either. Annie, however, had become the young woman's champion.

Paul closed the chart, rapped lightly on the door of the examining room.

A throaty "Come in" was followed by a phlegmy coughing fit.

He opened the door and paused. He had expected to see a fresh-faced young woman with intelligent eyes and a ready smile—she was one of the Finnegan sisters. Sort of. Yet, aside from the eyes, nothing about Rose's appearance hinted at a connection to the Finnegans. She was thin to the point of being gaunt and her face had a sickly pallor. Black liner emphasized the dark circles under her eyes. Her side-swept bangs were disproportionately long compared to the rest of her sleek, dark, short-cropped hair. She sat on the edge of the examining table wearing one of the clinic's faded blue gowns over tattered blue jeans and scuffed, black combat boots.

"Hi, Rose. I'm Dr. Paul Woodward. That's a nasty-sounding cough."

She nodded, clearing her throat.

Paul selected a tongue depressor from a glass jar and tore off the paper wrapper. "Open up and let's have a look at that throat."

As suspected, her tonsils were swollen and her throat an angry shade of red. She exhaled with the "ah," her breath a pungent blend of tobacco smoke and alcohol.

"I'll take a throat swab and send it to the lab," he said. "Just to be sure you don't have a strep infection going on in there." After he sealed the swab and labeled it, he reached for a prescription pad. "I'm going to prescribe an antibiotic. I want you take this twice a day for ten days. And no alcohol while you're taking it," he said, watching closely for her reaction.

"Oh. Sure. I don't drink much anyway."

Right. Except for prelunch cocktails that had her smelling like a bottle of gin. He tore the sheet off the pad, handed it to her. "What about cigarettes?" he asked.

She responded with a one-shoulder shrug.

With his stethoscope, he listened to her lungs rattle as she wheezed a couple of deep breaths in and out for him. "If you ever think about quitting," he said with as much gentleness as he could muster, "I can give you information about smoking cessation programs."

"Oh, I can quit if I want to."

Okay, then. "Fair enough. If you'd like to

stop at the desk and book an appointment for a checkup next week, I should have the lab results by Tuesday. And while you're at the drugstore getting the prescription filled, ask the pharmacist for a good cough syrup."

"Sure." It was all she managed to say before launching into another coughing fit.

"Good. I'll see you next week, Rose." He left the examining room and closed the door behind him.

He could see why the younger Finnegan sisters hadn't warmed up to their half sister, but he could also see why Annie had rushed to her rescue. This young woman needed all the help she could get.

CHAPTER THREE

ANNIE KNEW HER reaction to Isaac's fall that morning had been over-the-top. Still, she played back Paul's words over and over again. *You did the right thing, bringing him in to have him checked him out.* He had been gentle and patient with Isaac, and even gentler and more patient with her. Inexplicably, the back of her hand still sizzled from his touch. *That* reaction was also completely over-the-top.

She sighed, pressed buttons to preheat the two wall ovens. Her father had always said the kitchen was her domain. He was right. She loved this kitchen. She had planned and overseen the renovation down to the smallest detail and now it was, to her mind at least, the perfect combination of form and function, modern and vintage, all in a cheery combination of gleaming white with vibrant red and sunny yellow accents. This was the center of her universe, her very own command central, the one place where she felt completely secure and fully in charge. This was where everyone came to her for help and she gave it, no questions asked.

She lifted the flour canister off an open shelf, set it on the island next to the basket of eggs she had brought in from the coop not half an hour ago. From the fridge, milk and butter. Sugar, cocoa and baking powder from the pantry. From memory, she measured and sifted dry ingredients into a bowl. In another, she creamed the butter, eggs and sugar until they were pale yellow and velvety smooth. Isaac would have his favorite five-layer chocolate ganache cake for dessert tonight.

She pulled a set of cake tins from a cupboard, greased and floured all five and set them aside, ready for the batter. Folding the dry ingredients into the wet, she quickly stirred the mixture until it was smooth and poured the batter into the prepared pans and popped them into one of the ovens. After clearing away baking supplies and loading the utensils into the dishwasher, she turned her attention to dinner. Pot roast, she had decided earlier. A family favorite, and easy to make. She checked the temperature of the other oven and took out the roaster.

If she kept herself busy, she didn't have to think about Isaac getting hurt this morning or how she had blamed the fall on CJ or how she had behaved like a neurotic parent at the clinic. And maybe she could avoid thinking about that *thing* with Paul. She didn't need a shoulder to lean on. His familiar embrace had suddenly felt unfamiliar and new. It had caught her off guard, that's all. Thank goodness he hadn't noticed. But then, why would he?

She opened a bin, took out some potatoes. She had probably misinterpreted that moment with her husband's best friend. She could call it relief that it was Paul who would examine Isaac, but that didn't explain why she had invited him to drop by for coffee tomorrow morning. Nor did it explain why she had been secretly glad when he accepted.

But it was just coffee. Just Paul. He had been one of Eric's best friends. He cared about her and Isaac the way friends did. The same way Jack did. Having Paul drop by for coffee was not a big deal, and she wasn't the type to make something out of nothing.

So why was she overthinking this?

She browned the roast in a large skillet on the stovetop, transferred it to the roaster and slid it into the lower oven. Then she took a vegetable peeler from a drawer and attacked the mound of potatoes she had dumped in the sink.

She had loved Eric for as long as she could remember. Losing him in the spring had carved a huge hole in her life, one that left her aching and empty. Having Paul and Jack in Riverton would be good for her and Isaac. Especially Isaac.

Jack was about to become her brother-in-law and Paul was…just Paul, she reminded herself.

A movement at the veranda door caught her eye. Chester, the family's aging retriever, sat patiently waiting to be let in. Annie dropped the last potato into a pot of cold water, then crossed the kitchen to let in the dog.

"Hey there, golden boy." She gave his head a rub, fed him a biscuit from the jar on the counter. Chester crunched and swallowed the treat, ambled over to his water bowl for a drink, then carefully lowered his arthritic hips to the big red-and-gold plaid cushion that was his bed. For more than a year now, Isaac had been begging for a puppy. Annie had deflected his cajoling with a reminder that they already had a dog. Much as she hated to admit it, the old retriever wouldn't be with them forever. The Finnegan farmhouse had never been without a dog and Annie knew she would have to relent one of these days. Just not this one.

With Chester snoring softly in his corner, she went back to work. She always welcomed an afternoon alone in the kitchen. After they'd come home from the clinic and had lunch, CJ had gone to work in the stable and their father had taken Isaac into town to pick up a few last-minute back-to-school supplies. They would be home anytime, though, and her solitude would come to an end. She loved her son's boisterous boyishness, but she also cherished these moments of peace and quiet. There would be more of those moments once school started next week.

She could hardly believe her little boy was already in second grade. He loved school, especially reading and science and gym class, and already had a large circle of friends. He was so much like his father in so many ways, it made her heart swell with love and ache a little at the same time.

Eric would have been over-the-moon to have his two long-time friends in Riverton. With Jack about to marry Emily, he and Eric would have been brothers-in-law. He would have loved that. And now Paul was here, too. Still single and looking like a doctor on a Hollywood TV drama. What had they called that doctor on *Grey's Anatomy*? McSomething. McDreamy? That was it. And that was Paul.

The shock from the way she had reacted to his embrace that morning stung again. She felt guilty, too. His relationship with her husband made these feelings inappropriate and downright disrespectful. Eric deserved better.

As she finished readying the vegetables for the pot roast, she could hear the front door swing open and Isaac barreled through the house, yelling a greeting. "Mom? Mo-om! Where are you?" He was heading straight for the kitchen because everyone knew this was the first place to look for her.

"Guess what!" He burst into the room, blue eyes alight, blond curls bouncing, grinning from ear to ear. "You'll never guess!"

"Then you'll have to tell me." She pulled him close, carefully avoiding his bruised shoulder. "Using your inside voice."

"We went to the hardware store 'cause Auntie CJ needed us to pick up a bridle for the new horse she's boarding. And you know the dog that's always at the store? Izzie?"

"I do," Annie said, leery of the direction this conversation was headed.

"She has puppies! Five of 'em."

Annie already knew this. She had gone into the hardware store earlier in the week to pick up paint for the chicken coop, and had immediately been drawn to the makeshift pen behind the sales counter, where Izzie had been sprawled on a blanket, nursing her impossibly adorable puppies. Having a soft spot for animals, especially an animal in need of a home, Annie had refused to let herself be drawn to those puppies. She already had all the strays she needed.

Isaac had other ideas. "A dog would be a good thing to get."

"We have Chester."

"But he's not *my* dog, and he's *old*."

Both were true. Since Isaac was a toddler, Chester had tolerated him. Now he mostly ignored him. But a puppy? Puppies made messes on the floor and chewed the heels off shoes. Puppies needed to be housebroken and crate-trained.

Puppies were also a boy's best friend. They taught kids to be considerate and compassionate and responsible.

"I *need* a puppy, Mom."

"I'll think about it," Annie said.

"Yay!" Isaac raced back to the front door. "Gramps! We're getting one of those puppies and we're going to name him Beasley."

Annie sighed. "Use your inside voice, please," she called after him, but she knew he hadn't heard. When it came to her son, she was a pushover, but he was all she had left of Eric and there was nothing she wouldn't do for him.

Her father rolled into the kitchen. Isaac had climbed onboard and was sitting on his grandfather's lap. He'd been doing this since he was a baby, but not for much longer.

"The way you're growing, you'll soon be too big to ride with Gramps," she said.

Isaac flung his arms around his grandfather's neck. "Then I'll stop growing."

Annie exchanged smiles with her father. "So what's this I hear about a puppy?" he asked. His attempt at innocence didn't fool her for a second and she immediately knew what she was up against. It wasn't just Isaac who wanted a puppy, it was Isaac *and* his grandfather.

"I said I would think about it."

The co-conspirators in the wheelchair exchanged a wink.

"So…" her father said. "Isaac tells me you saw Paul at the clinic this morning. Said the two of you have a date tomorrow."

"It's not a date. He's just dropping by for coffee." Annie felt her nose turn red as she debated which conversation was more awkward—dogs or dates.

EARLY SATURDAY MORNING, Paul fixed his father's breakfast and served it to him at the kitchen table. Two soft-boiled eggs that Geoff Woodward deemed to be too hard, dry toast that wasn't dry enough, coffee that was too strong. Afterward, Paul settled the cantankerous old man in his favorite chair with a newspaper, the television remote and a thermos of tea.

"I have patients I need to see this morning," he said after he had washed the dishes and set them in the drainer to dry. Saying he was on his way to the clinic wasn't quite true, although he did have to get there eventually. First he wanted to see Annie. He'd thought of little else since yesterday. If he was being honest, he didn't just *want* to see Annie, he *needed* to see her.

"Fine," the old man said. "Go ahead and leave me. You're just like your mother."

Paul knew better than to remind his father that Margaret Woodward had not walked out on her husband, she had died. Feeling a sense of abandonment was normal after the loss of a spouse—there was no point calling her a loved one, since he didn't believe his father had ever experienced that emotion—and these feelings could be more pronounced in an Alzheimer's patient.

"Walt Evans from across the street will stop by after lunch. He said he was hoping to have a cup of tea and a game of cribbage."

"I hope he doesn't mind me beating the pants off him."

"I'm sure he won't." Their lifelong neighbor and the father of one of Paul's oldest and best friends in the world knew as well as anyone that Geoff had always been a sore loser. Now if he lost, he was likely to toss the board across the room, pegs and all, and fling the deck of cards in its wake. Luckily for all concerned, Walt had been one of the few people who had managed to forge a genuine friendship with Geoff over the years. No surprise there. Jack's father was always as cool as a cucumber, and Paul's father was as approachable as a porcupine.

For now, Paul was comfortable leaving his father on his own in the house, knowing he didn't yet have a tendency to wander. The disease would progress, though, and that day would come. Paul would deal with it when it did, but for now he could go about his day, confident that his father would still be here when he returned.

At first glance, Geoff was the same man he had always been—tall in stature, almost as tall as his son, hair not gray but silver, with the fit body and angular facial features of a man in his sixties. Of course, he *was* in his sixties. It was his mind that had decided to age prematurely.

It was the eyes that betrayed him. Sitting as he was now, ensconced in his recliner, remote in hand, staring vacantly at the dark TV screen...this was the man his father had become, and the speed with which the change had come about had been shocking.

Paul knew he should feel compassion for this man who was his father, but all he felt was resentment. For his entire career, Geoff had been a compassionate physician with an exemplary bedside manner. At home, he had ruled his family with a sharp tongue and an iron fist. Paul had looked forward to the day when he could flaunt his own medical successes in his father's face and call him out on the years of verbal abuse. The Alzheimer's had robbed him of the chance. It would have been one thing to have a mental sparring match with his father while he was sharp-witted and mean. Now, sadly, the old man was just mean, and having that conversation would be pointless.

For the millionth time in the past few weeks, Paul contemplated his fate and for the first time decided the fates had been fair after all. Riverton's clinic needed a new doctor, his father needed someone to look after him and Annie was a single woman. None of these things would be easy, he knew that. He already missed practicing medicine at a big hospital. He'd had no idea how to relate to his father when he was in his right mind, let alone like this.

As for Annie, Paul had no idea how he would stop himself from acting like a fool. He knew one thing for sure, though—his shift didn't start for two hours and Annie had invited him to drop by for coffee, so that's exactly what he was going to do.

CHAPTER FOUR

TEN MINUTES LATER, Paul was behind the wheel of his car and heading out of town along River Road. The drive from town to the country brought back a lot of memories, most of them bittersweet.

As kids, he and Jack and Eric had ridden their bikes out here during summer holidays. That had been before they knew about Finnegan Farm or the oldest Finnegan girl, who'd been destined to earn the love of not one but two good men. In those days, they'd been more interested in doing what boys do best when there was no adult supervision—competing to see who could ride the farthest without touching the handlebars, who could spit the farthest when they were munching on sunflower seeds and who could string together the longest series of swear words. Fortunately for the women of the world, boys eventually grew into men.

Jack had been the first to get his driver's license, and that summer had been a blur of illicit parties. By then, Jack was dating a girl named Belinda and Eric was dating Annie, leaving Paul on the sidelines. The girls he ended up being paired with were friends of either Annie's or Belinda's. Sometimes there was the occasional girl he'd mustered the courage to ask out himself. None of them had turned into girlfriends, though. He'd been preoccupied with Annie and his futile hope that she would realize he was a far better catch than Eric.

She hadn't, of course. But that was then and this was now. He knew better than to think she could miraculously stop grieving the loss of her husband and realize Paul was the second love of her life. But now that she was single and he was home, he intended to rekindle their long-time friendship. After seeing her so upset at the clinic yesterday, he could tell she was struggling a little—maybe more than a little. He would be there for her. His might even be the shoulder she leaned on when the going got rough.

Just ahead he spotted the white gazebo on the riverbank. Situated on the narrow strip of public land that ran between River Road and the Mississippi, it had been built by Annie's grandfather. There was a small parking area where anyone passing by could stop and enjoy the view. The landmark would always be known to locals as Finnegan's gazebo. To Paul, it would always be the place where Eric had proposed to Annie, and where Annie had said yes.

Paul signaled, slowed and swung into the driveway then drove up the sloping, fence-lined gravel drive that separated two paddocks, one of which had a series of jumps set up in it. At the house, he parked in the roundabout next to a large white van and in front of a painted wooden sign, both embellished with the Finnegan Farm Bed & Breakfast name and logo.

The two-and-a-half-story farmhouse had been built at least a hundred years ago. As a teenager, Paul had spent a fair bit of time here. After Eric had married Annie and moved in, he hadn't set foot in the place.

The clapboard exterior was still a crisp white and the trim was barn-red, just as he remembered. The wraparound screened porch was furnished with wicker and painted wood furniture. The white lace curtains in the windows, the old yellow dog sleeping on the welcome mat at the front door—it was as if time had stood still. Even the wheelchair ramp adjacent to the front steps had been there for as long as Paul had been coming here. Everyone in Riverton knew about Thomas Finnegan's acts of heroism during Desert Storm and about the lives he had saved while almost giving up his own. Soon after he'd come home to his family in a wheelchair, his wife had abandoned him and his daughters. Annie, the oldest of the three, had taken on the role of caregiver and Paul knew she continued to fulfill it. The big question for Paul had always been…who took care of Annie?

ANNIE LOVED WEEKEND mornings. Every Saturday, her sisters gathered around the big kitchen island for coffee and muffins and sisterly conversation. The three of them had always been close, but after Eric died, she had valued these get-togethers more than ever. This morning she was anticipating another visitor, a little too eagerly, perhaps. She was sliding a pan of lemon-cranberry muffins into the oven when she heard the knock at the front door.

Paul! She hastily set the timer and made her way to the door. She opened it and felt her breath catch in her throat.

"Paul."

"Good morning, Annie. I hope I'm not too early. When you invited me, I might have forgotten to mention that my shift at the clinic starts at ten o'clock."

"Not a problem, and it's definitely not too early. Come in, please."

He stepped inside, seemed to hesitate before he opened his arms. She stepped into the awkward hug and instantly felt the same zing of awareness she'd had yesterday. CJ's insistence that this was a date rushed through her mind.

Paul leaned down and planted a kiss on top of her head.

Definitely not a date, she reminded herself.

"Come to the kitchen. There's fresh coffee, and I just put a second batch of muffins in the oven."

"Wow," he said as he followed her. "Eric wasn't exaggerating. You really have made some big changes in here."

"We renovated about five years ago, after I decided to open the B and B. The old kitchen was quaint but it sure wasn't functional. We kept the original cabinets, but we painted them, and we kept these old farmhouse-style door and drawer pulls."

"Those are original? They look as though they could have been installed yesterday."

"You know what they say—everything old is new again." She often congratulated herself on that decision. Now, when she checked out design magazines, she could see they were once again in vogue. The same could be said for Great-Grandmother Finnegan's metal canisters, still lined up along the counter, their red lids with the paint chipped from years of use, the cherry-cluster decoration on the fronts faded but still cheery. Their contents still matched the stenciled labels—flour, sugar, coffee, tea.

"I wanted modern conveniences without sacrificing family tradition," she said. The cabinet drawers were filled with fresh linens and towels and all the modern gadgets she used every day to prepare the meals she served to her family and guests. Nestled among them, though, were the old wooden rolling pin her grandmother had used to roll countless pie crusts and strudels, and the old hand-crank eggbeater that Annie and her sisters had been allowed to use before they could be trusted with an electric appliance. She indicated the upper cabinets. "We added these glass doors because I wanted to display this vintage crockery and glassware. They've been in the family for generations."

"I'm impressed. I remember Eric's emails about the work you were doing. It was hard to imagine him in a tool belt, though, wielding a hammer."

"Eric was…helpful," Annie said, giving a weak laugh. "Although I'm not sure the contractor would have agreed with that statement."

Paul laughed, too. "That sounds like Eric, all right. How's Isaac this morning?" he asked, taking a seat at the island.

"He's fine." She took a mug out of the cupboard, filled it with coffee and passed it to Paul. Her hand grazed his and gave her a little jolt.

"Thanks." His smile had the same effect on her heart.

"After we came home yesterday, I tried putting an ice pack on his shoulder like you suggested, but he wouldn't sit still long enough for it to do any good."

"That's a good sign."

"It is. I'm sorry I was such a basket case yesterday, but I was so worried."

"Annie, don't apologize. Your reaction was completely understandable."

"He's already down at the stable with CJ. They're saddling the horses for the kids who come every Saturday morning for riding therapy."

"And your father?"

"He's down there, too. He often rides with them."

"Impressive. I'd like to come and watch sometime."

"We can go down and check out the class this morning if you'd like."

"Thanks. Maybe another time. I'm good right here for today."

She was oddly pleased that he had opted to stay in the kitchen with her. "How's your father doing?" she asked.

Paul sighed. "As sharp-tongued as ever. Now he just can't remember why. Although, come to think of it, I'm not sure he ever had a good reason."

"I'm sorry. I know a lot of people in town were surprised to hear that he was retiring, but everyone was shocked to hear he has Alzheimer's. He seems too young for that."

"Most people think of it as a geriatric condition but the truth is that as many as five percent of patients are afflicted before they turn sixty-five."

"I had no idea," Annie said. "That's so sad."

The timer pinged. She pulled the pan from the oven, dumped the muffins into a cloth-lined basket. She set out side plates and knives, butter and a small pot of her homemade strawberry-rhubarb jam, and placed the basket on the island. "Help yourself," she said. "Lemon-cranberry, fresh from the oven, obviously, but they'll cool quickly."

"You won't have to twist my arm," Paul said. "They smell amazing, but I'll only have one if you pour yourself a cup of coffee and sit with me."

"Of course." She wasn't accustomed to sitting still in her own kitchen, but she refilled her mug and settled onto a stool, careful to leave an empty one between her and Paul.

"These taste as wonderful as they smell," he said, after his first bite of the piping hot muffin he had sliced in half and generously slathered with butter and jam.

"I'm glad you like them. I bake muffins every Saturday morning. My sisters and I have a coffee date after CJ's riding class is over, and I freeze the leftovers for family and guests who come to stay."

"How's that going?" he asked. "The bed-and-breakfast? It sounds like a lot of work."

"It can be, but I'm already cooking and cleaning and making beds for the family, so it's not a lot of extra work to do it for a few more people. And we're only open through the summer and for the holidays, from Thanksgiving through Christmas. Not a lot of people book a holiday on a Wisconsin farm in the middle of January. And if they do…" She smiled at him over the rim of her cup. "They won't make the same mistake twice."

They both laughed at that.

"Makes sense," Paul said. "I guess folks are searching for sun and surf at that time of year."

He was easy to talk to and she loved that he made it easy for her to laugh, that he made it *okay* for her to laugh again. It was all so easy that she was startled when Paul checked his watch and stood to leave.

"Annie, this has been great but I need to get going. Otherwise I'll be late for my first appointment."

"I'm glad you came out this morning. It's good to have you back in Riverton." She meant it. She hadn't realized how important it would be to have Eric's friends around.

Paul stood, picked up his dishes and carried them to the dishwasher.

Annie rushed to her feet. "Don't worry about those. I'll take care of them."

He gave her a quizzical smile. "I know how to load a dishwasher. I've been taking care of myself since I went away to college."

"Right. Well, thank you." He was a doctor. He took care of other people for a living, so without question he could look after himself. She just wasn't used to being around men who did. Or if they did, she wasn't accustomed to letting them.

"Walk me out?" he asked.

"Of course." As they made their way down the hall to the door, she found herself wondering about Paul's past. He seemed to be single, but there must have been girlfriends, serious relationships even. For all she knew, he was still involved with someone in Chicago. She could ask, but she wasn't sure she wanted to know.

Outside on the screened veranda, they stopped and Paul turned to face her. "Thanks for coffee."

"Anytime, Paul. I mean it."

He placed his hands on her shoulders, leaned in as though he was going to kiss her forehead the way he always did. As he moved, she inexplicably tipped her head back and looked at him. His lips made contact with hers. The kiss lasted a millisecond—brief but electrifying. They both pulled back, startled, gazes locked.

Paul was the first to find his voice. "Um, I'm sorry."

"No, I'm sorry."

"I only meant to—"

"I shouldn't have——"

"I didn't mean for that to happen," he said.

Neither had she. Or had she? That would explain why right now she wanted to grab the front of his shirt, pull him close and kiss him again, for real. The mortifying thought set the tip of her nose on fire.

"It's not a big deal," she said. *Liar.*

They stood in awkward silence for a few beats and she wished she knew what he was thinking, but his expression gave nothing away.

"You'll have to join us for Sunday dinner sometime."

The invitation seemed to startle him. "Oh. Sure. Leaving my dad on his own for dinner will depend on what kind of day he's having but…sure. We'll play it by ear."

"Right. I'm sorry, I forgot. I just thought, since Emily and Jack will be here, you might like to see them. And your father is welcome to come, too."

Paul looked downright surprised by that suggestion. "He has a tough time now with new situations, new people. I'm afraid it might be too much for him. Maybe for everyone."

"I see. I'm sorry."

Paul shoved his hands in his pants pockets.

"No need to apologize. It is what it is. I'll see what I can do, though. It would be good to see Jack and Emily."

"Do you have someone come in to look after him while you're at the clinic?"

He shook his head. "He's pretty good in the daytime, and Jack's father drops in every day around lunchtime. If I can work something out with the Evanses, I'll let you know."

"We'd like that."

"Okay, then. I'd better get going." He pushed through the screen door and ran down the front steps to his car.

Annie stood on the veranda. She touched her fingertips to her lips as he drove down the driveway, onto River Road and out of sight.

PAUL DIDN'T REMEMBER a lot after that kiss. He recalled pulling out of the Finnegans' driveway onto River Road. But his mind was a blur of images from the past and the present, so he had no recollection of making the drive to the Riverton Health Center. Yet here he was, parked in the space that, for years, had been reserved for Dr. Woodward. The name plate was now as worn and faded as the mind of the man who had parked his various Volvo sedans here over the past forty odd years. On Paul's first morning here, Edna Albright, the clinic's long-time office administrator, had declared how convenient it was for the health center that the sign didn't have to be changed.

At the time, he had refrained from telling her that his being here was not a permanent solution. Coming home to care for his demanding, ungrateful father and cover for him at the clinic was meant to be a short-term fix. Eventually, the old man would move into a care facility, the clinic would find a permanent replacement for him and Paul would return to his position at the hospital in Chicago. He had been generously granted a one-year leave of absence. The clock was already ticking.

But being home meant being close to Annie, and he felt as though that brief kiss had already upset his carefully laid plans. He hadn't meant to kiss her. She was his best friend's wife. Strictly off-limits. For as long as he could remember, she had passively accepted his casual embrace, the light touch of his lips to her forehead. This morning, there had been a subtle, almost imperceptible change. This morning, she had altered the pattern by looking up at him, eyes awash with emotion, lips parted ever so slightly with an invitation he couldn't have refused to save his life. And so he had kissed her, even though he hadn't meant to. Now he couldn't wait for an opportunity to do it again.

CHAPTER FIVE

AFTER PAUL LEFT, Annie didn't know what to do with herself. So she made more muffins—carrot-pineapple this time. Then she whipped up a batch of cream-cheese frosting to slather on them as soon as they had cooled. Baking was easy. Reconciling herself with that kiss was not. Her sensible side doubted she could ever face Paul again. Her closely guarded inner self couldn't wait to see him. In spite of that one unexpected moment they had shared, she liked the feeling of actually... feeling. Having him care for Isaac yesterday had made her feel safe. Being alone with him this morning was like dropping a match in a tinder-dry hayloft. As exciting as the heat of these initial flare-ups might be, she needed to be careful not to burn down the barn.

She put on a fresh pot of coffee and while the scent of it filled the kitchen, mingling with the aroma of fresh baking, she iced the muffins and arranged them on a footed Depression glass cake plate. Soon her sisters would join her and she liked having everything ready before they arrived.

"Hello! I'm here." Emily let herself in the front door and breezed into the kitchen as Annie poured boiling water over the decaf coffee grounds she had spooned into the bottom of a Bodum.

"Is that for me?" she asked, pulling Annie into a sisterly hug.

"It sure is."

"You're the best. I've been dying for a cup."

"You do know there's no caffeine in it."

"Doesn't matter. I let the smell and taste of it trick me into believing it's the real thing." Emily set her oversize bag on the counter. "I have something for you."

"You do?"

"Remember when I asked you about writing a weekly column for my blog? And you said you'd give it a try at the end of the summer after Isaac was back in school?"

Right. The *Ask Annie* column. Annie had not forgotten, but she had hoped her sister would.

"Jack gave me a new camera for my birthday, and it's amazing. You should see the photos it takes." Emily ran a hand over her belly. "This will be the most photographed baby in the world."

Annie smiled at her sister's enthusiasm over a gift that other women might find overwhelmingly unromantic from a man who had recently proposed. Not Emily. Since childhood, she had dreamed of becoming a journalist. Now she was a reporter for the *Riverton Gazette*, and a popular blogger with a recently signed book contract.

Emily pulled her old camera out of her bag. "I thought you might like to have my old one. For illustrating the column, although you can use it for anything. Isaac's birthday parties, school events, whatever."

Annie eyed the camera suspiciously. "You said you wanted me to answer a question about running a busy household, a farm, a bed-and-breakfast. You didn't say anything about taking pictures."

"Oh. I guess you don't have to. I thought you might *like* to."

"I don't know the first thing about photography."

"That's the beauty of the digital age. You don't need to know anything. I've put all the settings to auto, which means that as long as the light is reasonably good, the camera will do all the work. You simply have to point and shoot." Emily thrust the device into her hands.

Annie cringed as she studied the undecipherable symbols that presumably indicated what the various buttons and dials were for. "What do you want me to take pictures of?"

"Whatever you like. Whatever will work with the column you're writing."

"I'm not a writer, remember? I have no idea what I'm going to write about."

"Fine. We're calling the column *Ask Annie*. Would you like me to give you a question to answer?"

"I think you'll have to." For the life of her, Annie couldn't think of anything she did from day to day that anyone else would want to read about.

Emily glanced around the kitchen as though pondering what to ask, and then her gaze settled on the kitchen window and beyond. "Chickens. Farm-fresh eggs. That'll be your first question. Is there any advantage to cooking and baking with farm-fresh eggs?"

"In a word, yes."

Emily made a face. "Now you're being difficult. Tell us about your chickens—what you feed them, how many eggs you get every day, what the eggs taste like. Maybe include a recipe or two."

Annie found herself wishing she had never agreed to this. Emily's posts on her blog were hugely popular, filled with humor and insight and charm about life in a small town. Why would her readers want to read about chickens and eggs? She had long accepted that Emily was a brilliant writer and that their younger sister was an accomplished horsewoman. Annie herself had none of those exceptional skills. She raised a family, prepared food, kept house. She loved what she did. Taking care of her family was enormously satisfying, but there was nothing earthshaking about any of the things she did.

As though Emily could read her thoughts—and given how close they had always been, she probably could—she gently took the camera from her and switched it on. "Just line up whatever you want to take a picture of in the monitor and push this button. Let me know when you're ready to upload them to your computer and I'll show you how. For the first column, I only need about two hundred and fifty words. Then we'll take it from there."

Never one to go back on a promise, Annie gave a reluctant nod. "Fine. I'll give it a try. Now can we talk about you?"

She gave her sister a good look up and down. Her flowing tan-colored top, worn with a pair of off-white jeans and accessorized with gold hoop earrings and bangles, suited her perfectly and did an excellent job of disguising her expanding midsection. "You're looking gorgeous this morning. New outfit?"

"Newish."

"Your baby bump is getting very—"

"Bumpish?" Emily suggested.

Annie smiled. "It's going to be more and more difficult to disguise this under a wedding dress."

Emily shook her head. "Honestly, I'm not trying to hide. It's not as though people don't already know. But I did find a dress online that I really love. It has an empire waist with a full skirt. Really pretty."

"White?"

"More ivory with just a hint of pink. They call the color champagne."

"That'll be perfect with your complexion. Is it a full-length gown?"

"Knee-length. I didn't want anything too formal. I'll show you a picture when CJ gets here."

"Rose is joining us, too."

The excitement in Emily's eyes dimmed.

"She is our sister," Annie reminded her.

"I know. I'm just not ready to share my wedding arrangements with her."

"Fair enough. But you do realize you have to invite her, right?"

Emily sighed and gave a reluctant nod.

Rather than push the point, Annie changed the subject. "Have you set a date?"

"We have, finally. The last Saturday in September. We've decided to get married outdoors, in the gazebo, because we want to take advantage of the fall color."

"Oh, my." The gazebo. The place where Eric had proposed to her. Overcome with nostalgia and a fierce longing for her old life, Annie's chest tightened and her breath clogged her throat. It was also the place where Jack had proposed to Emily, she reminded herself. She recovered before her sister noticed, she hoped, and pasted on a smile. "The end of September. Wow. Your big day will be here before we know it. Doesn't give us a lot of time for planning."

"There's no need for a big plan. We want to keep the wedding simple, and we didn't want to hold it until Jack's mom was feeling up to it and his sister, Faith, could make it from San Francisco."

"Makes perfect sense. How's his mother doing?"

"She's good. It's taken her some time to recover from the fall she had at the start of the summer. The cast came off her arm last Wednesday and she'll be starting physio soon.

Jack and his dad and I will take turns driving her to appointments."

"She must be so happy to have her son at home with her, even if it's just until the two of you find a place of your own."

"Well, that might already be taken care of."

"You've found a place?"

"Not yet. His mom has always been a homebody and never wanted to travel, but after breaking her arm and having to rely on everyone else's help, she's decided she likes having other people take care of her. So his parents have decided to take a cruise this fall, right after the wedding. Go figure, huh?"

"Wow. That's huge. Have they decided where they are going?"

"The Panama Canal, leaving from New York, I think, and ending up at Faith's in San Francisco. She made all the arrangements for them. After they disembark, they'll stay with her until Christmastime. They'll be back in Riverton before the baby is born, and Jack and I are going to stay at their place, for now, while we look for a place of our own."

"That'll be perfect. What about a honeymoon?"

"We're thinking next summer, maybe. Jack is barely settled into his new job with the police department and it's too soon for him to take time off. And I want to finish my book before the baby's born. For now it'll feel good to move out of my apartment and into Jack's place and be…" Emily's stared dreamily into her coffee cup. "You know."

"Husband and wife. A family. I totally get it, and I am so happy for the two of you."

Annie was really and truly excited about the prospect of having one of Eric's best friends for a brother-in-law, and especially about being an aunt. She had honestly given up hope of that ever happening. Now they were going to have a Christmas baby—a baby boy or girl who would be a much-loved addition to the Finnegan family.

Annie looked up and found Emily smiling at her. "I've been hoping to get you alone so I could ask you something."

"Ask away."

"I know the three of us had this thing worked out where I was your bridesmaid when you married Eric, and then CJ would be mine and you would be hers. That way everyone gets a turn."

"That's right. I'd forgotten all about that."

"Me too, until CJ reminded me. The thing is, though, I'd really like you to be my maid of honor. It just feels right somehow. And then maybe CJ could be yours when…if you get married again."

Taken aback, Annie stared at her sister. "That is not likely to happen."

"Don't be silly. Not right away, but you're young and gorgeous and you're sure to meet another man someday who'll fall madly in love with you and your apple strudel."

Annie's thoughts inexplicably turned to Paul.

Emily reached across the island, took her hand and squeezed it. "It would mean the world to me if you would do this."

"Of course I will. I'll be honored."

"Thank you." Her sister sat back and smiled, seeming to look a little more smug than necessary.

Then, too late, Annie realized she might have landed herself in a bit of a sticky situation. "Who has Jack asked to be his best man?"

"Oh. Paul, of course. Have you heard? He's back in Riverton now."

The sound of CJ's footsteps on the back veranda saved Annie from having to answer. For once, her little sister's timing was impeccable.

CHAPTER SIX

PAUL ARRIVED AT the clinic in time to see his first patient of the morning and to find out the next two had called to cancel. Feeling at loose ends, and not wanting to return to the house to hear his father's newest complaints, he fired off a quick text message to Jack.

Morning schedule has been cleared. Any chance you have time for coffee?

His friend's response arrived a moment later.

Sure do. Meet you at the café.

Café was shorthand for the Riverton Bar & Grill. As he pulled out of the clinic parking lot and drove downtown, he considered all of the positive aspects of living in his hometown. He hadn't expected there to be so many, he thought, as he passed the old town hall that was now home to the library and county museum, the Big River Theater, Baxter's Pharmacy and Henderson's Hardware before he angled into a parking space in front of Morris's Barbershop.

Initially he had balked at the idea of having to take care of his father. The old man had always been difficult to live with but his forgetfulness had made him surprisingly easy to manage. He still tested Paul's patience, although in a different way.

Paul had also worried about seeing Annie again, about having her nearby and yet completely out of reach. This morning's coffee date now topped the list of pluses. Getting together with his long-time friend Jack was a close second.

He stepped out of his car and crossed the street to the Riverton Bar & Grill. This was one of those timeless places that never seemed to change. Not even after the name had changed from the Riverton Café and the menu had been updated to include salads made with organic greens—no one called it lettuce anymore—and topped with things like dried cranberries and candied pecans. He was pretty sure dried cranberries hadn't even been invented when he was a kid.

Jack was already there and sitting in a booth near the window. Paul slid onto the opposite bench. They bumped fists across the table.

Jack already had a cup of coffee in front of him. "Good to see you," he said. "All settled in?"

"Pretty much, thanks. How are things with you?" Strangely enough, he and Jack were both living in their childhood homes. They had kept in touch but seldom saw one another while they'd both been living and working in Chicago. Paul expected that to change now that they were here.

"The new job's keeping me on my toes," Jack said.

"So...you've taken up ballet."

His friend laughed. "Feels like it some days."

"How's Emily?"

"Amazing, brilliant, stubborn. She's got this book deal, the blog, her job at the *Gazette*. I keep saying she should slow down, take things easy." Jack shrugged.

"How far along is she?"

"Five and a half months, give or take."

Since they knew exactly when this baby was conceived—the night of Eric's funeral—there wasn't much giving or taking. Paul figured it would be wise to keep that observation to himself.

"Does she still have her own apartment?"

"Until the wedding, she does. Annie suggested she move out to the farm, take some of the pressure off, but she likes being in town, where she's close to the office. Did I mention stubborn?"

"You'd almost think she was a Finnegan sister." Paul glanced around, hoping to catch the eye of a server. "What does a guy have to do to get a cup of coffee around here?"

Jack waved at the waitress, who was engaged in a conversation with a customer who was sitting on a stool. "Rose? Could we get another coffee here, please?"

She shot him a look before she slowly reached for the coffeepot.

"Is that the Finnegans' other sister? The half sister?" Paul asked, although he already knew the answer to his question.

"Yes, that's Rose Daniels. How did you know?"

"Just a guess," he said, wishing he hadn't let that slip.

Jack appeared to consider that. "Or maybe you've already met her? Treated her at the clinic?"

"That I can't say."

"I get it. Doctor-patent confidentiality. Rose has a nasty cough. Annie and Emily both told her she needed to see a doctor. I'm hoping maybe she took their advice, for once."

Paul shrugged. "You know I can't discuss patients."

"Fair enough."

Rose appeared and set a cup of coffee on the table. "Can I get you anything else?"

"Thanks but no, this is good."

She looked from Paul to Jack and back to Paul. "You're the doctor I saw at the clinic."

The corner of Jack's mouth twitched.

"I am. How are you, Rose?"

"Good." She coughed into her elbow. "I'm taking the meds but I still haven't shaken this cold."

"These things take time." It had only been twenty-four hours. If he had to guess, she hadn't shaken the booze and cigarettes, either.

"If you change your mind and feel like ordering something, let me know. I'm off shift in a few minutes, though." She skewered Jack with a defiant glare. "I've been invited out to the farm to have coffee with my sisters."

She swung around and as she walked to the counter, Paul was struck by how thin she was. She was dressed completely in black. Ridiculously skinny jeans, a lacy, long-sleeved top, over-the-knee, suede boots. Far from a small-town waitress's typical attire.

"Interesting," Paul said.

"It wasn't Emily who invited her, I can tell you that much."

"And I take it you're not one of her favorite people," Paul said.

"Not even a little bit." Jack's smile suggested that he didn't care one little bit, either. "She likes you, though."

"I'm inclined to go with indifference. She seems far more interested in the guy sitting at the counter."

Jack glanced over his shoulder. "She's attracted a following among the young guys in town. I have no idea who that is." Jack picked up his cup, took a drink. "Speaking of interesting, how's Annie? I hear she had to take Isaac to the clinic yesterday." Jack flashed him a wicked grin.

"She did, and I went out to the farm for coffee earlier this morning. She invited me out for coffee." And he had kissed her. Accidentally, but still, his lips had touched her lips and he hadn't been able to stop thinking about it.

"I think it's great, you and Annie."

"There's no 'me and Annie.' We're friends." *Just* friends, according to her.

"Sorry, man. I didn't mean to give you a hard time, but we—Emily and I—think it's good for Annie to have someone, namely you, in her life right now. We're worried about her. She works all the time. Be good to see her have some fun once in a while."

"And I'm...fun?"

They both laughed. "Maybe I should have said she needs a distraction."

Paul wasn't so sure he wanted to be anyone's *fun distraction*. He wanted his friendship with Annie to be deeper than that, but talking about it wasn't going to make it so. "We're just friends," he said. "What's new with you and Emily?"

"Well, I've finally convinced her to set a date—the last weekend of September—and I imagine that'll be the sole topic of conversation when the Finnegan sisters convene over coffee this morning."

The young man who'd been sitting at the counter talking to Rose checked his watch, then abruptly jumped up and left as though he was late for something. Rose immediately took out her phone and started tapping away.

"And the groom's part in all of these wedding plans?" Paul asked.

"We'd be married by now if I'd had anything to say about it. But we've talked about the details and we're both on the same page.

Family and friends at a small ceremony and reception at the farm, nothing fancy."

Paul pushed aside his envy. "And the best man's role in all of this? I take it I'm throwing the stag?"

Jack shook his head. "Emily is saying no to stags, stagettes and couples showers."

"Gee, missing out on a couples shower has to be disappointing."

Jack laughed. "Yeah, right. I'm still busy with work and to be honest, when I do have a free evening, I want to spend it with Emily."

Paul ignored another stab of envy. Just because he was alone didn't mean he begrudged his friend's happiness, or the fact that he was actually marrying one of the Finnegan sisters.

"I hear you," he said instead. "How's Emily feeling these days?"

"She's feeling great and Dr. Cameron says the baby is doing well, too."

"Glad to hear it. Emily's in good hands. Alyssa Cameron has a lot of maternity experience."

"We were kind of hoping she could be your patient."

Paul shook his head. "I wouldn't be comfortable with that. We've been friends for so long, we're practically family."

"I get it," Jack said. "We both do."

The door opened and a man walked in. He looked vaguely familiar to Paul, and he waved at Jack, which meant he probably was, and then he strode up to the counter to talk to Rose. Right away her eyes lit up, as much as they had when she'd been chatting with the previous guy.

"That's Emily's friend, Fred Morris," Jack said. "Remember him?"

"Right, right. From the barbershop. I thought I recognized him."

"That's right. For reasons no one can figure out, Fred has a thing for Rose. And for reasons that are blatantly obvious, she tolerates him because he'll do favors for her. It makes Emily a little crazy."

"Isn't he a little old for her?"

Jack quirked an eyebrow. "And a little on the buttoned-down side to be hanging around with someone who dresses like a vampire."

Paul watched the interaction between the two. He considered himself a good judge of character and from what he could see, Fred had it bad.

"Emily and CJ don't trust this newfound half sister of theirs," Jack said. "I'll confess that I had the green-monster thing going on when Em first got so overprotective of Fred, but now I think she's right."

Paul lowered his voice. "How do you feel about the newest addition to the Finnegan clan?"

"I don't trust her, either. To say she had a troubled childhood is a gross understatement. She has the poor-me attitude down pat, and some people—single young guys in particular—seem to fall for it."

"People like Fred."

Jack nodded. "And then there's Annie. She won't listen to anything negative when it comes to Rose. Says that after everything this poor kid's been through, everyone should cut her some slack."

"What do you think?" Paul knew there were things Jack, as police chief, couldn't tell him, but as the young woman's future brother-in-law, he could talk about the family connection.

"I think Rose has a drinking problem. A serious one."

Based on Paul's own assessment, he completely agreed. He just couldn't say so.

"There's no question that she knows how to play the sympathy card, but I think the kid also has a self-destructive streak."

"You mean suicidal?" Paul certainly hadn't picked up on that.

"No, more like reckless abandon. For one

thing, she thinks nothing of drinking and driving."

"Has she been pulled over?"

"She has. Last time she sweet-talked one of my rookies into letting her go without a Breathalyzer."

"That's manipulative, all right."

Jack glanced at her across the restaurant. "She'd better watch herself. I've had a talk with my staff about this. Next time she won't get off so easy."

Paul watched Fred fish a set of keys out of his pocket and hand them to the young woman. She waved goodbye to the other waitress, who had just stepped out of the kitchen, then walked around the counter with a black messenger bag slung over her shoulder, dropped the keys into it and gave Fred a quick hug and a peck on the cheek.

"You're a doll," she said to him. "I'll have your car back by the time you close up shop this afternoon."

Sporting an ear-to-ear grin, Fred strolled toward the door with her. "If you'd like, I can take a look at your car tonight," he said. "See if I can figure out why it won't start." They walked out before Paul could hear Rose's reply.

He picked up his cup and drained it. "I see what you mean."

While he had known who Rose was when he treated her, he had not realized how invested Annie was in this young woman's life. He was concerned about Rose as a patient, that was his job. But Annie was something else. She had an inherent goodness and she cared about everyone around her, especially family. Paul could accept that she saw him as "just a friend," even though his feelings for her ran a lot deeper. Heaven help anyone who intentionally set out to take advantage of her.

CHAPTER SEVEN

ANNIE WAS STILL contemplating the intricacies of Emily's hand-me-down camera when CJ burst through the French doors and into the kitchen, filling the space with her energy.

"Oh my gosh, I'm starving and it smells so good in here." She shrugged out of her brown barn jacket and tossed it on the bench by the door. Her long, blond hair was pulled into a high ponytail, as was customary when she was giving riding lessons. She wore a scoop-necked yellow T-shirt with faded, form-fitting jeans tucked into black riding boots. She ogled the muffins. "Are those carrot-pineapple?"

"They are."

"With cream-cheese frosting?"

"Of course."

"I thought you were making lemon-cranberry muffins this morning."

"I did."

"*Two* batches of muffins in *one* morning?"

Annie watched her sisters exchange a look. *Here we go.*

"Did something happen?" Emily asked. "Is something wrong?"

"Of course not. Why would you ask?"

CJ had already bitten into a carrot-pine-apple muffin and was swiping frosting off her lips with her tongue, but that didn't stop her from talking. "Because you were making muffins before I went out to the stable this morning. Since you didn't stop baking, it's a sure sign something's wrong."

"Nothing's wrong." Which was technically not a lie.

Emily started on her second muffin. "All right then, what's *bothering* you? Are you still worried about Isaac?"

"No, not at all. Isaac's fine. He spent most of the morning with CJ's therapeutic riding group, then he was going into town with Dad. They've probably left already. I think he's hoping his grandfather plans to stop at the hardware store."

"Still has his eye on one of those puppies, does he?"

"He does."

Relieved to have the conversation steered away from her baking spree, Annie poured a cup of coffee and slid it across the counter to CJ's customary place at the island.

"How was your class this morning?"

"Good. Really good, actually. Remember me telling you about Monica Cooper, the little girl with spina bifida? Her mom brings her from Wabasha every Saturday?"

Emily nodded.

"Well, she's been doing great all summer. Her mom's been bringing her twice a week— every Saturday for the group class and every Wednesday afternoon for a private session. She's my first student with spina bifida so I've been doing a lot of reading on this condition."

Annie watched CJ's eyes light up with enthusiasm. Her two younger sisters were so dedicated to their chosen careers, and so accomplished. Earlier in the summer, Emily had been approached by a major New York publisher, inviting her to turn her blog into a book. She had even appeared on a national television talk show and people were saying she was the next Garrison Keillor.

CJ had segued her lifelong love of horses into a thriving business. Here at Finnegan Farm, she bred and boarded horses, taught riding lessons—one of her former students had recently qualified for the national equestrian team—and operated one of the most successful therapeutic riding programs in the state, possibly even the country. Annie watched her now, as she talked about her young student, and felt a stab of envy. Would she ever feel this excited about something?

Since losing her husband, Annie felt as though she was making her way through familiar territory after a dense fog had settled in. She used to love running the bed-and-breakfast. Now she practically cringed every time the phone rang or another email reservation came in. She had always loved cooking, and especially baking. Everyone in town said her apple strudel was legendary. Yet this morning, as she had prepared one batch of muffins after another, her baking frenzy had been more compulsion than joy. Something was missing from her life. Eric was gone, of course, but it was more than that. She had no direction, no purpose—if she had ever really had one—and she had no idea how to find it.

The truth was that she had always done what was expected of her, required of her, even demanded of her, but she had never simply done what she wanted. She had been living up to everyone else's expectations for so long, she wasn't sure she had any of her own.

In the months since Eric's death, her family and friends had urged her to take time to grieve, to talk about her feelings. Until this morning, she had steadfastly denied the need to do that. Paul had changed her view. He had made her want to open up, but he was the last person she should be turning to. And the very last person she should be kissing.

"Annie?" CJ's question dragged her back to the here and now.

"Yes?"

"You're a million miles away. What's up?"

Should she tell them? She would never hear the end of it if she did. If she didn't, they would keep after her until she spilled the details of Paul's kiss. Luckily, Rose's late arrival saved her from making the confession.

"Sorry." Rose coughed against the back of her hand. "My stupid car broke down. Again."

"What's wrong with it?" CJ asked.

Rose shrugged. "I don't know. It won't start."

Emily polished off her muffin and wiped her fingers on a napkin. "Maybe it's the battery."

"Could be."

Annie poured a cup of coffee and slid it toward Rose. "If your car won't start, then how did you get here?"

"That guy Fred who runs the barbershop let me borrow his."

Emily bristled. "I could have given you a ride."

Rose shrugged again. "He didn't mind. Said he wouldn't be using it today so I might as well take it."

Emily and Fred had been best friends since first grade, and Annie knew it irked her to no end that Fred had developed a crush on the newest and youngest member of the Finnegan sisterhood. Not that Rose appeared to notice. She had an insular quality that was both endearing and off-putting. Annie wasn't convinced that Rose was taking advantage of Fred so much as Fred was throwing himself under the bus for her.

"More coffee?" Annie asked, reaching for the pot in an attempt to redirect the conversation.

CJ nudged her cup forward. "Love some. Now, getting back to all the baking you did this morning. You should have one of these muffins, by the way." She passed the basket of lemon-cranberry muffins to Rose. "They're delicious. So are the frosted ones."

Rose selected one from the basket and set it on a plate. "That's a lot of muffins."

"She's been baking all morning," Emily said. "We all know what that means."

Rose looked from one sister to the next. "I don't."

Here we go again, Annie thought.

"Well…" CJ paused for dramatic effect. "If Annie is worried or upset, she bakes."

"She also bakes when she's happy and excited about something," Emily said.

"True. But muffins usually mean worried or upset."

"Good point. Happy baking usually yields apple strudel or blueberry pie."

Rose followed the volley of their conversation like a cat watching a ping-pong ball.

"Enough, you two. Who knew my kitchen productivity was a barometer for my emotions?"

Emily and CJ grinned. "We did," they said in unison.

"And since it's a two-kinds-of-muffins morning, something's got you going." Emily sipped her decaf and smiled smugly.

"Let's hear it," CJ said.

Annie hesitated.

Emily set down her cup. "You might as well spill. You know we're not letting up until you do."

"See what I have to put up with?" Annie said to Rose.

Rose responded with her usual shrug.

Annie took a fortifying gulp of coffee. "Paul kissed me." She regretted the admission the instant the words were out.

Emily looked stunned. "He...*what*?"

CJ clapped her hands together. "When?"

"Who's Paul?" Rose asked.

"He's an old friend of Eric's." CJ knocked the Cheshire cat out of the running for the world's widest grin.

"And Jack's," Emily added.

Annie wished she hadn't said anything. "He dropped by for coffee this morning—"

"Way to go, Paul! He didn't waste any time." CJ had gone from grinning to downright giddy.

Emily was still dumbfounded. "He came for coffee and he kissed you? Like, *kissed you* kissed you?"

"I don't know what that means," Annie said.

"Oh, I think you do."

Annie felt herself blush.

CJ pounced. "Ah ha. What did I tell you after we left the clinic yesterday? He's interested."

"He is not interested."

"Seriously?" Emily said. "He has *always* had a thing for you."

"Still not sure who this Paul guy is, or why this kiss is such a big deal." Rose's voice had taken on the slightly sullen tone she reserved for times when she was desperate to fit in, but felt as though she was left to sit on the sidelines.

"Dr. Paul Woodward," Emily said.

"Junior," CJ added. "His father—Dr. Geoff Woodward—used to work at the clinic but he had to retire." She triple-tapped her temple with her forefinger. "Cuh-raz-ee."

"CJ! The poor man has Alzheimer's."

"Okay, I'm sorry. Lighten up. Anyway, he's retired and his son—Dr. Paul Woodward—has come home to take over the clinic."

"Oh." Rose covered her mouth with the back of her hand, coughed and cleared her throat. "I see."

"That's still a nasty-sounding cough," Annie said. "You should get it checked out."

"I did. I saw Dr. Woodward at the clinic yesterday. It's just a cold. I'm practically over it." Rose glanced at her but her gaze darted away as soon as Annie made eye contact. "So, tell me more about our Annie and this Dr. Paul."

"There's nothing to tell." Annie grabbed

the coffeepot and refilled everyone's cups but Emily's. "Would you like me to make more decaf?"

"No thanks. I want more details about the kiss."

"It was not a big deal."

"You spent all morning baking enough muffins to feed half the town."

Annie sighed. No sense denying defeat when it was staring her in the face. "All right, all right. It was mostly...no, not mostly, *totally*—it was a totally innocent kiss."

She glanced at her sisters' eager faces.

CJ opened her mouth to say something. No doubt something inappropriate.

Annie held up her hand, palm out, cautioning CJ to keep it to herself.

"Yesterday, I invited him to come out here for coffee. Today, he dropped by. We had coffee, we talked, it was...nice. Really nice. Then he had to leave so I walked him to the door. He always gives me a kiss on the forehead."

CJ set her empty cup on her plate. "Oh, that's right. He does."

Emily's head bobbed. "He always has done that, now that you mention it."

Rose looked disinterested.

"We were saying goodbye and I knew

that's what he was going to do because he's *always* done it, but…"

"But?" Three voices, in unison, breathlessly demanded details.

She knew what they were thinking. They were thinking Paul had made a move on her. As if he would.

"I didn't keep my head down. I looked up at him and he ended up kissing me…" She raised her fingertips to her lips.

Rose looked bored. "An accidental kiss. What's the big deal?"

Emily and CJ exchanged a look.

"Oh, that was no accident," Emily said.

CJ clapped her hands again. "You wanted him to kiss you."

"I did not." But if Annie didn't believe that, how could she expect her sisters to buy it?

"You are such a liar," CJ said.

Emily high-fived CJ. "Wait'll I tell Jack!"

"He probably already knows," Rose said.

They all stared at her. "Why would you say that?" Annie asked.

"Because Jack and the doctor were having coffee at the restaurant when I left to come here."

Oh, for heaven's sake. Would Paul tell Jack that he kissed her? She knew without a doubt the answer was yes. Her sisters knew and it wouldn't be long until they shared the news with her father. Pretty soon the whole town would be talking.

"It was just a kiss. A casual kiss between friends, and it won't happen again." A thought that was surprisingly disappointing. "Now I need everyone out of my kitchen so I can start on lunch."

"It'll happen again," CJ quipped over her shoulder as she headed up the stairs to her room in the attic. "I'd put money on it."

This time Annie was happy to let her little sister have the last word, and found herself hoping she was right.

CHAPTER EIGHT

ANNIE WAS FIGHTING off a headache as she cleared away the Sunday morning breakfast dishes. "Please don't tell me I'm catching Rose's cold," she said to the mountains of suds in the kitchen sink. "I don't have time to be sick."

A week had passed since the ill-fated kiss and she hadn't seen Paul, although they had exchanged a handful of polite text messages.

She still had a dozen things to do before it was time to make Sunday dinner, and one of those was to write an illustrated chickens and eggs article for Emily's blog. The idea had been weighing on her since Emily had presented her with the camera, but she had agreed to do it and now she needed to get it done. .

"It's just chickens and eggs," she reminded herself. "A maximum of two hundred and fifty words plus a handful of photographs." Provided she remembered Emily's instructions for using the camera. She looped the strap of the dreaded device around her neck and carried her ancient but still serviceable wicker egg basket to the chicken coop, let herself into the pen and secured the chicken-wire gate behind her.

All five of her motley clutch of laying hens were in the yard, preening in the early morning sunshine, carving the ground—still damp with morning dew—with chicken scratching in their quest for grubs. Annie felt a ridiculous rush of affection for these girls of hers. She set the basket on the ground and fumbled with the camera until it emitted a faint whirring sound and the lens emerged from the case.

In one corner of the enclosure, Ginger had settled herself into a shallow well she had carved into the dirt and was alternately sending up a shower of earth and wiggling on one side, working soil particles into her feathers. Annie snapped several pictures of the dust bath in progress, then switched modes so she could review them.

"Huh," she said to herself. "Not half-bad." One photo in particular actually seemed to capture Ginger's ecstasy as she writhed in the dirt.

Next Annie turned her attention to Salt and Pepper as they squabbled over an earthworm. After several attempts she was especially pleased to see she had managed to snap one photo of the two hens having a tug-of-war with the plump worm one of them had unearthed.

Fluff had settled herself partway up the ramp that led to the raised coop and was preening her wing feathers. Fry, the Rhode Island Red who had been the most recent addition to the flock and who had immediately established herself at the top of the pecking order, was strutting around the perimeter of the pen as though she owned the place. Annie snapped a series of photos of both hens.

Feeling reasonably satisfied with the pictures she'd taken, Annie picked up her basket, let herself out of the pen and went around to the back of the coop. She swung open the access door to the nesting boxes and snapped a few more photos of eggs nestled in straw. All five of her girls had produced an egg for her, and she took one last photo of them grouped in the bottom of her basket. All in a day's work for her and for her girls.

PAUL HAD WANTED to drop by Annie's before now, but somehow a week had passed and he hadn't worked up the courage. They'd exchanged several rounds of text messages and he had hoped she would suggest he pay another visit to the farm, but she hadn't. He hadn't been able to put her or the kiss out of his mind, and he suspected the same might be true for her. He just wished he knew if she felt the same way he did, or if she was only experiencing regret. He knew the longer he put it off, the more awkward seeing her again would be. So he found himself driving along River Road on Sunday morning and before he knew it, he was parked in the roundabout in front the farmhouse.

He knocked lightly on the door, chiding himself for feeling so nervous. Annie was a good friend. The kiss had been an accident, albeit a pleasant one. He just had to make sure it didn't happen again. Besides, he'd found a great book about dinosaurs, which was now tucked under one arm, that he wanted to give to Isaac. He was rehearsing what he would say to Annie when the front door opened and he was greeted instead by her father.

"Paul Woodward, as I live and breathe. Come in, come in. Good to see you."

"Good to see you, sir."

Thomas Finnegan backed his wheelchair away from the door and Paul stepped inside.

"Did you come out to see Annie?"

"I did. And Isaac," he said, hoping it didn't

sound like an afterthought. "I found a book he might like."

Thomas examined the cover. "Dinosaurs, eh? That'll tickle his fancy, all right."

Paul followed the man into the kitchen. The scents of pumpkin and allspice hung in the air, and he suspected the muffins on a glass-domed plate at one end of the kitchen island were responsible for that. With any luck, he'd get to sample one before he left.

"Isaac's down at the stable with his aunt but Annie's just out back." Thomas wheeled himself into place at the kitchen table, where a coffee cup sat next to a newspaper. "She said she was going to the chicken coop to collect the eggs. Been out there a while, though. Must be something besides the eggs keeping her busy."

Paul set the book on the kitchen island. "I'll leave this here, then, and run out to say hello."

With a nod and a knowing smile, Thomas picked up his cup and turned his attention to the newspaper.

Paul stepped through the open French doors onto the veranda and stopped. Across the yard, Annie sat on a white-painted bench. Wearing jeans and a dark blue-and-white plaid shirt, a broad-brimmed straw hat framing her beautiful face, a wicker basket resting beside her on the bench and the chicken coop forming the perfect backdrop, she looked every inch the country woman. A throwback to a time when life was more laid-back, natural, simple. The only modern influence in this vignette was the digital camera in her hands, and she was studying it intently. He was tempted to use his phone to take a picture of her, then thought better of it.

He walked down a few steps to the lawn, strolled toward her and was rewarded with a wide, easy smile when she glanced up and saw him.

"I didn't know you were a photographer." He lowered himself onto the bench, keeping a safe distance between them.

"More like the furthest thing possible. Emily asked me to write a weekly column for her blog and I agreed. It's called *Ask Annie*, and all I have to do is answer a question she gives me. It sounded simple, and she has so much going on. She's working on a book right now and planning her wedding, and with the baby on the way, I said I'd be happy to help any way I can. Then she gave me this." She held up the camera for inspection. "I have no idea how it works. All I can do is turn it on and snap a picture."

"Can I take a look?" Paul reached for the

camera. She happily relinquished it, and he managed to take it without getting his fingers tangled with hers. He quickly scrolled through the pictures she'd taken and with each shot, he turned his head to compare the photos with her subjects. "Annie, these are good. Really good."

He could tell she didn't believe him.

"I mean it. This one, for example." He leaned a little closer and angled the camera so they could both see the monitor.

"Oh, that's Ginger giving herself a dust bath."

"Yes, but it's more than that. It's humorous and filled with…" He wanted to say *love*, but could anyone really love a chicken?

"Affection?" Annie asked.

"Yes, absolutely."

"That's good, then, because I'm really very fond of these girls."

And apparently he was wrong. Love might be overstating it, but apparently some people felt fond affection for a dusty chicken.

The next photo featured a bizarre-looking bundle of white fluff that vaguely resembled the shape of a chicken.

"That's Fluff," Annie said. "She's a timid little thing, which puts her at the bottom of the pecking order, but she's very good-natured about it."

"She's aptly named." He studied each of the photos and listened to Annie's vivid descriptions of the two leghorns she called Salt and Pepper, and the Rhode Island Red whose name was Fry. Isaac named them, she explained, and at the time Fry arrived on the scene, her son had chosen the name because fried chicken was his favorite food.

"We only eat their eggs," Annie quickly explained. "Fry is not going to end up being dinner."

Paul laughed. "I'd say you've just written your first blog post."

"Do you really think so?"

"Absolutely. These pictures are perfectly suited to everything you just told me. You just have to write it down."

"Emily wants me to say something about eggs, too."

"Maybe that can be next week's article."

A smile lit up Annie's face and for a second or two, he thought she might hug him. Or maybe that was wishful thinking. Instead she took the camera from him, stood and picked up the basket of eggs. "Let's go inside. I have freshly baked muffins, and I can put on a pot of coffee."

He wasn't going to say no to that, or to her incredible baked goods.

"Are you working at the clinic today?" she asked.

"Not today. How's Isaac doing after that fall he had last week?"

"He's fine, just like you said he'd be. Good thing, too, because school started this week. And he's still practicing for the junior rodeo. He and CJ are down at the stable now."

Paul followed her up the steps to the veranda. "Is he happy to be back at school?"

"He is. He loves school and he's especially fond of his teacher this year. Her name is Ms. Potter. Olivia, but she likes to be called Libby. Her mother, Mable Potter, was our high school English teacher. Remember her?"

"I sure do."

"Ms. Potter, Isaac's teacher, told me she has taken her mother to the clinic to have her memory tested and that you referred them to a specialist in Madison."

"That's right. They'll be seeing the doctor who diagnosed my father," Paul said.

"Have a seat," she said. She set the egg basket on the counter next to the sink. "The coffee will be ready in a jiffy."

Paul sat on a stool and watched her while she made coffee. He wished he could walk up behind her, put his arms around her and hold her. For now, he would take what he could get, which, this morning, would be a cup of coffee, a muffin and some good company. He was happy he had shown up when he did because she'd given him the impression she was close to bailing on Emily's blog before she had even given it a try. That would be a real shame because for someone who claimed to be a novice, her photographs had been brilliantly executed.

At his friend Jack's suggestion, he had checked out Emily's *Small Town, Big Hearts* blog. He had found it completely engaging, and Annie's weekly column was going to fit right in. He was sure her photographs would garner some attention, and in his opinion that was exactly what she needed. She was always taking care of everyone else and making sure their needs were met. She deserved some of the limelight for a change.

He was selfishly pleased to see that Annie's father was no longer at the table. Paul knew it was too much to hope for a repeat of last week's kiss, but he was still not-so-secretly glad to have her all to himself.

CHAPTER NINE

AT THE SOUND of Annie's and Paul's footsteps on the veranda off the kitchen, Thomas had hastily wheeled himself out of the kitchen, down the hallway to his bedroom. He knew when it was time to make himself scarce. Paul had come out here specifically to see Annie, to spend time with her. Having coffee with her father would not have been part of his plan, Thomas was sure of that. And if anyone deserved someone's undivided attention and admiration, that person was his Annie.

While she was growing up, there'd been more times than Thomas could count when he'd felt guilty as all get-out for the burden he had placed on her. From the time she was six years old, she had taken responsibility for the care of their family—a single dad in a wheelchair and two small girls, one of them barely a toddler. He'd had little choice but to rely on her, the eldest child, and she had never let him down.

His daughters had grown into amazing

women, and over the years they had teamed up and tried to use themselves as a human shield to protect him from the outside world. They also seemed to think that because he couldn't navigate the stairs, he didn't know what went on in the world of the teenage girls—who eventually grew into women— who were ensconced on the second floor and in the attic. But he had eyes and ears, and he was a lot more tuned in to their tomfoolery and conspiracies than they ever imagined. This past spring, when Emily discovered she was pregnant, was a case in point.

To start with, Isaac had come to him and asked what a "prennancy test" was. No keeping secrets with a six-year-old boy in the house. Seemed to Thomas that pregnancy tests shouldn't be in any young child's vocabulary, but it turned out he'd discovered one in an upstairs bathroom. At first, Thomas had figured it must be Annie's, that she had conceived before Eric's unexpected death.

Then he'd had suspicions about Emily when, as a self-proclaimed caffeine addict, she had abruptly stopped drinking coffee. Those suspicions were confirmed several weeks later when Jack Evans had paid Thomas a visit and asked for his permission to ask her to marry him. It had been touch-

and-go for a while there, Emily being the classic middle child, full of unwarranted insecurities and longing for things she could never have while the perfect man was carrying a ring in his pocket and wearing his heart on his sleeve. Emily was settled now, and it was Annie's turn for a little romance.

Paul Woodward was back in town and this was his second visit to the farm in a week. A visit to Annie, to be precise. Didn't take a mind reader to figure out what was going on in that fellow's head. Paul and Eric had been best friends, though. Eric had been a good man, no question about it. A good husband and a wonderful father. Annie had all but revered her husband and those feelings should have been mutual, but Thomas had always felt Eric was a little too self-absorbed to reciprocate. Not that he'd ever breathed a word of that to another living soul, and he certainly had no intention of interfering in the lives of his adult daughters. Still, he'd always thought Annie was being shortchanged.

Paul was an entirely different matter. He looked at Annie like she was the only woman in the world. Thomas was equally certain that his daughter was completely oblivious to the man's feelings. Thomas wouldn't be the one to point out the man's inclination, though. He didn't need to. That's what sisters were for.

Before leaving the kitchen, he had peered through the French doors to see what the two of them were up to. They'd been sitting together on the bench on the edge of the garden by the chicken coop. Annie had been staring intently at the camera she held with both hands. Paul only had eyes for her, his attention focused, as though he was trying to absorb her essence through his pores.

Thomas wished he hadn't wheeled himself out of the kitchen in such a hurry. In his haste, he had left his newspaper on the table and now it was too late to retrieve it. He should have gone to the living room, or maybe out onto the front veranda. From there he could have skirted the house and taken the paved trail down to the stable to see what CJ and Isaac were up to, maybe talked them into taking a trail ride. Instead, he was stuck here until Paul left.

He rolled over to his desk and turned on his laptop to check his email. The first message caught his eye. It was from his old army buddy, Nate Benson. He quickly opened it and perused the content. Nate and his wife, Angie, lived on a ranch in East Texas. They had three adult children, just as Thomas did.

The two of them, Nate and Thomas, had joked when they first met that maybe someday when Nate's sons and Thomas's daughters were grown, they might meet and some of them might even get married. That hadn't happened, of course. Thomas had come home from Desert Storm in a wheelchair, returning to Wisconsin to recuperate on the family farm. Nate had finished out his tour of duty and returned to Texas. Still, they'd kept in touch all these years and Thomas still considered Nate to be one of his best friends.

Two of Nate's boys had joined the service. His eldest was in the marines, currently stationed in Southern California. The youngest was in the army and on his second tour in the Middle East. The middle boy had stayed on the ranch to work with his father.

With carjackings and suicide bombings, military service was potentially even more deadly than in his day. Thomas heaved a huge sigh when he reached the end of the email. No bad news this time. He scrolled to the beginning of the message and began to read again, slowly this time, so he wouldn't miss anything.

Angie's keeping busy these days planning our middle son's—Jake's—wedding to his high-school sweetheart. I'm leaving the decisions about bridesmaid dresses and flower arrangements to Ang and the DIL-to-be. The womenfolk have a lot of opinions about these things but me—not so much.

Thomas cringed a little, knowing how his daughters would react to the *womenfolk* reference. He could relate, though, and he would be sure to tell Nate that Emily and Jack were getting ready to tie the knot.

Course my wife's got her sights set on being a grandmother. Jake and his bride haven't given any indication that's where they're headed, but Ang has been dropping hints all over the place.

Thomas had some news to share in that department as well. Not that he was trying to one-up his old buddy, but he was about to become a grandfather for the second time.

Everything's status quo with our other two boys. Cody's stationed at the marine corps base in San Diego. Matt's on his second tour in the Middle East. He's our biggest worry right now but you know we're praying hard for him.

Thomas felt a tug of sympathy. A second tour was always worse than the first, a bigger worry for the family, since they could count on luck only for so long. And yes, a soldier was more experienced, but sometimes that could work against him or her. In Thomas's case, he was plain grateful his girls had chosen to stay close to home. His biggest concern right now was Annie. He'd been keeping a close eye on her since Eric passed away. Granted it had only been half a year ago and she was still recovering from the shock of her husband's unexpected death, but he wished she would slow down and take care of herself. She was thinner than she ought to be, more tired looking and less like herself. It was as if a spark in her had been extinguished. It might be wrong to wish for it, but he secretly hoped Paul would light it again.

He hit the reply button and spent the next ten minutes using the hunt-and-peck method to respond to Nate's message. Thomas mentioned Emily's wedding coming up at the end of September, and the second grandchild due at Christmastime. With the day-to-day out of the way, he decided it was time to share the difficult news, the thing he had not wanted to open up about until now.

I haven't mentioned Scarlett in a long, long time, but there's news. We found out this summer that she passed away in the spring. Murdered, along with two other women. I wasn't altogether surprised, given what I knew about her lifestyle, but it was a shock to my girls. And maybe an even bigger shock…it turns out I have a stepdaughter and they have a half sister. Her name's Rose. After her mother passed, she came to Riverton to check us out, and Annie convinced her to stay.

Thomas reread what he'd written. To-the-point, honest without being maudlin. He had his suspicions about Rose—the girl was too much like her mother for her own good. But again he mostly worried about Annie. She was quick to see the good in everyone and a little too willing to take on everyone else's problems.

I won't lie to you, Nate. I have misgivings. Rose is her mother's daughter, no two ways about it, and I sure hope Annie isn't taking on too much. Time will tell, I guess.

It was good to hear from you, old friend. We'll have to swap wedding pictures after the big events. You be sure and tell your boy,

Matt, we're praying for him to stay safe and get himself home in one piece.

As Thomas signed off and shut down his laptop, he heard a car door close and an engine start out front. He wheeled himself to the window in time to see Paul drive away. That meant the coast was clear, so he headed for the kitchen. He could use another cup of coffee, and it'd be interesting to hear how the visit went. Annie wasn't one to be too open with her emotions, but he knew how to read her. If she was already busy baking, that was a good sign.

He rolled to a stop at the entrance to the kitchen. Annie stood at the island, creaming butter and sugar in a big yellow crockery bowl.

All right, Thomas thought to himself. *Paul Woodward, you are one lucky man. Let's hope you're also a patient one.*

CHAPTER TEN

OLIVIA POTTER SURVEYED the flat tire on her pearl-gray Lexus LS. After moving to Riverton, she never should have kept the ridiculous, ostentatious car with its obsidian leather interior and every automotive bell and whistle known to mankind. Meanwhile, what was a woman to do? She was reasonably self-sufficient—not that she'd had a choice after her ex had traded her in for a much younger model last year. That said, changing a tire was well outside her skill set.

And in today's outfit, it was completely out of the question. For meet-the-parents' day, she had settled on a red skirt with a softly gathered waist and paired it with a tan-colored tank top and an ivory blazer. She had slipped a set of ivory, tan and gold bangles on her wrist, fastened on matching earrings and completed her outfit with a red-and-ivory handbag. The effect was eye-catching yet still practical for the classroom. The shoes—tan peep-toes with two-inch heels—were not designed for walking, especially not while carrying her handbag and briefcase and an extra-large cupcake carrier.

For as long as she had been a primary teacher, she had purposely set out to create a wardrobe of stylish clothes in bright, happy colors. Before that, and even now when she wasn't in the classroom, her tastes tended to casual styles in a more subdued palette. Her teaching wardrobe, though, served two purposes: dressing up for the classroom boosted her self-confidence; it also set the tone for the students.

That said, she was *not* dressed for auto repairs.

"Well, Libby? What are your options?"

Change her clothes and try to figure out how to change a flat? Not in this lifetime, let alone that it wasn't something she could accomplish before the morning bell.

Call a taxi? Did this sleepy little town even have a cab company? She couldn't remember.

Put on a pair of sensible shoes and walk the eight blocks to school? That was probably her best option.

"No, Libby. That's your only option."

Five minutes later she was hurrying onto Cottonwood Street with her bag slung over her shoulder, her briefcase in one hand and the bright pink cupcake carrier in her hand. Of all the days to have car trouble, it had to be meet-the-parents' day. Just her rotten luck. She picked up her pace so she would arrive at her classroom before the bell, and hoped she wouldn't look completely frazzled when she did.

She had only walked a block and a half and was already wishing her bag was a little lighter when a large white van slowed and stopped. Her heart did the jitterbug when she spotted the lettering scrolled down the side panel.

Finnegan Farm Bed & Breakfast.

It was a silly reaction. It probably wasn't even him. It was probably—

The driver's side window slid down and... there he was. Thomas Finnegan.

"Libby? Libby Potter?"

"Thomas. Hi. Yes, it's me. I mean, I've been Libby Lawrence for a long time but I'm back to using Potter now because, um..." *Oh, Libby. Shut. Up.*

"Good to know." He smiled. No, it was more like a grin.

In spite of the hardships—and she knew he'd been hit with more than his fair share— the years had been gentle on this man. He still had a full head of thick, sandy-brown hair that looked as though it had been effortlessly finger-combed into unruly waves that curled around his temples. Maybe it had. Back in high school he'd had a careless Patrick-Swayze-in-*Dirty-Dancing* thing going on. Some things clearly didn't change. Sometimes they improved with age.

"Need a lift?"

"I'm on my way to the school," she said, then realized she hadn't answered his question.

"So are we." His words and his easy smile caught her off guard. For the first time since he'd stopped, she realized he wasn't alone.

"Hi, Ms. Potter." A little boy waved at her from the passenger seat. "Gramps is coming to parents' day."

"Isaac. Hi." Isaac Larsen was one of her students. His parents were…she wracked her brain. Isaac had told her that his mother, Annie, ran a bed-and-breakfast. His father, Eric, was dead. And he, Isaac, was getting a puppy named Beasley.

Finnegan Farm Bed & Breakfast.

That would make Thomas Finnegan his—

"You're Isaac's grandfather." Which was stating the obvious in the dumbest way possible, given that the child had just called him Gramps.

"That I am. And a stand-in for parents' day, since Isaac's mom is feeling a little under the weather this morning."

Libby found herself wondering how many grandchildren Thomas had, and wished she didn't feel so absurdly envious.

"So, about that ride," he said.

"I'd really like that," she said. "I'm loaded down with books and cupcakes, and my car has a flat."

"Isaac, help Ms. Potter put her things in the back of the van, then you let her sit up front, okay?"

"Sure, Gramps." The boy cheerfully flung open the passenger door and scrambled out as the side door slid open automatically, revealing a wheelchair on a hydraulic lift. Isaac climbed in, dove into the backseat and buckled up. Libby set the cupcake carrier on the floor next to the wheelchair.

"Is that everything?" Thomas asked.

She nodded and stepped back, saw him press a button on the dash and then watched the side door slide shut on its own.

She climbed into the bucket seat next to him, set her book bag on her lap and closed the door.

Thomas sat tall, feet flat on the floor, and

used the hand controls mounted on the steering wheel to accelerate away from the curb.

Libby had wondered how she would feel when she saw him after all these years. She knew he'd been a wheelchair since Desert Storm. She knew his wife had run off soon after he'd come home—unthinkable!—leaving him to raise their three young girls on his own. She had not expected to see him sitting confidently behind the wheel of a car, driving his grandson to school.

"I really appreciate this," she said, annoyed with herself for feeling flustered, unable to think of anything else to say.

"Don't mention it. Isaac's been talking about meet-the-parents' day all weekend." He gave her sideways glance. "This morning his mother woke up with a headache, thinks she might be coming down with a cold, so I volunteered to come along instead."

"That was nice. I hope it's not too much of an inconvenience for you. Especially since, I mean…never mind, I'm sorry." *You idiot! He probably thinks you think that because of the wheelchair—*

Which, truth be told, was exactly what she was thinking.

Thomas, apparently unfazed by her blunder, simply grinned. "I've spent more of my life in that chair than out of it. I drive, as you can see for yourself. I help out around the farm, ride a horse, babysit." He glanced at his grandson in the rearview mirror, eyes brimming with affection.

She was horrified with the direction her thoughts had taken. And she was beyond impressed with him. Horseback riding? She had no idea how he managed that, but seeing him like this: strong, competent and still so ridiculously handsome. She could easily picture him in the saddle. She was sure the image would still be on her mind when she fell asleep that night.

"And that chair—" he angled his head in the direction of the wheelchair "—it cuts a pretty good rug. I danced with Isaac's mother at her wedding, and I'm about to do it again with my middle girl, Emily. Still can't do stairs, though."

She glanced at him sharply, found him laughing, maybe even at her expense. Well, she could hardly fault him for that. She hadn't known what to say, and the reality was that she hadn't had to say anything. Thomas still had the same quirky humor and zest for life he'd had when they were teenagers, when the shy, insecure wallflower she'd been then had secretly pined for the athlete, the leader of the pack and the best-looking boy in school. The first boy she had imagined herself being truly and deeply in love with.

They pulled into a parking space in the lot next to the school.

"Now it's my turn to apologize," he said before she could muster words of her own. "My daughter Annie, Isaac's mom, gets after me for what she calls my 'handicapped humor.' Says it's off-putting for a lot of people."

Libby shook her head. "Not at all," she said, finally finding her voice. "I'm the one who should apologize. I do apologize. I'm so sorry. And now I really do have to get these things to my classroom before the bell rings. I'd offer to stay and help you out, but I can tell that's not necessary."

"Thanks, and you're right. I'll see you inside."

She pushed the door open but before she could step out, Thomas took her hand. "It's good to see you in Riverton, Libby. And good to see you looking so...good."

She flushed at the compliment, not sure what to make of it.

"Thank you. You look good, too."

She gathered her things and hurried into the school, ridiculously pleased by the simple compliment while warning herself not to make more of it than it was. Back in high school, everyone had known everyone else. That was both the beauty and the curse of living in a small town. But like any high school, there had been the typical teenage hierarchy: the jocks who swaggered through the hallways and the gorgeous girls who cheered them on; the brainiacs who owned the honor roll and competed for debate trophies and SAT scores; the kids who struggled with school and sometimes life in general, spending the bulk of their time in detention, smoking cigarettes and drinking bootlegged beer behind the rec center every Friday night.

In those days, Libby hadn't fit into any of the groups. She had been painfully shy and unsure of herself, with no real friends and no idea how to make any. To make matters worse, she was the daughter of the school's no-nonsense English teacher. Mable Potter had doled out top marks to the students who worked hard in her classes, and detentions and failing grades to those who sloughed off. For Libby, being in the first group had been the only option. Thomas had good-naturedly fit into the second, usually handing in assignments after half-heartedly finishing them in the detention hall.

Now he was a family man, a grandfather,

a war hero, a paraplegic. He had never done anything by half measures, and being in a wheelchair hadn't changed that.

THOMAS WHEELED HIMSELF into the school and down the corridor to his grandson's classroom. Only the second graders were hosting meet-the-parents' day, but the whole school was abuzz with the extra energy. A group of mostly moms milled in the hallway outside the door to the classroom, but the crowd parted to let him through. In many ways, the wheelchair was like a free pass, and it was one he didn't like to overuse.

"Good morning, ladies." He knew many of these young mothers because his daughters had grown up with them.

"Hello, Mr. Finnegan."

"Good to see you."

"Where's Annie this morning?"

"She's coming down with a cold," he told them. Not surprising, either, given how much time she spent with Rose. He understood Annie's need to take care of everyone around her, but it when it came to that young woman, he wished his eldest daughter shared her younger sisters' innate reluctance to put too much trust in their long-lost half sister.

Inside the classroom, the desks had been

rearranged to make room for extra seating. Three little girls hovered around Libby, listening eagerly to the instructions she was giving them. Four boys, Isaac among them, were kibitzing at the opposite end of the room. Boys will be boys, Thomas thought.

Many times over the years, he had wondered what it would have been like to raise a son. Not that he ever would have traded his three beautiful daughters for all the sons in the world. They had been the center of his life even before their mother had walked out on them. Only when Isaac was born had he acknowledged—privately, of course—that a deep-seated need had been filled. He watched Isaac now, with his mother's stunning good looks and his father's passion for life, and felt the kind of love that accompanies a deeply rooted sense of kinship.

Across the classroom, Libby turned away from her cluster of students and locked gazes with him. Then she smiled and walked toward him.

"Thank you again for the lift, Thomas. You're a lifesaver."

"Don't even mention it. Anytime you need a hand with anything, let me know. As long as it's not changing a tire."

This time his offbeat humor made her

laugh. "I'm guessing you'd figure out a way to change a tire if you had to."

"Like making a call to Triple A."

This time they laughed together. He liked that she was comfortable having this conversation. He couldn't remember the last time he'd had a conversation with an attractive woman. Come to think of it, it had been a long time since he'd found any woman attractive. Libby Potter—the shy, awkward girl he'd gone to school with but had really only known as the English teacher's daughter—had matured into a graceful, elegant woman. She wore her hair—the same shade of chestnut with subtle hints of auburn—in a no-nonsense bob that suited her face and gave her a youthful appearance. Moments ago, he had watched her slip off her suit jacket and drape it over the back of her chair at the front of the classroom. Now she stood there in a red skirt and sleeveless beige top that were both classy and appropriate for a second-grade classroom, and still managed to cause a hitch in his breathing.

And there's no fool like an old fool, he reminded himself. Women felt many things for a man in a chair—pity, indifference, sometimes even resentment—but never attraction. No. His heartthrob days ended the day the earth had exploded around him, beneath him, within him.

He picked up the Tupperware container resting on his lap and handed it to Libby.

"Annie baked a batch of oatmeal-raisin cookies. And she sends her regrets, of course."

"We all thank her for these," Libby said, accepting the contribution. "Isaac says his mom is the best cook in the world."

"Well, now, he has that right. Annie feeds us well."

"After school started, she invited me and my mother to Sunday dinner. That was very generous of her, but we would hate to impose."

Thomas felt himself brighten. "Feeding family and friends is never an imposition. You should come. My daughter Emily and her fiancé, Jack Evans, always join us. I know Emily and your mother have formed a special friendship."

Libby laughed. "That they have. Before I was able to move home, knowing Emily was checking in on my mother was a godsend."

Isaac tugged on his forearm. "Gramps, move your wheelchair over here where the parents are sitting. Me and my friends cleared a space for you."

Libby smoothed a hand over the boy's head. "That was a really good idea, Isaac. Thank you for doing that." Suddenly all business, she clapped her hands twice and called out, "Children. Can I have your attention, please?"

The energized buzz in the room quieted to a low hum as the students quickly turned their full attention to their teacher.

"Welcome, parents. And grandparents," she added with a smile. "Thank you for joining us this morning. Your children and I want to welcome you to the second grade at Riverton Elementary. Please take a seat." She waved at the double row of primary-school-size chairs arranged in a semicircle at the rear of the classroom.

As mothers laughingly settled themselves onto the too-small chairs, Thomas rolled into the space that had been readied for him at the end of the row. For the next thirty minutes, he and the other adults were entertained by a science experiment that created weather in a mason jar, an art exhibit of boldly colored finger paintings, an explanation of how a terrarium works, the introduction of Sampson, the classroom's guinea pig, and finally a song about greasy, grimy gopher guts. If anyone besides Thomas thought the song choice juxtaposed with the class rodent was a bit on the maudlin side, they didn't let on.

After a few words from Libby, it was time for refreshments and the classroom was once again abuzz with adult conversation intermingled with high-pitched children's voices. At the sound of the recess bell, the children cleared out, leaving the grownups to have a few final words with one another and Ms. Potter.

Thomas watched her move from one group of mothers to another, then realized she was making her way toward him.

"It's been so good to see you again, Thomas. It's been a long time."

"It has." Too long, he decided. "I hope you'll accept Annie's invitation to dinner." He meant it. He'd like to see her again. To be honest, he'd rather spend time with her alone. But he had no idea how a guy his age, and in a wheelchair, no less, asked a woman like Libby out on a date. What was the point? She would only say no. Dinner with the family was safer. "It'll be good to catch up."

"I'd like that." And in spite of her lightly applied makeup, he could see she was blushing.

Huh. Maybe he'd work up to that date, after all. It's not like he and Libby were teenagers, and it didn't have to be a *date* date. He could invite her to meet him for coffee somewhere—neutral territory—and see where that took them. He already knew where he wanted it to go. Coffee, and just the two of them, would give him a chance to figure out if she was willing to go along for the ride.

CHAPTER ELEVEN

AFTER SPENDING an entire week recuperating from a cold—and now convinced she had caught the bug from Rose—Annie saw Isaac safely onto the school bus on Monday morning and pulled her shopping list from beneath a magnet on the fridge. She skimmed the page to make sure she hadn't forgotten anything, added "chicken feed" and tucked it into her handbag. She had been up early and baked a batch of lemon-cranberry muffins—Paul's favorite. But then he'd texted to say he wouldn't make it out to the farm that morning.

Taking the early shift at the clinic. Should be able to make it tomorrow. Paul.

Feeling disappointed didn't make sense, but that didn't stop her from feeling it.

"Dad?" she called down the hallway. After breakfast he always spent an hour or so in his room, checking email and reading online news reports. "I'm going into town to run errands. CJ's at the stable and has her phone with her if you need anything."

"I'll be fine, Annie."

Of course he would. Monday was her errand day and she always spent the morning in town, and everything at the farm was always fine when she returned. "I'll be back in time to make lunch."

Thomas appeared in the doorway of his room. "Why don't you treat yourself to lunch in town?"

"Oh, I shouldn't." She really shouldn't. "I don't have anything ready for you and CJ."

"That kitchen is full of food, and Cassie Jo and I are quite capable of putting some of it on a plate. You should get together with one of your friends. Maybe that young Woodward fellow is free."

"Really, Dad?" Bad enough her sisters were practically tripping over themselves to push her and Paul together, but now her father was in on it? His expression of mock innocence made her laugh out loud. "I am not asking Paul to have lunch with me."

"What about Emily? You could have lunch with her, talk about wedding plans."

That was actually a good idea. If she had

thought of it sooner, she would have left something ready for her father and her sister.

"Call Emily. CJ and I will make ourselves sandwiches," he said as though he was reading her thoughts.

"Fine. I'll call Emily. There's a fresh loaf of bread in the pantry, ham and cheese in the..."

But her father had returned to his room and quietly closed the door and she was left talking to herself. He was right. They could take care of themselves and she did deserve to treat herself to lunch out. On her way out to the car, she dialed Emily's number before she changed her mind.

PAUL'S DECISION TO take the early shift at the clinic had an upside: his father. Geoff was reasonably cheerful after a good night's sleep and a breakfast of soft-boiled eggs and wheat toast cut into soldiers—buttered, crusts removed, and cut into fingers. This was a throwback to his childhood, having been brought up by a British mother whose rigid ways had extended all the way to her stiff upper lip. As a child, Paul had seen very little of his paternal grandmother and hadn't liked her much when he did.

The downside of the early shift was not starting his day over coffee in Annie's kitchen. For the past week, she hadn't been feeling well and he had used that as a reason to check in on her. Those meetings were fast becoming the favorite part of his daily routine.

By eleven o'clock, he was updating the last patient's chart when his cell phone buzzed.

Can I buy my best man lunch? Riverton Bar & Grill, 12:30? Jack.

Paul was more than ready to take a break and the timing was perfect because it gave him a chance to drop by the house to check on his father and fix him some lunch. Paul could have the old man fed and settled into his recliner for an afternoon of TV talk shows and intermittent naps and still have time to meet his friend at the appointed time.

Best offer I've had all morning. See you there. Paul.

A better offer would have been lunch with Annie but she would never agree. According to her, they were still "just friends." Meeting him at the café would seem too much like a date, and that wasn't going to happen. At least not anytime soon.

ANNIE'S LAST STOP of the morning was Henderson's Hardware. She had just enough time to pick up the remaining items on her list and load them into her station wagon before she met Emily for lunch at the Riverton Bar & Grill. She pushed her cart along the aisles, tossing in boxes of lids for her canning jars, a package of lightbulbs, a roll of duct tape for her father, ticking items off her list as she went. What was it with men and duct tape? Her father claimed he could fix anything with a pocketknife and a roll of tape. She briefly considered buying a roll with the cupcake print—he was not a fan of cupcakes, saying he didn't understand why anyone would settle for a small cake when they could have a large one—but she decided he was unlikely to see the humor in it, so settled for the original gray instead. She dragged bags of dog chow and chicken feed onto the bottom of her cart, finally picking up the new push broom CJ had requested for the stable.

Mel and Marjorie Henderson were waiting for her behind the counter. Mel and his wife had taken over the store from his father, and now their son managed the lumberyard and their two grandsons worked as stock boys on weekends.

"Annie, it's so good to see you," Marjorie

said, ringing in items and adding them to Annie's canvas shopping bag. "How's everything at Finnegan Farm these days?"

"Good. Busy, of course, with Emily's wedding coming up in a few weeks."

"That's right. We heard all about it the last time your father was in with Isaac. Leave those bags of feed on the cart," Marjorie said. "Mel can load them in your car. What a handsome little boy you have there. The spitting image of his father. Oh. Oh, dear, I hope you don't mind me saying that, after what happened to your husband."

"Not at all. We talk about Eric all the time." Annie did her best to muster a reassuring smile but she was actually remembering something her father had once said about Marjorie, *That woman could talk the hind leg off a mule.*

Mel stepped around the counter and loaded Annie's shopping bag into the cart. "Isaac took a real shine to Izzie's puppies when he was here."

"He hasn't stopped talking about them since he saw them." Annie had been doing her best to ignore the enclosure behind the counter, where a black-and-white border collie was sprawled with her puppies on a red plaid blanket. She looked at them now and tried to harden her heart. One of the pups had woken up and was stumbling across its litter mates. "He's desperate to have one, but I don't know. Puppies need a lot of attention and I'm afraid I don't have the time to devote to training one right now."

Annie paid for her purchases and dropped her wallet back into her handbag.

Mel swung the cart toward the door, then paused. "If your boy really wants a dog and you don't want a puppy, then we just might have a solution for you."

"You do?"

"One of the pups from Izzie's litter last year was adopted by a family here in town. Unfortunately, their toddler has developed an allergy to pet dander and they can't keep him. He's housebroken, knows basic commands. Sit, stay, that sort of thing. And he's looking for a new home."

"Oh." She did not need to be hearing this right now. When she'd said "we'll see" to Isaac, she had hoped to buy some time, come up with a good argument for not getting another dog right now. She had also hoped if she stalled long enough, the puppies might find other homes. Mel's offer was a deal changer. This gave her the chance to fill a void in her son's life without making hers unmanageable. "Thanks for letting me know. I'll think about it."

"His name's Bentley," Mel said. "Nice dog, real good with kids."

What little resistance Annie had slipped away. "That's good to know. I'll talk it over with my family tonight and give you a call tomorrow."

She unlocked her car and, as he stowed everything in the back, she checked the time. Perfect. All her errands were done with five minutes to spare.

"Thanks, Mel." She locked her car and set off down the block and across the street to the café, where she was meeting Emily for lunch. Her father was right. Annie worked hard and she deserved to treat herself once in a while.

PAUL STIRRED CREAM into his coffee. Morning coffee with Annie would always be his first choice. And while lunch with Jack was a definite second place, Paul was glad for the invitation. Their lives in Chicago had been fast-paced and they had both been driven to progress in their respective careers. Now here they were in sleepy Riverton, finally making a concerted effort to stay in touch regularly.

Annie's half sister, Rose, wasn't working the lunch shift today. This was a good thing, he decided. They didn't need her eavesdropping on their conversation.

His cell phone pinged with an incoming message.

Something's come up at the station. Can't make it after all. Sorry, buddy. Jack.

Well, that was disappointing, but understandable. Paul was debating whether he should order lunch or just finish his coffee and leave, when Annie walked in.

ANNIE GLANCED AROUND the interior of the café. No sign of Emily yet. Then her gaze landed on the last person she expected to see.

"Paul, hi." She looked as surprised to see him as he was to see her. "What are you doing here?"

"I was meeting Jack for lunch but he can't make it. What about you?"

"I'm having lunch with Emily. We're going to do some wedding planning."

"I see. Would you like to join me?"

"You want to listen to us talk about food and flowers?"

He laughed. "Okay, not really, but you're welcome to sit with me until she gets here."

"Sure." She slid into the booth and sat

across from him. "What time was Jack supposed to be here?"

"Twelve thirty, but then something came up at the station at the last minute."

"I see."

"What time is Emily supposed to be here?"

"Twelve thirty."

"Ah. I see."

Did he? she wondered. Because she was pretty sure she did. This was a setup. She took out her cell phone and checked for messages. Sure enough, there was a text from Emily, sent a minute ago.

Can't make it. Sorry. My publisher called. Needs me to take care of something right away. TTYL. Em.

"Everything okay?" Paul asked.

"It seems my sister can't make it, either. Something to do with the book she's working on."

"So we've both been stood up?"

No, we've been set *up.* "I guess we have," she said.

He handed her a menu. "Then we might as well order some lunch."

She scanned the menu, glancing up at Paul several times, finding him doing the same.

Each time, their gazes connected for a split second before they quickly looked at their menus. This was silly. And awkward. Did he suspect her family of matchmaking? Or did he think this was purely a coincidence?

How could they? Even her father had been in on this, encouraging her to stay in town for lunch. Emily had readily agreed to meet, and then she'd promptly dragged Jack into it. As for CJ, she had no obvious role in this particular caper, but Annie knew she was involved. She may even have been the mastermind.

Annie should have worn something more appropriate. She had pulled a pale blue hoodie over her T-shirt and she was still wearing the same jeans she'd worn while making breakfast, vacuuming the house and cleaning out the chicken coop. And because she had planned to run errands and have lunch with her sister—in other words, nothing special—she had only waved a little mascara at her lashes and dabbed her lips with gloss. The gloss was long gone.

Paul had rolled the sleeves of his white dress shirt almost to the elbows, but it still looked crisp in spite of his having worked at the clinic all morning. He wore a paisley tie in subdued shades of dark green and brown. A perfect match for his eyes, she thought, and wondered if he had chosen it for himself. Maybe he hadn't. Maybe a woman he'd been dating in Chicago had picked it out for him. Not that it mattered who he had dated then, and she was sure he wasn't seeing anyone now. Jack wouldn't have joined in on this matchmaking conspiracy if his friend had another woman in his life.

"Annie?"

"What?"

"Do you know what you'd like to order?"

"Oh." She looked up to find Paul and the waitress, Heather Wilson, watching her intently. Heather was married to Jesse Wilson, who had dropped out of high school the year before Annie, Paul, Jack and Eric had graduated. Jesse worked at the feedlot in Pepin and spent a good chunk of his paycheck on booze and cigarettes. He and Heather lived in the Cottonwood Trailer Park on the east side of town. Jesse's sister, Becky, was a hairdresser and owned the Clip 'n' Curl, the hub of Riverton's rumor mill. By that afternoon, everyone who went in to have their hair done would know Annie Finnegan Larsen had been seen having lunch with Dr. Paul Woodward. By tonight, everyone in the trailer park would have heard, and by this time tomorrow, the whole town would be talking.

"Do you have a lunch special?"

"Liver and onions."

The thought alone was enough to make her gag. "I'll have the BLT wrap."

"Soup, salad or fries?"

"The salad, please."

"Ranch, Italian or balsamic vinaigrette?"

"The vinaigrette. And coffee, please."

After unsmilingly peppering Annie with options, Heather turned on the charm for Paul. "And what can I get for the handsome doctor?" She was all but purring.

If Paul noticed, he wasn't letting on. He smiled at Annie instead. "The BLT wrap with a salad sounds good. Make that two." He closed the menu and handed it to Heather without making eye contact.

She snagged Annie's menu and hustled off to the kitchen in a huff. Paul's slight would do nothing to dampen the rumor mill but Annie didn't care. If it wasn't for the table between them, she would have hugged him.

"Did we go to school with her?" Paul asked.

"We did. That's Heather Hobbart—Wilson now, since she married Jesse Wilson."

"Okay, him I remember. Jack, Eric and I got ourselves into some trouble, hanging out with him."

"Oh, right. I'd forgotten about that. Didn't you have to spend a couple of Saturdays washing cruisers at the police station?"

Paul shook his head. "More than a couple. And our parents grounded us for a month. It taught us all a lesson—several lessons, actually. One, egging police cars wasn't cool. Two, Jesse wasn't cool. That's when Jack developed an interest in police work, though, and look at him now."

"I know. We're so proud of him and so happy for Emily. They're going to be amazing parents."

"I'm pretty sure it runs in your family. Your dad's a good man and I see his good traits in all of you."

He reached across the table and patted her hand just as Heather reappeared with a cup of coffee for Annie.

Wonderful, she thought. More fuel for the rumor mill. But at the same time, his touch was reassuring and she was grateful for that. He didn't take his hand away until after Heather left, and she could have sworn his eyes actually twinkled. He'd done the whole touching-hands-across-the-table thing on purpose, and Annie surprised herself by feeling glad he had.

"How's your father doing?" she asked, deciding a change of subject was in order.

"He has ups and downs and we're taking things day by day. His specialist in Madison has him on some new medication that seems to be helping."

"That's a relief for you, I'm sure." She sipped her coffee, which was surprisingly good. She thought again of what Mel had said about the dog in need of a home. "There's something I'd like your opinion on. I'm giving some thought to letting Isaac have a dog of his own. What do you think?"

"Ah, yes. One of the border collie puppies from Henderson's."

"He told you about it?"

Paul laughed. "He's mentioned it a time or ten."

Annie laughed along with him. "He's definitely obsessed."

"Research shows kids who are pet owners learn responsibility, that's a given. There's also a lot of evidence to show they're healthier, happier, have better self-esteem and maybe even perform better in school."

Annie sighed. She knew these things intuitively, but she still questioned whether or not this was the right time to add another animal to the menagerie. "We have the horses and chickens," she said. "And Chester."

"True, but CJ manages the stable and the riding programs and looks after the horses, and you take care of the chickens."

"True, and poor Chester is too old and arthritic to be a companion for an energetic little boy."

Heather appeared and set two plates on the table. "Here you go," she said, smiling at Paul. "Can I get you anything else?"

"Looks good." He gave her a polite smile in return and shifted his attention to Annie. "Do you need anything?"

"No, thank you. This looks really good."

"Well then, I'll leave the two of you to enjoy your lunch," Heather said before moving on to another table.

Paul bit into his wrap and gave it a nod of approval.

Annie seldom ate anything she hadn't prepared herself and she had to admit the food looked amazing. She took a bite of hers and agreed. It was as delicious as it looked.

"So," Paul said after devouring some of his food, "it sounds as though you've pretty much settled on the puppy."

"Not necessarily." She explained the situation with the older dog that was housebroken and crate-trained. "And he's graduated from obedience 101, which is an added bonus. Isaac is too young to take on the responsibility of training a puppy and I don't have time to do a proper job of it myself. I've had the B and B on hiatus so I can help with the wedding, but I'll be reopening later in the fall, in time for the holidays."

"Sounds like a win-win—for you, Isaac and the dog."

"So you think I should do it?"

"Oh, no," he said. "Picture me sitting on the fence here. Get the dog, don't get the dog. It's your decision."

"Because that way if I make the wrong decision, I have to own it."

"Pretty much." He grinned at her. "Seriously, though, there is no wrong decision. If this is the right time for you to get a dog, you'll know. If it doesn't feel right, then you'll wait."

"So you're saying I should relax and go with the flow."

"Pretty much."

Annie had never been good at accepting advice—yes, she could admit that about herself—but she'd needed to hear this. "Thank you," she said. "That's the best non-advice advice anyone's ever given me."

She held up her coffee cup and he raised his and the rims clinked.

"These wraps are really good," she said, starting on the second half. "So tell me, did you have pets when you were growing up?"

"Have you forgotten I was raised by Geoff Woodward in a home his wife had been expected to keep just so? Or else? So, no, there were no pets. Not a lot of anything that resembled family fun."

Annie reached across the table and covered his hand with hers. She couldn't stop herself. "Eric told me it wasn't a very…happy house. I'm sorry."

But Paul was smiling. "It wasn't all bad. My mother did what she could to soften his sternness. She used to tell me and my sister we were lucky in some ways because when we grew up and got married, it was our chance for a do-over. To make a happy home."

"She actually said that?"

"She did." The affection he still had for his mom, even though she was no longer with him, was written all over his face.

"I wish I'd had a chance to get to know her. I think I would have liked her."

"And I know the feeling would have been mutual."

Slowly, she drew her hand away and caught a glimpse of her watch as she did. "Oh, my. Look at the time. I should go. My family will start to worry."

He leaned across the table. "Can I let you in on a little not-so-secret secret?" he asked, shielding his mouth with the back of his hand.

"What's that?"

"Your family knows *exactly* where you are."

So he had figured out what her father and sisters and Jack were up to. "I'm sorry. I don't know what they were thinking."

He pushed his empty plate to one side, leaned back in the booth, crossed his arms. "How does this sound? Next time we should make this easy for them."

"Easy?" She hated to say it, but they hadn't had to put much effort in to this.

"You do errands in town every Monday, right?"

"I do. How did you know?"

He avoided the question with a shrug.

"I'm that predictable?"

"I'd call it reliable, dependable," he said. They both laughed.

"Thank you for that. So, what did you have in mind for—"

Heather chose that moment to appear.

"Will there be anything else? No? Just the check then?"

She dropped the slip on the table and sashayed away. Annie wished she had the nerve to toss her crumpled napkin at the woman's back. She reached for her purse instead.

"I'll get it." Paul tossed a couple of bills on the table. "About next Monday. How about we meet here after my shift at the clinic and after you finish your errands? That way if they try to pull a fast one on us, wc can tell them we already have plans. What do you say?"

"I say…" She'd like to say the whole lot of them deserved to be one-upped but the truth was, she no longer cared. The food here was surprisingly good and the conversation even better. "I say I'm in."

He stood, extended a hand to help her up. "Then it's a date."

Speaking of *dates*… "Everyone's coming for dinner on Sunday. Even my son's teacher will be there. We'd love to have you join us, too."

He held the door for her as they left the restaurant. "I'll be there. What about morning coffee this week?"

"Drop by anytime you'd like."

"Great. I'll text you when I have a free

morning." He glanced up and down the sidewalk. "Where are you parked?"

"You do not have to walk me to my car," she said as they left the café.

"Maybe not, but I wouldn't be much of gentleman if I didn't."

The sentiment made her smile. Paul was the dictionary definition of a gentleman and she was lucky to have him for a friend. He planned to drop by again for coffee, he was coming for Sunday dinner, and they were meeting for lunch again next Monday. She wouldn›t call it a date, exactly, but she was secretly pleased he had. She was equally grateful to her family for the set-up, although not in a million years would she give them the satisfaction of hearing her say so.

CHAPTER TWELVE

LIBBY HAD BEEN invited to Sunday night dinner at the Finnegan family farmhouse, and she felt as nervous as a schoolgirl on a first date. She hadn't been on a date in more than thirty years. And now she fervently wished the thought hadn't crossed her mind because it made her feel just plain old. She glanced at her reflection in the rearview mirror and tried not to notice the telltale lines at the corners of her eyes. The thing was, though, that Thomas had those lines, too, and they looked good on him, especially when he smiled.

She reversed out of the driveway, easing over the curb so as not to disturb the contents of the big Tupperware cake carrier on the passenger seat. Being invited to Sunday dinner was intimidating. Having grown up an only child, and then having a childless marriage, her family dinners had been quiet and small.

She gave the cake a nervous glance. Thomas's daughter, Annie, had a reputation for being a stellar cook and baker—the goodies she'd sent on meet-the-parents' day had been delicious. And Libby was sure tonight's dinner table would further attest to Annie's reputation.

Still, Libby couldn't show up empty-handed, so she had enlisted her mother's help. Mable's signature red velvet cake was known and loved by everyone in town, and in the back of her mind, Libby couldn't shake the old saying that the way to a man's heart was through his stomach. It was a silly notion, wishing her now-middle-aged, high-school crush might be willing to give his heart to a recently divorced schoolteacher who hadn't been able to catch his eye when she was young and wrinkle-free.

Of course—and this time she avoided examining her crow's feet as she exchanged glances with herself in the mirror—a woman could do a lot worse than having a man like Thomas Finnegan as a friend. And he had suggested the two of them meet for coffee sometime, she reminded herself. He had also encouraged her to accept Annie's invitation to Sunday dinner. Those had to count for something.

The invitation had been extended to her mother as well, but at the last minute, Mable Potter said she was feeling poorly and decided it was best to stay home. She insisted Libby go without her, saying it would do her a world of good to get out into the Riverton community again. Libby had agreed, pushing aside the niggling guilt at leaving her mother alone because she looked forward to an evening spent in the company of Thomas Finnegan. Besides, Mable had been managing on her own until Libby had moved from St. Paul. Her mother also had Banjo, a rascal of a dog of indeterminate breeding and a definite lack of manners, for company. So Libby assured herself she was entitled to a night out. Her mother would be fine on her own.

The drive along River Road to the farm was always a pleasant one and today, now late in the summer, was no exception. The Finnegans' gazebo came into view and she slowed to admire it, noticing as she did that it had been outfitted with a wheelchair ramp. It would have to be, of course. She had heard rumors that Thomas often marshaled the Riverboat Days parade on horseback. She, for one, looked forward to seeing that next year. Just thinking about it sped up her pulse.

She signaled and carefully pulled into the long driveway leading to the house, so as not to send the cake sliding off the car seat. It was impressive that a man in a wheelchair managed to maintain all of this property.

"Stop it," she said to herself. "Stop it right now. He's not merely a 'man in a wheelchair.' He's Thomas Finnegan." He was heartthrob handsome, a loving family man with a big heart, a genuine smile and a wide circle of friends. He was smart and funny and had already proven there wasn't anything he couldn't do. Except stairs, she remembered with a smile.

No, Thomas Finnegan wasn't just a man in a wheelchair.

As a teenage boy, he had unknowingly stolen her heart, and she was well aware that she was in danger of surrendering it once again. This time was different. This time she had a feeling he might be falling for her, too. She had no idea how that would work, being with a man in a…being with a paraplegic. But did it matter? Not one bit, she realized. If she was lucky enough for a romantic relationship to develop, they would figure it out.

She pulled into the roundabout in front of the house and parked next to Thomas's van. A number of other cars were parked there as well. A dark-blue sedan she knew to be Annie's because she'd seen her pick up her son after school. A large white truck with

Finnegan Farm Equestrian Program embla-
zoned on the door. There was also a black
Jeep with Illinois plates, a silver-gray BMW
two-seater, a red-and-white Mini with Morris's Barbershop painted on the door and a
late model Honda Civic that may have been
black at one time, its dull finish marred by
an untold number of fender benders.

She hesitated before getting out of her car.
Exactly how many people had been invited
to this *family* dinner? She glanced at the
welcoming veranda, where a big yellow dog
lay sleeping at the front door, and decided it
didn't matter. She had been invited, and she
intended to make the most of the opportunity.

FROM HIS PLACE at the head of the dinner table,
Thomas surveyed the faces around him and
took in the lively conversations abundantly
laced with laugher. Life was good. At times
in the past it hadn't always seemed so, but
seeing his family and extended family come
together like this—this was good.

Impossible as it might seem, Annie always
seemed to outdo herself. Tonight's prime rib
had been roasted to perfection, the mashed
potatoes whipped to a cloudlike consistency,
the gravy rich and dark, just the way he liked
it. And the Yorkshire pudding… He savored

a forkful. Who needed gourmet fare when there was food like this in the world?

And then there was the company. His girls, their friends and significant others—as they liked to call them—his grandson. And tonight, a newcomer. Like everything else about the dinner, Annie was in charge of seating arrangements and she had seated Libby immediately to his right...probably because they were the two old-timers at the table and his daughter assumed they had enough in common to maintain polite conversation. To his left sat Emily and Jack.

Paul hadn't fared so well. Annie had seated him a safe distance away from where she sat at the opposite end of the table. At first he seemed to have taken it in stride, but then he had made the bold move of asking Fred Morris to swap places with him so he could sit next to Annie. Thomas could have hugged him.

"Does your family really do this every Sunday?" Libby asked.

"Every Sunday. Since I was a boy younger than Isaac, I have memories of those dinners. My mother was an amazing cook and Annie has inherited her skills. For a few years there—after my mother passed away and before Annie was old enough to prepare anything on such a grand scale—the dinners were pretty basic. You'd be surprised by what a guy in a chair and three young girls can do with a canned ham and some crushed pineapple."

Libby's smile made him a little breathless. "Oh, I don't think I'd be surprised at all."

Maybe not, but he could think of several things that might surprise her. "By the time Annie started high school, she had started pouring over her grandmother's cookbooks, pulling out the good china. Wasn't long before her boyfriend, Eric, and Emily's friend Fred started hanging out here. Teenage boys are not known to turn down a meal."

"I'll take your word for it. I must confess I don't have much experience with teen boys," she said. "Not even when I was a teenager myself."

The confession made her blush, and Thomas found himself grinning. "You're one of the lucky ones, then. They don't have a lot going for them."

Libby savored a forkful of mashed potatoes before she spoke again. "Annie's an amazing cook. And from what I've seen of her with her son, she's a great mom, too. You must be so proud of her."

Thomas glanced at his eldest daughter,

watched her scoop buttered peas onto her son's plate, her eyes and her actions brimming with tenderness. Proud barely scratched the surface.

"I am. I'm proud of all my girls." He glanced around the table, realized all three of his daughters were unabashedly watching him and Libby. As he caught them at it, they exchanged a look, a nod, a smile. Favorable ones.

When their mother had packed her bags and headed for the door, they had been too young to have memories of him and Scarlett as a couple. After he'd come home from the Middle East in this chair, they hadn't lived like a couple anyway. In all these years, tonight was the first time they'd seen him with a woman, a potential love interest. Now there was an old-fashioned phrase, and yet it seemed appropriate. In all those years, this was the first time he'd found a woman who had the potential to become a love interest.

CJ—his beautiful Cassie Jo—leaned toward them, grinning. "Do you like horses, Ms. Potter?"

"Please, call me Libby. And yes, I do. I guess. I mean, I've never ridden one but I do love to watch equestrian events—especially show jumping at the Olympic level—on television. The riders always look so elegant and they make it look so easy, although I know it isn't."

CJ picked up her water glass, swirled it until the ice cubes made a musical sound. "You should come out sometime and I'll show you around the stable. And I'd be happy to give you a lesson or two if you're interested."

"Oh." Libby touched her napkin to the corners of her mouth. "I'd love to look around. I'm not sure about actually riding, though. I think I'm a little too old to take up that sport."

Thomas knew his youngest well enough to know where she was going with this.

"My dad's *really* old and he rides," she said with a wink and a grin.

"CJ!" Annie admonished, but everyone else laughed, Thomas included.

"Yes," he said. "I'm pretty much the poster boy for grumpy old men on horseback. And although you and I are about the same age, Libby, I'm sure my lovely daughter didn't mean to imply you're old. Just me."

"Touché, Dad."

Libby humored them all with a wide smile and faint blush. "I'll definitely take you up on the offer to visit the stable. In class, Isaac has told us about your horses. I understand you run a therapeutic riding program?"

CJ's face lit up.

"And here we go," Emily teased. "My sister can talk your ear off about her kids and her horses."

"I can and I will, given the chance. But since everyone else at the table has heard this a thousand times and since you'll be dropping by soon…maybe next Saturday?"

Libby nodded. "I'd like that."

"Perfect. And now I won't monopolize the dinner conversation. Why don't you tell us about yourself, Libby."

"Oh." That seemed to catch her off guard. "Not much to tell, really. I grew up in Riverton but moved to St. Paul after college. I got married and taught elementary school there for many years. Now I'm *not* married and I'm back in Riverton to take care of my mom." She angled her head in Paul's direction, gave him a smile. "I'm sorry to say she's in the early stages of Alzheimer's, but she's being very well taken care of by Dr. Woodward here."

Thomas sat back and listened as Libby was swept into an easy conversation that touched on Paul's work at the clinic, Emily and Jack's upcoming wedding, Annie's bed-and-breakfast, which was now on hiatus until Thanksgiving, and the new column she was writing for Emily's blog.

Thomas was impressed. This woman was as engaging with a group of adults as she was with her young students, and she and his family seemed to have an easy, seamless fit. He liked that. He liked *her*. And after he'd finished a second helping of Annie's incredible dinner, and eased himself and his chair out of the way so the table could be cleared, he liked that Libby jumped up and started stacking plates, gathering cutlery. She handed the stack of china to Annie, absently smoothed her hand over Isaac's head, paused to exchange a few quiet words with Paul.

Thomas let his thoughts drift to how the rest of the evening might play out after coffee and dessert were served. Would Libby need to rush home to her mother? He hoped not. He wanted to invite her to sit with him out on the screened veranda that wrapped around the front of the house. Truthfully, what he really wanted was to kiss her. His being seated while she was standing put him at a distinct disadvantage when it came to initiating a kiss. If he could get her to sit with him, he'd have half a chance. He hoped.

CHAPTER THIRTEEN

PAUL HAD BEEN DISAPPOINTED that Annie's seating arrangement had him sitting well away from her. Normally, he was a go-with-the-flow kind of guy, but he had not wanted to sit between Libby Potter and Rose, at the opposite end of the table from Annie. So he'd been willing to risk being a terrible dinner guest by shaking things up a little.

He'd asked Fred Morris to trade seats with him. Fred was happy to comply, since the switch meant he would still be sitting beside Rose, and Paul was next to Annie. Win-win. Paul's audacity earned him a wink from Thomas, a fist pump from CJ and two thumbs up from Emily. If he annoyed Annie, she wasn't letting on.

It had been years since he'd been here for dinner. While Annie's kitchen was now a model of modern efficiency, the dining room was a throwback to the farmhouse's origins. From the chandelier overhead to the Turkish carpet on the floor, the dusky floral wallpaper, sturdy old oak furniture, delicate china and gleaming silverware, it all came together to tell this family's story.

Annie was as comfortable here as she was in the kitchen, getting up from time to time to move a bowl to the sideboard or retrieve a platter, making sure everyone had all they needed. On several occasions her knee bumped his, making her blush. Her movements were so fluid and effortless that no one else seemed to notice as she anticipated what one of them might want or need even before they knew it themselves. The conversation flowed from horses to weddings to blogs, periodically interspersed with references to the weather, the economy and Isaac's favorite new dinosaur, "a plant-eating titanosaur with a ginormous body and a long neck that it waved around like a weed whacker."

Paul could get used to eating like this. Family-style, the table laden with bowls and platters, a centerpiece of early fall flowers from Annie's garden. The only thing better than the food was the company, he decided, taking in the faces around the table.

Across from him, Jack had his arm draped protectively across the back of Emily's chair. From time to time she looked up at her fiancé, her eyes filled with affection. It made

Paul's chest tighten. Their wedding was just a week away, and Paul was looking forward to the event. He was happy for them, of course, but even more, he looked forward to Annie being maid of honor to his best man. And if she thought his switching places at the dinner table had been a bold move, then she was in for a few more surprises.

Isaac's teacher was engaged in a quiet conversation with Thomas. Easy to see what was happening between the two of them. Apparently they had known one another in high school and gone their separate ways. Now they were reconnecting and, if Paul had to guess, neither of them was fighting the attraction. Not unlike his current situation with Annie, with that one important exception. If she could feel the pull of attraction, and he was sure she could, then she was having an easier time denying it than he was.

CJ sat next to her nephew, fully engaged with everything the little chatterbox had to say, from dogs to dinosaurs to dodgeball, which was his new favorite sport at school. The child was bright and energetic, full of mischief, no doubt, but also respectful of his mother and extended family. He had been raised well and with love, and it showed. Paul was completely taken with the little boy's exuberance.

The one exception to the convivial group was Annie's young half sister, Rose. She sat between Paul and Fred. It was obvious Fred had more than a passing interest in Rose, and it was equally obvious those feelings were not reciprocated. Rose still had the crackly cough, and in spite of a generous application of cologne, her clothing carried the scent of cigarette smoke. And although the only beverages at the table were sodas and sparkling water—plus milk for Isaac and Emily—there was no mistaking a hint of alcohol on her breath.

She had returned to the clinic for a follow-up appointment, as he had requested the first time he saw her at the clinic. The throat swab had ruled out a strep infection but she did have a nasty case of bronchitis. Blood work indicated severe anemia and she was underweight, symptoms he was sure were due to alcohol abuse and poor nutrition.

Tonight, he noticed, she served herself small portions and spent more time pushing the food around the plate with her fork than consuming it. Annie encouraged her to try the yam casserole, to help herself to a second serving of mashed potatoes and gravy. Yet no amount of Annie's gentle cajoling could convince her to eat. Paul found her overall demeanor to be more childlike than adult, and he had to wonder what it was Fred saw in her.

As the dinner plates were cleared, Paul saw an opportunity to catch a few minutes of alone time with Annie.

"Let me take those," he said to Libby, picking up the stack of dinner plates and carrying them into the kitchen. Annie went ahead with serving bowls in each hand. Somewhat to his dismay, CJ followed with a platter and the gravy boat. Once inside the kitchen, though, she smiled and gave him a cheeky wink when Annie wasn't looking. "You two go ahead and load the dishwasher and I'll finish clearing the table," she said before she disappeared with a tray tucked under her arm.

Paul liked both of Annie's sisters, her whole family, for that matter. But right now, intentionally leaving him alone in the kitchen with Annie made CJ his hands-down favorite.

He opened the dishwasher. "Annie, thank you for dinner. That was the best meal I've had in ages."

While he rinsed plates and loaded them into the dishwasher, Annie turned on the coffeemaker and took the lid off a large plastic container that was sitting on the island. "I'm glad you were able to get away. How's your father?"

"Today was a relatively good day. Jack's parents asked him over for dinner and thankfully he agreed to go." Otherwise Paul might have had to stay home with him. "He's known them for years and has been to their home many times. His long-term memory is still pretty well intact and he feels comfortable there. And it's good for him to have company."

"It must be a worry for you, having to leave him on his own while you're at the clinic."

Luckily, his father had always preferred solitude, even when he was healthy. "The Evanses have been checking in on him— they've always been wonderful neighbors— but I won't be able to rely on them for long."

"Emily tells me they plan to do some traveling after the wedding."

"Yes, finally. They've worked hard and deserve to enjoy their retirement while they can. I have lined up a caregiver who starts on Wednesday. A young LPN—his name is Jordan—who'll come in for four or five hours a day."

"A male nurse? That's great, and having him there will be a huge relief, I'm sure."

"It is."

Truthfully, finding any nurse would have been great but Paul was happy to have found a man who was willing to take on the job. His father tended to be demanding and even difficult with the staff he'd worked with at the clinic, particularly with women. Jordan had a no-nonsense approach to patient care, and his height and build were an added advantage for coping with a difficult patient. Not that Paul expected his father would need to be restrained. If and when that time came, Paul would have to arrange permanent care in a nursing home. In the meantime, his father was less likely to be verbally challenging with another man, especially one who towered over him by a good four inches. That would make everyone's life easier. And on his father's more difficult days, Paul was confident that Jordan would take the old man's unpredictable behavior in stride.

But for now, Paul didn't want to talk about his father. "Your dad looks good. And he and Libby seem to be hitting it off."

"I didn't realize they knew each other so well."

From what Paul had seen, they intended to get to know one another even better. He wondered how Annie would feel about that.

"Anyway," she said, as though she'd read

his thoughts and wanted to answer his question. "I think it's great. My dad was born and raised here and he's always had lots of friends but never anyone special, not since my mom. I hope Libby's really okay with him being in a wheelchair and not just being nice."

"Oh, I'd say she's more than okay with it."

Annie's cheeks went a little pink, all but obliterating the faint dusting of freckles he'd always found so delectable.

"Good. It's weird to think of my dad dating, but it's kind of adorable at the same time."

Paul wondered how Isaac would feel if *his* mother was dating someone, half hoping that Annie was still following his train of thought.

She wasn't. She was slicing into the cake Libby had brought with her and was transferring generous wedges onto dessert plates.

"Look at this cake. No one in Riverton bakes a red velvet cake the way Mable Potter does. Except maybe her daughter. And this boiled frosting…" She swiped her finger along the back of the knife, closed her eyes as she tasted the white icing. "Mmm…so good."

Paul was sure his heart skipped a few beats before it sped up.

"Try some."

He did, and agreed the frosting was delicious. It might have tasted better from the tip of her finger than his own. He wished the idea hadn't entered his head, and then he *really* hoped she wasn't reading his thoughts.

"If the cake tastes half that good, I think I'm going to like it."

"You've never eaten red velvet cake?"

He shook his head.

"You'll love it. Everyone does."

CJ returned from the dining room with a tray loaded with dishes and set them on the counter. "Is that Libby's mom's red velvet cake?" she asked.

"It is, and Paul's never had it before."

"Seriously?" CJ quickly transferred the dishes from the tray to the dishwasher. "I've been watching Dad and Libby. If the two of them hook up, we can have her mom's cake more often."

"CJ!" Annie carefully set five dessert plates onto the newly emptied tray, then placed the remaining plates on another tray. "What a thing to say."

"What? I love cake. And I call it as I see it. There's something going on with Dad and Libby. I think it's cute." CJ grinned. "In fact, I think we should all get to have our cake and eat it, too."

Paul wholeheartedly agreed.

AT THE END of the evening, Libby helped Annie clean up the kitchen. The rest of the group had drifted. Paul left first, saying he needed to check on his father. Libby felt badly for him, knowing firsthand how devastating an Alzheimer's diagnosis was for everyone involved. She also gathered from what Paul had said the disease was more advanced with his father. Emily was feeling tired so Jack had driven her home, and Rose and Fred had left at the same time. CJ had taken Isaac upstairs to supervise his bedtime routine, and then she had gone out to the stable for a final check on her horses.

Only Thomas had remained in the kitchen and Libby kept glancing over to where he sat at the kitchen table with a newspaper spread in front of him and a pair of reading glasses resting low on his nose. He was a fascinating man with diverse interests and carefully considered opinions on a wide range of subjects.

Annie snapped the lid on Libby's cake carrier and set it on the end of the island. "That cake was delicious. Please thank your mother for us," she said. "And please let her know we'd love to have her come to Sunday dinner sometime."

"Thank you. That's very thoughtful."

"Not at all. As you can see, we love having people join us."

"I'm not sure my mother could cope, unfortunately. She's good in one-on-one situations, sometimes even with two or three people if she knows them well. But in a large group she tends to get confused and then she gets frustrated even though she doesn't understand why she's confused and frustrated."

"I'm sorry to hear that. Paul is going through a similar situation with his father."

"We've talked a bit about that." Somehow, hearing about his circumstances made her feel a little less alone in hers. "We're very lucky to have him as our doctor."

"I think the whole town is happy to have another Dr. Woodward in its midst." Annie set a stack of plastic containers next to the cake carrier. "Here, I packaged up some leftovers for you take home. That way you won't have to cook dinner after school tomorrow."

"Oh, you didn't have to do that," Libby said. "Although honestly, I'm grateful you did." Tomorrow it would be a real treat to come home after a long day and not have to prepare a meal.

She reached out and gave Annie a hug and was surprised when the young woman whispered in her ear. "Thank you for putting some sparkle back in my dad's eye."

Libby stepped back, felt her face grow warm and gave Annie a long look. Was Thomas's daughter giving her the stamp of approval?

"Looks like you're ready to go," Thomas said, looking up from his paper. "I'll see you out."

Annie answered her silent question with a wink. "Good night, Libby. I hope you'll join us again soon."

"I will. Thank you." Libby gathered up her things and followed Thomas out of the kitchen and through the house to the front door.

He held her cake carrier and the containers of leftovers on his lap while she retrieved her coat from the closet and slipped into it. On the screened veranda, he swung his chair next to a wicker armchair and patted the seat cushion. "Sit for a bit before you go?"

"I'd like that." She set her things on a side table, realizing as she sat just how close he had positioned himself to her chair.

The porch itself wasn't lit, but a warm glow from the living room filtered through the lace curtains. The night air was crisp but not cold, and she realized that at some point after dessert, Thomas had put on a sweater, as though sitting out here had not been a spur-of-the-moment decision.

"Warm enough?" he asked.

"Yes, thanks."

"I'm glad you came tonight."

"Thank you again for inviting me. You have a wonderful family and I enjoyed getting to know them a little. Isaac is a very lucky little boy."

"Family is important," he said.

"It is." For the umpteenth time, she wondered how she had allowed her own life to drift so far away from that all-important principle. His daughters were beautiful, inside and out, and their mutual love and respect for one another and for their father had literally lit up the dining room tonight. "Not having a family of my own is my biggest regret."

Thomas reached for her hand and held it between both of his. For a second or two, she closed her eyes as the warmth of his touch seeped into her skin. She opened them to find him leaning close.

"Life is too short for regrets." He moved his hands, big and strong and gentle, to the sides of her face and kissed her. Her own hands, fingers splayed, found the firmly muscled contours of his chest. A soul-deep heat like nothing she had ever experienced flared through her. These emotions were new and raw and real, exciting and comforting and satisfying. It was as though she had struggled her whole life to put together a jigsaw puzzle, only to realize, too late, that a piece was missing. Suddenly that one last, errant piece had been found and finally, easily slipped into place.

"Oh, Thomas," she breathed after the kiss ended.

He stayed close, looking at her as he smoothed her hair. Even out here on the dimly lit veranda, she could see the intent in his eyes and again her only thought was...*finally.*

"I'd like to see you again," he said.

"I'd like that, too."

"Tomorrow."

"I have school tomorrow."

"I know. If I pick you up at seven, does that give you enough time to have dinner with your mother, get her settled?"

"You could have dinner with us."

He shook his head. "I have something else in mind."

Libby considered what he was saying. He wanted to pick her up, take her out, as though... "Is this a date?"

"Sure, we can call it that."

"Are you going to tell me where you're taking me?"

"No." But there was a promise in his smile that she found irresistible.

"So, it's a surprise?"

"We can call it that, too." He took her face in his hands and kissed her again, and there was a promise there, too.

CHAPTER FOURTEEN

THE MORNING OF Emily and Jack's wedding dawned with a blue sky lavishly brushed with pink and orange, creating a dramatic backdrop for the fiery red and gold and orange leaves of the poplars and maples and birch trees scattered across the farm and along the riverbank. It was one of those mornings that tricked a person into believing winter was in the distant future.

Annie stood on the back veranda with her hands wrapped around her favorite coffee mug, inhaling the scented steam between sips. The early morning air had an autumn crispness to it, but the afternoon forecast was for warm, late-summer sunshine. This was hands down her favorite time of day. It always started with a cup of coffee, sometimes two, which she savored while the rest of the house still slumbered. She used this time to plan her day, making mental to-do lists of all the things she intended to accomplish.

Today, however, was different. She felt

oddly out of sorts and couldn't quite put her finger on why.

Emily had planned everything down to the last detail, and then she had typed it all into her laptop and printed it. The master list was now on the fridge door, held there by a magnet that read, "I Do!" The magnet had been tucked into the bridal shower gift—a pair of his-and-hers coffee mugs—that Libby had given to Emily.

Annie had committed Emily's entire list to memory. The photographer would arrive at eight thirty to record every aspect of the day. Having photographs of the bride eating breakfast and the crew setting up the big outdoor tent and tables for the reception seemed excessive to Annie. Emily insisted on capturing every moment. She intended to blog about every one of them, and her huge readership no doubt expected it.

At eleven o'clock the bride and her three sisters were having their hair done at the Clip 'n' Curl in town. Back to the farm by twelve thirty for lunch. Annie had baked bread yesterday. This morning she would whip up an egg salad for sandwiches, and there was strudel for dessert.

At one o'clock, forty white folding chairs would be assembled by the gazebo on the riverbank, each with a sweeping blue bow tied to the back. The rest of the afternoon would be taken up with makeup and manicures and "sister stuff," as CJ called it. Their father had been tasked with keeping Isaac occupied and out of mischief, and keeping him clean after he was dressed in his tuxedo. At four o'clock, the wedding party would climb the steps of the gazebo to the exact spot where Jack had proposed to Emily, and the ceremony would begin.

Throughout the planning and preparation, Annie had tried not to think about her own wedding day. This morning, though, she found it impossible to keep the memories at bay. Maybe that's what had her feeling a little blue. They were happy memories and she wanted to keep them separate from the grief of losing her husband, her high-school sweetheart, her son's father. Now, with the sun-lightened sky and the first sounds of morning spreading around her, she slowly opened her mind to their special day and let herself remember.

She had wanted to get married here at the farm with just family and close friends gathered with them, but Eric had insisted on having their wedding in town—a ceremony at the church followed by formal photographs at

Riverside Park and a reception for a hundred and fifty at the community center. Annie, who had always been a bit of a homebody, had found the day overwhelming. Eric, surrounded by both their families, friends, acquaintances and a few people he hadn't met before that day, had been in his element. By the end of the evening, she was sure he had spoken with all of them, sweeping her along with him. That night she had been happy to hang on his arm, smile and thank their guests for sharing their special day. Looking back, she knew she had put his wants and wishes ahead of her own, and by doing that, she had set the tone for their marriage.

It had been a good marriage, she reminded herself. She had thought she might have to dig in her heels about living at the farm but Eric had readily agreed. He had been hired as the physical education teacher and it made sense, he'd told her. She wouldn't have to work—he had never viewed cooking and baking and laundry and housework as real work—and they could use his meager salary to buy a car and pay for winter trips to nearby ski resorts and summer boating excursions and water-skiing on Lake Pepin. Eric had loved athletics and the outdoors, and as usual, he had swept her along with him. Perhaps he'd been having too much fun to notice she'd been sipping hot chocolate and reading in the ski lodge or sequestered under a beach umbrella with a book. Or maybe he had assumed that's how she wanted to spend her time.

Annie gave herself a shake. This line of thinking was never productive, and it was downright dangerous on a day like this. Eric had been a good husband and a great dad. They had rarely argued and they'd never had what anyone would consider a real fight. Of course, CJ said Annie was too easygoing, but she'd proven herself to be stronger than anyone thought. Instead of simply being a stay-at-home wife and mother who also provided a home for her father and youngest sister, she had turned the house into a successful bed-and-breakfast.

This summer had been the first time since opening the B&B that she had closed her doors to guests. After Eric's death, Emily had found out she was having Jack's baby and accepted his marriage proposal, so there had been a wedding to plan Around that time, their half sister Rose had arrived on the scene, and Annie had helped her settle into Riverton. She had thought she might miss having guests around since they kept her busy. But she had enjoyed being able to devote all of her time to family. With the wedding day finally upon them and Rose settled into a steady job and a small apartment in town, Annie had already decided she would reopen for the holidays and spring break and summer vacation.

She was in the process of considering her options in the form of a mental pros-and-cons list when a sound from the kitchen caught her attention. She turned, glanced through the French doors. Emily, dressed in the faded yellow flannel nightgown she kept at the farm for occasions when she spent the night, and the Cookie Monster slippers that Annie and CJ had given her for Christmas when she was fourteen, was moving through the kitchen, opening and closing cupboard doors.

Annie experienced a wave of sisterly affection tinged with motherly devotion. Which was silly because she was only two years older than Emily. But ever since their mother had left them, she had always felt more than sibling responsibility.

"Good morning," she said, pushing through the doors and closing them behind her. "Sleep well?"

Emily swung around, her mother-to-be glow exceptionally...glowy this morning. "Like a log. No, more like a baby." She grinned.

Annie crossed the room, set her mug on the island and drew her sister into a hug. "You look lovely this morning."

"I'm getting married. Me, little Emily Finnegan, is getting married! Can you believe it?"

"Yes, I can believe it. And you haven't been 'little Emily Finnegan' in years." Annie put her hands on her sister's shoulders, held her at arm's length and looked at the beautiful woman she had become, slippers and nightgown notwithstanding.

"But I'm marrying Jack Evans. *Jack. Evans.* We're going to be husband and wife, I'm having his baby, and I'm not freaking out. Not even a little bit."

"You have no reason to freak out. Jack loves you."

Emily's grin widened. "He does, doesn't he?" She resumed her search of the kitchen cupboards.

"What are you looking for?"

"Decaf."

"Sit." Annie led her to a stool at the kitchen island. "I'll make some."

Emily sat. "How long have you been up?"

"For a while." If she was being honest, she would admit to not being able to sleep. She had been looking back on the past with regret, and looking ahead, somewhat self-ishly, to how this day might unfold for her. "I stepped outside to enjoy the sunrise. We're going to have a perfect day for the wedding."

"That's good. I know it was risky, planning an outdoor wedding in September, but it's what we wanted."

Annie poured water into the coffeemaker, dumped grounds into the basket, switched it on. *It's what* we *wanted.* She envied them. Emily and Jack discussed everything, disagreed on a lot of things, and almost always found a compromise that worked for both of them.

"Oh, and I can't remember if I mentioned this or not, but Paul said he'd be here by eight thirty."

Annie swung around. "Paul? He's coming here? But he's the best man. He should be spending the day with Jack."

Emily shrugged. "Jack is going to shower, shave and put on his tux. Knowing him, he'll probably spend the morning at the station. He and I aren't supposed to see one another until the ceremony, so he certainly can't be here setting up the chairs at the gazebo and the tables for the reception."

"I thought Fred was going to help."

"Oh, he is, but it's a big job so I asked Paul if he would, too, and he said yes."

Of course he did. If there was one thing she knew about Paul, it was that he would do anything for his friends.

CJ straggled into the kitchen, yawning, and waved at the coffeemaker. "Too early. Need coffee. Is this the real thing?"

"Decaf," Emily said.

"There's regular coffee in the carafe. Have a seat and I'll get it."

CJ ignored her, took a mug from the cupboard and filled it. "You're very sweet, but I can pour my own coffee."

"You can pour mine, too. I don't feel like getting up," Emily said, and then turned to CJ as she settled onto the stool beside her. "I was telling Annie that Paul's coming this morning to help with setup."

"Such a great guy." CJ paused to gulp coffee. "Hard to believe he's still single."

And let the matchmaking begin, Annie thought. Out loud she said, "Since you're so taken with him, I'll let you oversee the setup while I organize the centerpieces."

"Can't," CJ said. "I have to get to the stable and check on the horses. That'll keep me busy until it's time to get our hair done."

"Don't look at me," Emily said. "I'll be too busy being queen for the day."

Their schemes to put her and Paul together were blatantly transparent and she should feel annoyed with them, but her traitorous heart was suddenly aflutter and her low spirits lifted. She set a skillet on the stove, took out eggs, milk and bread for French toast. She wouldn't give her meddling sisters the satisfaction by telling them this, but if she got breakfast out of the way now, she would have time to change her clothes and fix her makeup before Paul arrived.

PAUL EXCHANGED A look and a nod with Jack as they stood with the minister in the Finnegans' gazebo, facing the group of family and friends seated on the sweep of lawn along the riverbank. Ordinarily they would've given one another a one-armed hug and a back pat, but the occasion felt too formal for that. He didn't think he'd ever been happier for his buddy, or more envious. As always, Jack appeared calm and self-assured, and Paul knew it wasn't an act. Riverton's chief of police was as solid as they came. And he was marrying one of the Finnegan sisters, which also made him one of the luckiest guys alive.

At the stroke of four o'clock, Fred pressed

Play on the portable music system set up behind the gazebo. The strains of Pachelbel's Canon in D filled the air, its melody soothing to the spirit and just a little haunting to the soul. The wedding party appeared as if out of nowhere. CJ and Rose walked, with Isaac between them, along a narrow carpet forming an aisle between the chairs. Annie followed them, wearing the most incredible dress he'd ever seen. Or maybe it wasn't the dress. Maybe it was simply her. She could make anything look incredible.

And then the bride and her father appeared. Happiness radiated from her as she pushed his chair along the carpeted aisle. Among those gathered, Paul noticed more than a few of them reaching for tissues. As the bridesmaids and ring bearer climbed the steps, Emily wheeled her father into place in the front row next to Libby, then bent to kiss his cheek. Jack went down the steps, shook hands with Thomas, then tucked his bride's hand into the crook of his arm and led her into the gazebo to face the minster.

Paul glanced at Annie. Their gazes met and held for several heart-stopping seconds, and then she looked away as she reached for her sister's bouquet.

Later, from what he could remember of

the ceremony, it was traditional and, happily, quite short. Several of the minister's quips created ripples of laughter, others brought on a few tears. The bride and groom had written their own vows, and it was somewhat surprising that Jack's words generated the strongest reaction. As he spoke about finding a life and catching a wife here in Riverton, Paul even found himself tearing up.

What he remembered most, though, was Annie, standing next to the bride, her deep blue, knee-length dress emphasizing an hourglass figure, the square neckline forming a frame for a sapphire pendant that lay against a backdrop of ivory skin. He prided himself in being a practical man, yet as these images of Annie registered in his mind and transformed into thoughts, he was startled to find they were almost poetic.

He couldn't take his eyes off her, and he liked that she kept glancing his way. Sometimes hastily before looking away with a flutter of long lashes, but other times their gazes held for long seconds at a time. He couldn't wait to sit with her at dinner, to dance with her once the music started. For now, as the happy couple were pronounced husband and wife and the rousing notes of Mendelssohn's "Wedding March" filled the air, he offered his arm to Annie. She accepted with a slim hand and a ready smile, and as they followed Emily and Jack down the stairs, he was content with the knowledge that the evening was just getting started.

CHAPTER FIFTEEN

ANNIE HAD GIVEN her toast to the bride before dinner and now she couldn't remember the last time she'd felt so relaxed and—yes, she could say it—so happy. The food was wonderful. She had offered to do the catering herself but Emily and Jack graciously declined, insisting they wanted her to enjoy the wedding, not work at it. She was more than grateful they had.

The tables had been draped with white linen and set with silver-rimmed white china and silver flatware and elegant stemware provided by the caterers. Emily wanted some fall color so Annie had helped her make the centerpieces—shallow white vases filled with bunches of yellow and orange and gold chrysanthemums, and decorated with blue satin ribbon that matched the bridesmaids' dresses.

She and Paul were seated next to one another at the head table, and she now appreciated CJ for stepping aside as maid of honor and insisting Annie take on the role instead.

Her meddlesome sisters were being match-
makers, no question about it. This morning
they had come up with reasons to excuse
themselves from setup, which had left her
to work with Paul and Fred. Given that Fred
had kept making himself scarce, he had obviously been in on the plan. If Paul noticed,
he was either too polite or too mortified to
say anything.

Tonight, he was being attentive, charming,
polite. "More water?"

"I'd love some."

He tipped the pitcher and filled her glass.
"I've been following your *Ask Annie* posts
on Emily's blog. They're good. Really good."

"So you expect me to believe Paul Woodward, the dedicated doctor, is interested in
chickens?" she asked. "And eggs?"

His smile crinkled the corners of his eyes.
"I am now. If I wasn't being a best man this
weekend, I'd be home building a chicken
coop."

"Now you're making fun of me."

"The *dedicated* doctor is guilty as charged."

"Touché. Seriously, though, I know how
busy you are at the clinic and at home with
your dad, so I'm surprised you'd find time to
read *Ask Annie*."

He gave her a long, thoughtful look. "Apparently I'm not alone. There were forty-seven comments on your story about the chickens."

"I know." She couldn't keep the excitement out of her voice. "It's unbelievable. People I don't even know, people from places I've never been, like Eugene and Sarasota, were saying how much they liked my photographs and the stories about my silly chickens."

"The photographs are good, Annie. Really professional."

"That's not possible. I'm not a photographer. I've never owned a camera until Emily gave me hers."

"Then you're a natural with an eye for color and composition."

She felt herself blushing. "I don't know about that, and I have no idea what I'm going to do for this week's column. I've been so busy with the wedding."

"I think you just found your answer. You were taking pictures while we were setting up this morning. I bet you'll find a few gems in there."

"From chickens to weddings?" she asked. "Won't that seem strange?"

"Small-town living is the theme of Emily's blog, right? That covers a lot of territory."

He was right. That's exactly what she

would do, and of course Emily's fans would love to see photographs of her wedding. With that settled, she should probably take a few photographs now that the reception was in full swing. "Excuse me for a few minutes?" she asked. "I'm going to dash inside and get my camera."

He stood, always the gentleman, and helped her to her feet, holding her hand a beat longer than necessary. "I'll be right here when you get back."

She hurried into the house, brushing the tips of her fingers over the back of the hand he had held, hoping dinner would be over soon. Traditionally, the maid of honor's first dance was with the best man. She couldn't wait for the music to start.

In the kitchen, she pulled the camera from the desk drawer where she kept her laptop, address book and calendar for the B&B. She turned on the camera and quickly scrolled through the photographs she'd taken while she and Paul and Fred had arranged tables and chairs inside the tent. She had captured some nice close-up images of the flowers and the elegant place settings but, to her chagrin, Paul was in most—no, make that all of the wide-angle photographs. Fred had made it into only one.

Her face felt flushed. Was she really so focused on her husband's best friend that she had unconsciously pointed the camera at him every time she'd snapped a picture? The truth was...she didn't know what the truth was. She still loved Eric. Yes, she was angry with him for not taking better care of himself, for leaving her alone, but she missed him like crazy.

Paul had been his friend, but he was rapidly becoming her best friend, too. A closer friend than they'd been during and after high school. She enjoyed his company. He made it okay for her to share stories about Eric, to admit to being overprotective with Isaac. He made it okay to laugh again. But if she was being honest with herself, she loved the way he made her feel cared for, admired and capable of accomplishing things she never would have tried on her own. Emily had her own reasons for wanting her to write the *Ask Annie* column on her blog, but Paul simply believed in her.

She turned off the camera and returned to the reception as the emcee, Logan Kane, stood and welcomed everyone. He was a friend of the groom's, a detective with the Chicago PD as Jack himself had once been. He was every bit as tall and good-looking as the groom, with the same confident stance all police officers seemed to possess.

"Good evening. Emily and Jack hope you enjoyed the meal—I know I certainly did—but now they think it's time to get this party started. Before we do, the bride and groom are going to cut the cake, but I think there's another matter we need to attend to." He picked up his dinner knife and tapped the edge of his glass several times. Most of the guests enthusiastically joined in.

Annie watched her sister and her new brother-in-law share an intimate smile, then Jack stood, drew Emily to her feet, put his arms around her waist. She wound hers around his neck, and then he gave her a long, deliberate kiss.

Annie's gaze involuntarily swept the space and found Paul. He was watching her, his gaze so intense that even from a distance, her skin warmed and her heart fluttered. Amid the applause for the bride and groom, she made her way to her seat next to Paul. There would be no kissing in her foreseeable future but tonight she would dance.

THE BRIDE AND groom waltzed across the small dance floor to the melody of an Etta James classic. And while Jack's lonely days were over, Paul wasn't so sure that would ever be the case for him. He also sensed Annie was expecting him to invite her onto the dance floor. He had a different idea.

He stood and offered his hand. "Take a walk with me?"

"Oh." If she was disappointed, she quickly recovered. "Sure. I'd like that. A stroll by the river is always nice on an evening like this."

Perfect. The river walk ended at the gazebo, which was the destination he'd had in mind all along. He could see it from the sweeping lawn in front of the house, where the huge tent and makeshift dance floor had been set up, its outline strung with tiny white lights, beckoning.

Annie accepted his hand and he helped her to her feet. The air had cooled after the sun had set, so he pulled her shawl off the back of her chair and wrapped it around her shoulders.

"The bridesmaids' dresses are an amazing color," he said. "The three of you look great."

"Thanks. Emily picked out the dresses for us and I love that she chose a different style for each of us. I wasn't sure about this shade of blue, but she insisted. She wanted something that would stand out against the fall foliage, and Jack's favorite color is blue."

"Blue is every guy's favorite color," he said.

"Noted," she said, laughing.

Noted. He wondered what she meant, but didn't ask. "The ceremony was nice," he said instead. "Simple, traditional, not too long."

"And this was the perfect place for it, here in the gazebo. So many memories."

He wondered if she was thinking about the night her husband had proposed to her here, but her thoughts seemed to have taken a different track.

"My sisters and I used to play down here. We'd pretend the gazebo was a fort, a castle, a church, even a spaceship, and we would spend afternoons playacting one dramatic scene or another. Emily was usually the one to dream them up—she always had such a wild imagination. When Fred was old enough to ride his bike out from town, we co-opted him into being the groom for our wedding skits. At one time or another he was married to all three of us."

Lucky guy, Paul thought. He'd settle for one Finnegan sister. "And now Fred seems to have a thing for Rose," he said.

"I've noticed. I'm not sure she has, though."

"I spoke with her earlier," he said. "Asked her how she's settling into life in Riverton.

She had just stopped at the bar to have her gin and tonic refilled. She seemed a little tipsy."

"CJ mentioned that as well. I hadn't noticed."

"Did she drive out here?" he asked.

"She did. If she doesn't want to spend the night with us, I'll make sure she gets a ride back into town."

"I'll be happy to take her."

"That's sweet of you. I'll check with her when we get back to the party and let you know."

Right now Paul was in no hurry to get back to the reception.

As they approached the gazebo, Annie stopped and looked up at it. "It's so pretty with all these lights. With the ceremony being in the afternoon, I wasn't sure why Emily wanted them. Now I know." She reached for his hand. "Let's go inside and sit."

He hadn't anticipated her touch and it literally took his breath away. He walked with her up the steps and they sat together on the circular bench lining the perimeter, facing the farmhouse on the hill. Light filtered through its curtained windows. The big white tent on the lawn was aglow with soft lights and laughter. The dance floor was alive with swirling couples. They could hear the music from here—Frank Sinatra's "Fly Me to the Moon," the song he had asked the DJ to add to his playlist. Paul stood and reached for her. "Dance with me?"

Annie drifted into his arms, placed one hand in his, the other on his shoulder. "I thought maybe you didn't want to dance with me."

"Why would you think that?"

"Because when the music started, you asked me to go for a walk instead."

"And yet here we are," he said softly against her hair. *Here we are.*

For the first few steps, she felt stiff and uncomfortable and he held her awkwardly. Gradually, they both relaxed and found an easy rhythm that didn't involve anyone's toes being stepped on. Part way through the song he heard her sigh, sensed she might even have closed her eyes. He eased her a little closer and she didn't resist. By the closing chorus, her cheek had touched his shoulder and his rested on the top of her head. He held her even after the song ended, and she let him. Neither of them spoke and, for once, he felt words were not necessary. After that first awkward, accidental kiss, she had said she needed a friend but she wasn't ready for anything more. He had accepted that and agreed it would be best for things to stay as they were. He would have agreed to anything if meant he could keep seeing her. But standing here with her in his arms, this was more than friends. This was a turning point in their relationship. He needed to move carefully, he knew that, but he also knew he needed to make a move. It was now or never.

He shifted his weight and she responded by leaning away a little and looking up at him.

"We should probably get back before we're missed," she said.

"There's just one thing," he replied.

"What's that?"

"This."

He took his time lowering his mouth to hers. The accidental kiss a few weeks ago had caught them both off guard and come dangerously close to interfering with their friendship. This time he didn't want there to be any question that he wanted to be more than a friend. Her lashes fluttered but she didn't back away.

The instant their lips met and held, and when she slipped her arms around his neck, he decided she'd been worth waiting for. Finally kissing Annie for real and on purpose was heaven. Having her kiss him in return was a miracle. He knew this—whatever *this* was—wasn't going to go any further tonight, and probably not for many nights to come. For this night, though, it was enough and he didn't want it to end.

Annie had other ideas.

"Paul," she said, part gasping for breath and part whisper. "What is this?"

"This…" He touched his lips to hers, lightly, one last time. "This is what I'd call an incredible first kiss."

She gave him a quizzical look.

"In fact…" He smiled down at her. "As first kisses go, on a scale of one to ten, that was an eleven."

"You kissed me once before," she reminded him.

"Not intentionally," he said. "And you didn't kiss me back. This time, you did."

"And that makes it a first kiss?"

"It's a first for us."

She unwound her arms from his neck, rested her hands on his chest and her cheek on his shoulder. "I don't know if I can do this."

He closed his eyes, forced himself to breathe. "Do what?"

"This—us. You're Eric's best friend. It's only been six months since…since he's been gone. What will people say?"

Paul could well imagine what people would

say and he couldn't care less, but this wasn't about him. If Annie was willing, he could wait. "Those people don't need to know. No one needs to know right now, unless you want them to know."

"My sisters will figure it out."

"Are you worried about what your sisters will think?"

The question actually made her laugh. "No. They already think you're…well, they adore you. No worries there."

He thought they might be on his side and he liked having that confirmed. "Your dad?" he asked.

She shook her head.

"Isaac?"

"He's crazy about you."

Paul was tempted to ask if she worried what Eric would think, but he didn't want to hear the answer. Paul wished he could tell her no one else mattered, but he would have been wrong. Annie mattered more than anyone else, and she believed this wasn't the right time for them to be a couple. And that meant only one thing. He would wait. She had let him kiss her *and* she had kissed him back. Something he had long desired and yet believed would never happen. Well, he was a patient man and he would wait until she was ready, because if this could happen, anything could happen.

He picked up her shawl, which had slid off onto the bench when they stood to dance, and settled it around her shoulders, then tucked her hand into the crook of his elbow. "Ready to go back to the party?"

"I'm ready."

He cautioned himself about reading too much in to those two simple words while at the same time thinking he was beyond ready.

THOMAS ROLLED HIS chair onto the dance floor with his middle daughter at his side. At the DJ's request, the guests had cleared the floor for the father-daughter dance. At Annie's wedding, he had surprised her with both the dance and his song choice. There was no surprising Emily. She had her heart set on the same song and she had insisted on rehearsing ahead of time.

Now, as the opening notes of "Thank Heaven for Little Girls" floated through the air, she swept into as deep a curtsy as her expanding midsection would allow before putting her hand in his and following his lead across the floor. She was as light on her feet as he was on his wheels, and as they glided and swirled, as he raised his arm and she twirled beneath it, and as he spun under hers, the crowd around them clapped and cheered.

The song ended and Emily gave him a curious look after she leaned down and kissed him on the cheek.

"Are those tears?" she asked.

He nodded. "Happy ones. Thank you for the dance, sweetie. It's been quite a day, and Jack is a good man."

"I know he is, and he's going to be a great father, just like you."

"He's a lucky man, too. He's getting one of my girls."

Emily planted another kiss on his cheek. "I love you, Dad."

"I love you, too, Em. And I know you'll be happy."

As Jack approached to reclaim his wife, Thomas scanned the crowd, searching for Libby. He found her sitting alone. She had brought her mother to the ceremony because Mable was very fond of Emily. Afterward, Libby had driven Mable home because attending the reception would have been too much for the elderly woman. Now Libby was watching him with his daughter, smiling and dabbing the corners of her eyes with a napkin. More happy tears, he hoped.

One thing was certain. Libby looked amazing, like she could have walked off the page of one of those fashion magazines his daughters were so fond of. He had heard Annie and CJ gushing over Libby's dress when she'd arrived. He didn't remember the designer's name, but apparently the full skirt, narrow belted waist and bold floral print on a pastel background were said designer's signature. He'd also forgotten the name of this particular shade of pastel, but it looked light blue to him. Her classy elegance made her a standout, and at the same time she fit right in.

He closed the space between them and wheeled himself into the space next to her chair.

"Oh, Thomas. That was so touching. The song choice, the way you and Emily were in perfect step with one another, the love…" Again, the napkin fluttered up to touch her eyes.

"Didn't I tell you I cut a pretty mean rug?"

"You did, and you do. I'm impressed."

He reached for her hand. "Impressed enough to take a spin out there with me?"

"Oh. Oh, I don't know. I'm not a very good dancer."

"Doesn't matter. This is a wedding, not *Dancing with the Stars*. You're supposed to have fun. Besides, everyone knows someone's going to start doing the chicken dance, and that's never pretty."

Libby's smile brightened her whole face. "Yes, that is so true."

He leaned closer. "And I'll let you in on a little secret," he said in a stage whisper. "When you're dancing with a guy in a wheelchair, folks mostly notice he's not really dancing, and that makes you look like a pro."

Her easy laugh made him want to coax more of them out of her. She was beautiful when she smiled but her laughter made her glow. Based on the few things she had let slip about her marriage, he suspected there hadn't been a lot of levity. He'd like to change that, he decided, and doing the jive with a man on wheels sounded to him like a great place to start.

"Did I mention how beautiful you look tonight?"

She lowered her lashes and shook her head.

"Well, you do. Your dress is really something."

"Thank you."

"I have a question for you, though."

"Oh?" She looked up, startled. "What kind of question?"

"I've been wracking my brain for a memory of you back in high school. How could

I have spent four years in the same building with someone as gorgeous as you are and not remember anything about you?"

"That's easy," she said without hesitation, her gaze unwavering as it met his. "I was invisible."

"Not possible."

"Oh, but I'm afraid it was. I was an honor roll student and the English teacher's daughter. Queen of the geeks, or at least I might have been if I'd had any other geeky friends to hang out with. Since I didn't, I was a bit of a loner. Oh, and everything I wore was brown. When you're a teenage girl and you want to disappear, brown makes you invisible."

Were teenage boys really so dense they only noticed the girls who went out of their way to make themselves noticed? In a word, yes.

"Then I hope you never wear brown again. And now I'm going to swing by the DJ's booth and make a request. Meet me on the dance floor?"

"Oh." She folded her napkin and pressed it into a neat square. "What are you going to request?"

"Let me surprise you."

CHAPTER SIXTEEN

KISSING PAUL. The morning after the wedding, Annie drifted in and out of the dream before being startled awake by the sound of Beasley bounding down the hallway and Isaac chasing after him, loudly insisting they had to be quiet so they didn't wake Mom. Allowing her son to get the coveted border collie had made him the happiest boy alive, and he had promptly changed Bentley's name to Beasley. The dog's training and manners had been wildly overstated by his previous owners, but he had already waggled his way into Annie's heart.

She smiled and glanced at her clock, quickly flung back the covers and reached for her dressing gown. She'd overslept by almost an hour, something she rarely did even when she had forgotten to set an alarm. Normally she would feel guilty, but she was glad she had slept in this morning because she'd been dreaming about Paul. Until now, she hadn't been sure about his feelings for her, in spite of her sisters' insistence he had a thing for her. Last night he had let her know her sisters were right, and he had done it in a way that hadn't sent her running for cover. What he hadn't revealed was the depth of those feelings, which was just as well because that might have freaked her out.

Now she could acknowledge they shared a mutual attraction and enjoyed one another's company. The dancing followed by his kiss had simply been the icing on the cake that had been Emily and Jack's wedding. She and Paul had been caught up in the moment, and now everything about them and between them would go back to normal. It had to.

Downstairs, she corralled her son and the unruly dog in the kitchen before they woke the rest of the house, and then she put on a pot of coffee. Her father would be up soon enough. CJ liked to sleep in on Sunday mornings and have a leisurely breakfast before starting her day's work at the stable. As for Rose, there was no telling how late she might sleep.

Ever since Rose had moved to Riverton, everyone had been hinting she had a drinking problem. Annie was sure they were overreacting. Rose had not had an easy life, so the poor kid was bound to have issues. Annie would be the first to admit Rose had imbibed a little too heavily last night, but it was the first time she had seen her half sister tipsy. No, not tipsy. She'd been drunk. Paul had offered to drive her to her apartment, but she had barely been conscious by the end of the evening, and he and Jack had carried her upstairs to one of the guest rooms.

"What would you like for breakfast, Isaac?"

"Corn flakes." The book about dinosaurs Paul had given him lay open on the table in front of him. He held a plastic model of *Tyrannosaurus rex*, his all-time favorite, in one hand and *Brontosaurus* in the other.

"We don't have any corn flakes. I can make oatmeal."

Isaac scrunched his face. "Yuck." This was followed by "Rrraaawwwrrr!" as *Tyrannosaurus* lunged at *Brontosaurus*.

"Waffles?"

"Waffles! Wahoo, waffles!" The brontosaur swung its neck at its attacker, sending the *T. rex* tumbling across the pages of the book.

"I take it that's a yes."

"Yup."

Annie plugged in the waffle iron and assembled the ingredients. As she measured and mixed, she watched her son play out a

battle between the dinosaurs until the her-
bivore succumbed, listened to his endless
chatter that was partly anthropomorphic and
partly filled with facts he had gleaned from
Paul's book about the largest creatures to ever
have roamed the earth.

Before Isaac was born, she had secretly
hoped for a girl but from the moment her son
had been placed in her arms, red-faced and
wrinkled, his impossibly tiny fingers curled
into a fist, she had fallen head-over-heels in
love with him. And he was all boy, as rough
and tumble and full of energy as his father
had no doubt been as a child.

She whisked the wet and dry ingredients
together and set the bowl of batter aside. Then
she quartered an apple and poured a glass
of orange juice and set them out for Isaac.
Something to tide him over until everyone
else straggled in for breakfast.

"I'm going out to feed the chickens and
gather the eggs," she said, reaching for her
basket. "I want you and Beasley to stay in
the kitchen, okay? No running around the
house, please. Not until Gramps and Auntie
CJ are up."

"Okay. Rrraaawwwrrr!" *Brontosaurus* had
rebounded and trampled *T. rex*'s head.

Laughing, Annie slipped on a jacket,

opened the French doors and stepped out into the crisp autumn morning air. Inside the coop, she scattered feed and opened the door to release the hens, collected the eggs, and then sat for a moment on the bench. Thoughts about Paul tumbled through her mind. Sitting here with him, basking in his praise for her photographs. Being in his arms last night, swaying to "Fly Me to the Moon," knowing he had requested it, knowing he had planned to spirit her away to the gazebo for a private dance. Kissing him.

She could not stop thinking about his kiss, and she couldn't stop feeling guilty for thinking about it. Paul had been her husband's best friend, and now he was quickly becoming her best friend. But the kiss was a prelude to something that went well beyond friendship. She remembered Eric talking about Paul. He had been so proud of his friend's achievements at university, his success as a doctor. How would he feel about this? Annie would never know, of course. She would never really be sure because Eric's death had been so sudden. There had been no chance to even consider a future without him, let alone talk about it.

"Good morning," CJ called from the veranda. "Are you coming in for coffee?"

"I'll be right there." Grateful for the distraction, Annie picked up the basket of eggs and carried it into the house.

Her father was at the table with Isaac and CJ was at the counter, pouring coffee into mugs.

"Did everyone sleep well?" Annie asked. She set the eggs on the island and carried a cup to her father.

"Like a log," her father said.

"How do you sleep like a log?" Isaac asked.

"You get into bed, close your eyes and then the next thing you know, it's time to get up."

"I sleep like a log," Isaac said.

"That's a good thing because little boys need lots of sleep. That's when you do most of your growing."

Isaac considered this for a moment. "You mean I'm bigger when I wake up in the morning than I was when I went to bed the night before?"

"That's exactly what I mean."

"But my PJs still fit." Her son jumped off his chair, stood straight and tall with his arms extended. "See?"

His earnestness made them all laugh. Annie noticed, though, that while the pajamas did still fit, her son's ankles were exposed below the bottoms. He looked like an adorable little scarecrow. Isaac laughed along with them as he climbed onto his grandfather's lap. He'd soon be too big for that, too.

"Mom's making waffles for breakfast."

"My favorite," Thomas said, steadying his grandson with one arm.

"You say that about everything she makes."

"That's because she makes all my favorites. Now tell me, did you have fun at the wedding yesterday?"

While CJ set the table, Annie stirred the batter, made a small test waffle to make sure the iron was at the right temperature and listened to her father and her son talk about yesterday's celebration.

"My favorite thing was getting to carry the rings. Uncle Paul said I was the best ring bearer he's ever seen."

"What about the party? Did you like the food?"

Isaac made a face. "The chicken had cheese inside of it. That was gross. I liked the cake, though."

"So, not liking the chicken *cordon bleu*, but a big fan of the chocolate cake," Thomas said.

"We shoulda had Mom's fried chicken," Isaac suggested.

"Your Aunt Emily was going for something

a little more elegant," Annie said, "and a little less greasy finger food."

"Me and Gramps like greasy finger food. Right, Gramps?"

"It's another favorite to be sure, but there's a time and place for everything. What about the rest of the party? Did you like the music and the dancing?"

"Yup. You can dance pretty good in your wheelchair."

Annie watched her father affectionately ruffle her son's hair. He was an amazing man, he had been such a good father over the years and he had carried those skills into grandparenthood. At moments like this, she was overwhelmed with love and gratitude for the man who had steadfastly overcome one obstacle after the next and become an incredible role model for his daughters and grandson, and even their wider circle of family and friends.

"But why did it make people sad?" Isaac asked.

"Oh, honey. They weren't sad," Annie said. "Those were happy tears you saw when your grandfather danced with Auntie Em last night."

Isaac seemed to give the idea some serious consideration before moving on to his next question. "People were smiling when you danced with my teacher. How come that didn't make them cry?"

Annie and CJ exchanged a look while they waited for their father's response.

Thomas cleared his throat. "Well, I guess something about a father dancing with his daughter on her wedding day makes people kind of emotional."

"So why *did* you dance with Ms. Potter?"

Annie's father didn't fluster easily, but this question had definitely caught him off guard.

"He's actually blushing," CJ whispered into her ear.

Annie grinned as she lifted four golden waffles onto a plate and poured more batter into the waffle maker.

Thomas cleared his throat. "I danced with Libby because I like her. I knew her a long time ago. We weren't friends then, but I think we're going to be friends now."

"Is she going to be your girlfriend?"

CJ laughed outright and Annie tried to shush her, but there was no shushing CJ.

"Yeah, Dad. Is Libby going to be a girl *friend*, or is she your *girl*friend?"

Annie was sure she'd never seen her father so discombobulated. "All right, you two. Enough questions. It's time to eat."

She carried a platter piled with waffles

to the table. "CJ, if you'll get the butter and maple syrup, please, I'll pour the orange juice and refill everyone's coffee."

And she would be grateful that the subject of her father dancing with Libby had kept the focus off her and Paul. She wasn't sure how she felt about it, and she definitely wasn't ready to talk about it.

CHAPTER SEVENTEEN

TWO WEEKS AFTER Jack and Emily's wedding, Paul's life settled into an easy routine. He was out of bed early every morning to fix breakfast and spend some time with his father before he left for the clinic. Several mornings a week, he timed his departure so he could spend an hour at Annie's having coffee and some of her delectable baked goods before his shift started.

Now that Jack's parents had set off on their travels and he and his new wife were settled into his parents' home across the street, life was even a little easier. Emily frequently worked at home, and she had somehow managed to forge a relationship with Paul's father. The old man actually seemed quite smitten. Paul knew Emily visited Libby's mother as well, and Mable was also completely taken with her.

"Hello-o," Emily called out as she let herself in the side door and made her way into the kitchen.

"Good morning," Paul said, setting a cup of coffee in front of his father. "Look who's here, Dad."

"Good morning, Geoff," she said. His father insisted she call him by his first name rather than Doc Woodward, which was the way almost everyone had ever addressed him. "You're looking very handsome this morning."

His father preened, running a hand over his head, his neatly groomed hair now silver-gray but still thick and abundant. There weren't many things about his father Paul wanted to emulate, but he sure hoped he had inherited the man's hair genes.

This morning was Paul's early Monday shift at the health center, followed by lunch with Annie. Emily had offered to come over and see that his father had his breakfast, get him settled with his TV remote and anything else he needed, and then she would return at noon to see he ate his lunch. His father liked to have breakfast in his pajamas and bathrobe but this morning Paul had wanted him dressed for the day before Emily arrived. He had balked, of course, but the indignation was forgotten now that Emily was here and being charming. And if Emily knew he was meeting her sister for lunch, she didn't let on.

By the time Paul poured her cup of decaf, she was already at the kitchen counter and starting on breakfast.

"How do you like your eggs, Geoff?"

"Soft-boiled," he said.

"Me, too," she said brightly, but with her back to his father she made a face and stuck out her tongue as though she was gagging.

"Thank you for this," Paul said.

"Hey, you and Jack are practically like brothers. This is what families are for."

The way things had been going with him and Annie, he was beginning to have hope that someday the family connection might even be real.

"The numbers for my cell and for the clinic are on the notepad by the phone. Call me if anything comes up."

"I will."

"His lunch is in the fridge. There's soup to heat up and a tuna salad sandwich."

"Go, have a good morning. Everything will be fine." She gently pushed him toward the door. "And say hi to my sister for me," she said with a knowing smile.

So she did know about their Monday lunch dates. At least he thought of them as dates, although he was sure Annie thought of them as just lunch. He hadn't had another chance to kiss her since the wedding, aside from a chaste goodbye on the lips after morning coffee. He had given up hoping an opportunity would present itself. No such luck. If he wanted such an occasion to arise, he would have to create one. And that's exactly what he intended to do. Saturday was his day off and he was going to invite Annie to drive to the city with him. He would bring it up over lunch and hope for the best. Annie disliked crowds and shopping malls and excessive traffic, but thanks to a suggestion from Emily, he had found the perfect place to take her. All he could do now was keep his fingers crossed and hope she would be interested enough to say yes.

PAUL HAD ASKED Annie to spend the day in the city with him. It was a real date, no question about that. She wanted it to feel right, but something wasn't quite…right. She felt confused and conflicted and she wasn't sure why. The truth was…

The truth was that before Eric's death, their marriage had been starting to feel flat. One-sided. It's not that he had been a bad husband. In many ways he had been the perfect husband. He had kissed her goodbye every morning when he left for school. He had kissed her again when he came home and asked what was for dinner.

Eric had loved her cooking, that much she had known. He raved about the roast chickens and gravy, the omelets, the strudels. Paul seemed to like it, too, but there was a subtle difference in the way he talked about it. The other morning when he'd stopped by for coffee, she had offered him a slice of her apple-cinnamon coffee cake with the crumble topping and brown-sugar glaze. He had taken a forkful and set down the fork and then he looked directly into her eyes. "You are incredible," he'd said.

That had startled her. "Why do you say that?"

"You don't just cook. You're like an artist in her studio, creating one masterpiece after another."

The compliment had left her feeling flattered and oddly elated, a little light-headed even. "It's just coffee cake."

With his gaze still locked with hers, he had covered her hand with his. "It's never *just* coffee cake when you've made it." He had leaned in then and kissed her lightly on the lips. "Trust me. It's a work of art."

Even now, thinking about how Paul had looked at her left her breathless.

She tried to remember a time when Eric had looked at her that way—really, truly looked into her eyes as though she was the only person in the world. Sadly, she couldn't. He had always been getting ready to rush out the door or getting ready to watch a football game on television or checking baseball stats online or planning a field trip for his students at Riverton High.

"Stop," she said to herself. "Stop it right now."

What was wrong with her? She had never had these thoughts while Eric was alive. Now that Paul was in her life, she was becoming critical of someone who was no longer here to account for the way he had treated her. She was developing feelings for Paul. She couldn't deny them. A psychologist would probably tell her that having these thoughts about her deceased husband was her way of assuaging the guilt about falling for her husband's best friend.

"Penny for your thoughts."

She whirled around to find her father behind her. "Dad, I didn't hear you come in."

"I'm riding my stealth mobile today."

She laughed. He had always made up the corniest names for his wheelchairs.

"You looked like you were a million miles

away just now," he said. "With the weight of the world on your shoulders."

"Oh, Dad. Life would be so much easier if..."

"If it was easy?"

She nodded.

"It never is, though."

"It used to be. I thought I had it all. A great husband, an amazing family, this wonderful home..." She waved her hand. "I thought everything would stay this way forever."

"These things you're feeling are a natural part of grief. Trust me," he said. "I hate to sound glib but, been there, done that."

"I'm sorry, Dad. You're the last person I should be whining to about this."

"For starters, you're not whining. Second, I am your father, which makes me the first person you should be talking to when life gives you a backhand. And you also know better than to deal me the sympathy card. Yes, I lost the use of my legs. Yes, my wife walked out on me. And I made up my mind a long time ago those things were not going to define me. Now, when I look around, I see how lucky I am."

Annie slid off the stool and looped her arms around his shoulders. "You've always been the man we looked up to, me and Emily and CJ. Our knight in shining armor and a superhero cape."

"Now there's a picture for you." He gave her one of his deep, genuine laughs that always set the world right. "How about you pour your old dad a cup of coffee and tell me what's going on."

Annie did as he asked, refilled her own and carried both cups to the kitchen table. "It's Paul," she said. "He asked me to drive into the city with him on Saturday."

"Are you taking Isaac?"

"No, it's just the two of us. Isaac will have to stay at home."

Her father picked up his mug and studied her over the rim while he took a long drink. Then he set it down and leaned his forearms on the table. "I won't be here," he said. "I'm going out with Libby on Saturday."

"Oh." Not the response she was expecting, but she went with it. "That's nice. Where are you taking her?"

"To the veterans' retirement home."

"Seriously? Way to sweep a girl off her feet, Dad."

He laughed. "Believe it or not, this was her idea. We were there a couple of weeks ago and she had such an interesting time, she decided she'd like to go back. We just had to wait until Emily had a free day to stay with Libby's mother."

Annie realized her child-care options were rapidly diminishing. "I'll ask CJ to keep an eye on Isaac then."

"Now that you've sorted that out, why don't you tell me what's really on your mind?"

She brushed aside the temptation to deny that anything was bothering her. Her father would never believe her anyway.

"This thing with Paul feels like a date and *that* makes me uncomfortable."

"And you don't want to go on a date with him? I've been under the impression you liked him. A lot."

"I do, but it feels too...soon."

"Too soon to have a life? Too soon to have friends, *good* friends who you enjoy spending time with?"

"Not when you put it like that but—"

"Annie, it's your nature to overthink things, always has been. But sometimes you need to turn off those thoughts and just go with your heart."

"That's such a cliché."

"Maybe, but it's a cliché for a good reason.

So tell me, all thinking aside, what's your heart telling you to do?"

She sighed. "Everyone tells me I work too much, that I need to give myself a break and have some fun. I guess my heart is telling me they're right."

"And what is your heart telling you about Paul."

"He's a good person, a good friend." He was the kind of man she might be able to fall in love with if she let herself, but she wasn't sure she was ready to say those things out loud, especially not to her father.

"He is all of those things," her father said. "The way he's looking after his dad shows he cares about family. He's great with kids."

"That's true. Isaac loves him."

"And I see the way he looks at you." Her father's steely blue gaze was unrelenting. "If a guy like Paul is in a relationship…" Thomas said. "Seems to me he'd be the kind of guy who'd be all in."

Annie's nose was getting warm and it was no doubt turning red. Hearing her father talk about Paul was unexpected. He had never spoken about Eric this way and she felt compelled to defend him.

"Eric was a good man, too," she said softly. "A good husband and father."

"Of course he was, honey." He patted her hand. "There was never any question about that, and he was way too young when we lost him. The thing is, though…you're still here. You need to keep on living."

Another cliché. She let this one slide. "What about you? You didn't move on after my mother left."

Thomas chuckled. "Nice try, but that was different. Your mother and I were still married. I was recovering from a serious injury and getting used to life in a wheelchair."

"I'm sorry, Dad. I shouldn't have brought it up. I can't imagine how tough things must have been for you. Lonely, too."

"No, I'm glad you brought it up." He stared out the window but didn't appear to be looking at anything. "Memories are funny things. I don't remember it being so hard—I just did what I had to do to get from one day to the next—but I won't lie to you. There were times when it was lonely."

"And now?"

Her father looked at her and grinned. "And now, not so much."

"Libby is amazing. I'm so glad the two of you are…"

Thomas arched his brows, waited for her to finish.

"A couple?" she asked. She honestly wasn't sure.

"Me, too. I've been hoping it's not too weird for you and your sisters."

"Why would it be weird?"

He responded with an expansive shrug. "We're not exactly spring chickens, are we? We haven't known one another for long, and we both have some baggage."

Annie laughed at the image of two not-so-young chickens with too many suitcases. "Everyone has a past," she said. "It's what makes us who we are today, but we don't have to let our past set the course for our future."

"Wise words from a wise young woman." Her father's praise was warm and genuine. "So now the question is whether or not she'll listen to her own advice."

Good question. "So you think I should go into the city with Paul on Saturday?"

"It doesn't matter what I think. It's what you want that's important."

And what did she want? A year ago she would have wanted everything—including her marriage—to stay the same forever. The universe or fate or whatever had a different plan. Now she was on her own. Now a man she thought she had known forever had come back into her life, and it turned out she hadn't really known him at all. Paul encouraged her to explore new ways of looking at her everyday world. He made her believe her thoughts and ideas had value. The truth was that when she was with him, she felt vibrant and alive.

"And I want to spend the day with him." There, she'd said it.

"Go," her father said. "Call him."

"I should check with CJ first, find out if she can watch Isaac for me."

"Call him. Everything else will work itself out. Have a little faith."

She liked to have everything under control before she made a commitment, but her father was probably right. For once she would throw caution to the wind and follow her heart.

"Thanks, Dad." She gave him a hug, and then she went in search of her phone before she talked herself out of it.

CHAPTER EIGHTEEN

WITH HER PHONE in hand, Annie closed her bedroom door and settled into one of the two ivory wingback chairs that had been a splurge when she had redecorated five years ago. She had imagined herself and Eric sitting here in the evening, sharing some quiet time, perhaps reading or sharing details about their day. Or spending some intimate time over coffee on a Sunday morning, planning the week ahead.

Why hadn't those things ever happened?

Instead, she had come to bed dog-tired after a long day in the kitchen, the garden, the laundry room, and the hours spent taking care of her husband and her son, her extended family, her bed-and-breakfast guests. Eric had loved teaching and he'd been up and out the door early every morning, staying late after school to coach various sports teams, and would then come home with an armload of lesson plans and papers to grade.

And so the chairs had languished, mostly unused, except for when Eric had sat to lace up his shoes or had turned one of them into a catchall for a jacket or a gym bag.

Annie chased away the ghostly regrets as she kicked off her shoes and swung her feet onto the single ottoman shared by the two chairs. Before she chickened out, she sent Paul a text.

Would love to spend Saturday in the city. Thanks for suggesting it. Annie

Next she sent a message to CJ.

Hey, sis. I have a date on Saturday. Can you look after Isaac for me? We'll be back by dinner time. Please? Pretty please? A.
PS: Yes, it's a real date. Not a big deal.

Not a big deal. Who was she kidding? It was a *huge* deal. After she hit Send, her phone promptly played a tone to indicate she had an incoming message. It was from Paul.

You've made me one happy man. Pick you up Saturday at 9:30. FYI, now that you've said yes, there's no changing your mind. Paul

He must have been on a break or at least between patients to have responded so quickly.

His quip about not changing her mind made her laugh. She was in the process of formulating a witty response about a woman's prerogative when her phone jingled with another incoming message. This one was from CJ.

No can do, big sis. I teach therapeutic riding on Saturday morning and I've been asked to give a 4H workshop on halter and bridle training in the afternoon. CJ

Well, this was not working out as she had hoped. Her father and CJ both had plans. Emily had another commitment. Unless…
She tapped out a message to Emily.

Dad says you're spending Saturday with Libby's mom. Any chance you can keep an eye on Isaac, too? A.

As always, Emily responded right away.

Promised to take Mable to a whist tournament at the seniors' center. Good times! But no fun for a little boy. Sorry! E.

Okay, this was not going well at all. Annie had never expected, let alone asked, her family to put their lives on hold so she could live hers, and there was the problem. Until now, she hadn't asked. Ever. But now that she had agreed to spend the day with Paul, she wanted to do it and she didn't want to disappoint either of them by changing her mind.

Who else could she ask? If Isaac had been invited to a birthday party on Saturday afternoon, she could have CJ drop him off on her way to the 4H thing. But this weekend was remarkably commitment-free. Maybe Stacey McGregor? Isaac was friends with her daughter, Melissa, at school. No, that wouldn't work, either. They had chatted at the PTA meeting a few evenings ago and Stacey had said they were going to Madison for the weekend to celebrate her husband's parents' fortieth anniversary.

Annie scrolled through the list of contacts on her phone—her very *short* list of contacts—and stopped when she reached Rose's name. Rose! Of course. Rose worked the breakfast and lunch shifts on weekdays at the café. Isaac didn't know her very well, and to be honest, Rose hadn't exactly warmed up to him. For some reason, Annie felt a tad uneasy about asking her half sister to child-sit on her day off. But after all she had done for Rose, helping her settle into Riverton, get a job, find a place to live—not to mention going to bat for her with the rest of the family—she shouldn't feel guilty about asking. But was she feeling guilty, or was it something else?

The memory of Rose at Emily and Jack's wedding flashed across her mind: completely intoxicated, having to be carried upstairs; the young woman's bleary-eyed hangover the morning after. She remembered Jack and Emily cautioning her about putting too much faith in Rose because they thought she was covering up a substance-abuse problem. Even her father and CJ had reservations about her. All Annie saw was a scared and insecure kid—even though she was technically an adult—who had grown up in desperate circumstances and with none of the advantages the rest of them had enjoyed.

Come to think of it, Paul was the only person who hadn't offered any warnings about Rose. He had seen her at the wedding. He was a doctor and Rose herself had told Annie that she had seen him when she went to the clinic with that terrible bronchitis. If anyone would know about or even suspect a drinking problem, it would be Paul. And yet he hadn't said anything.

Annie brushed aside everyone else's concerns. She considered calling Rose, realized there was no point because she would still be at work, so she sent another text message.

Hi, Rose. I have plans with Paul on Saturday. Could you come out to the farm and stay with Isaac? Everyone else is busy. You'd be doing me a huge favor! Annie

There. It was done. If Rose was busy and couldn't make it, then Annie would have to cancel. What other choice did she have?

She set her phone on the narrow side table tucked between the two chairs, leaned back and flexed her ankles. She had forgotten how comfortable these chairs were. This would be a good place to sit while she worked on her weekly *Ask Annie* column. She quickly retrieved her laptop from the desk beneath the window and returned to the chair. She had started with two articles—or photo essays as Emily described them—on chickens and eggs. With the second one she had included her recipes for French toast and her asparagus-and-bacon frittata with photographs to illustrate the step-by-step instructions.

After those, she had switched things up with a series of articles about the wedding. The first had been about the decorations and table settings, which had been elegant and understated in spite of it being an outdoor country wedding. Her second article had focused on the bride who was, after all, the reason people read the blog in the first place. Even Annie had to admit that her close-ups of the flowers woven into Emily's stunning dark hair, their grandmother's vintage cameo pendant around her neck and the classic solitaire in her engagement ring were quite remarkable.

Her third and final wedding column had been about family gathered for the occasion. Emily and Jack gazing into each other's eyes during their first dance as husband and wife was a portrait of a match made in heaven.

The photograph she had taken of her father dancing with Libby had stolen the show. In addition to illustrating the joyfulness of the dance, Paul said she had captured the love blossoming between her father and this wonderful new woman in his life. If Annie had to make one prediction, it was that the Finnegan family would soon be celebrating another wedding.

She could practically hear CJ's and Isaac's laughter every time she looked at the picture of the two of them doing an offbeat hybrid of jive and line dancing. Isaac's curls, which had been tamed for the ceremony, were wildly tousled and his tie askew. CJ had kicked off her shoes and was dancing barefoot, her long blond hair flying around her.

Someone in the family—although no one would confess to having done it—had used her camera to take a photograph of her dancing with Paul. Annie had spent more time than she would ever admit studying that picture, examining the way her hand fit so well into his, how he was exactly the right height for her to rest her cheek against his shoulder, how his lips had brushed her hair at the exact moment the camera had captured their *moment*.

The only person missing from the family shots was Rose. Annie had poured over the photographs she and others had taken. In every single one of them, Rose had a wineglass in her hand, a wineglass to her lips, or she was at the bar getting another glass of wine. If her half sister had noticed she had been left out, she hadn't said anything. Annie felt beyond guilty—and even a little shocked to discover she had a self-righteous streak—but Emily had agreed it was her column and should reflect her values. Their readership expected no less.

Her phone jingled, announcing an incoming text message, pulling her back to the present. She picked it up and snapped her laptop shut.

Sure I can babysit. What time? RD

Annie considered responding, and then decided to call Rose instead. She must be on a break or maybe even finished for the day.

"Hey," Rose said when she picked up.

"Hi, Rose. Thank you so much. I really appreciate you doing this for us."

"Yah, well, I didn't have any plans so no probs."

No probs? Annie momentarily closed her eyes and took a long, slow breath. Her initial thought was to question whether this was the kind of influence she wanted for her son. Her second thought was to chastise herself for the first thought and to remind herself she needed to be more charitable, to give Rose a break. *The poor kid's had a tough go of things*, she told herself.

"Oh. Thank you, Rose. Do you need a ride out here in the morning? I can ask Paul to pick you up and give you a lift. Or would you like to come out on Friday and spend the night?"

"Nah. Thanks, though. I have, you know, plans in town on Friday. My car's running okay, though, so I can drive myself out in the morning. What time?"

"Nine thirty," Annie said. "I hope that's not too early."

"Nah, that should be fine."

"All right, then. I'll see you on Saturday. I'll be sure to leave lunch for you and Isaac."

"Sure. Whatevs. Oh, gotta run. Break's over."

Yah. Nah. No probs. Whatevs.

Annie sighed. While she understood Rose's life had been a tough one, she wasn't a kid anymore. She was a young woman in her early twenties with a family willing to support her. But before that could happen, she had to lose the attitude and then she had some serious growing up to do.

"Would you listen to yourself? 'Serious growing up to do.' When did you turn into an old lady?"

Isaac would be fine with Rose. She and Paul would be away only for the day. Just a few hours, really. He was taking her into the city, they were going for lunch and then he had a surprise for her. He had also promised to have her back here in time for dinner. What could go wrong in a few hours?

CHAPTER NINETEEN

ON SATURDAY MORNING, Paul congratulated himself as he drove up the driveway to the Finnegan farmhouse. He had a sense that this excursion was pivotal. Spending hours with Annie in a place that was unfamiliar to both of them—this was the day he would make it with her...or break it. And he had every intention of making this day the turning point in their relationship. He intended to pull out all the stops, and make her realize he was the one. The *next* one. But not second best.

He pulled into the roundabout, attempting to sing along to a familiar song on the radio by a band whose name he couldn't remember. He slowed when he spotted Rosc's rusted rattletrap. He parked next to her car and stepped out of his, noting the accumulation of empty junk-food wrappers, take-out boxes and cigarette packages littering her backseat, the overflowing ashtray in the front console. No bottles, empty or otherwise, that he could see, but even Rose had to be smart enough to keep those out of sight.

The sky was overcast and the morning air had a bite to it as he climbed the steps of the veranda. Chester was snoozing on the welcome mat. Paul opened the screen door and nudged the old dog, who slowly heaved himself onto all fours and made his way down the veranda in an arthritic amble and disappeared around the side of the house. Paul's knock was met by another dog's bark and a young boy's whoop. The door flew open and he was greeted by Isaac, who was gripping his dog by the collar.

"Uncle Paul! Down, boy," he commanded the dog. "Stay down."

"Hey, Isaac." He reached out, ruffled the boy's curls with one hand and scruffed the border collie with the other. "How's your new dog? Is he settling in?"

"Yup. Chester doesn't like him, though. Mom says he's too ramb—ramb…?"

"Rambunctious?"

"That's it. He's too rambunctious for an old dog."

"What's his name?"

"Beasley."

Paul smiled. "Good name. And I'm sure

Chester will come around, once you teach Beasley some manners."

"Auntie CJ is helping me train him. She trains horses, too."

Paul stepped inside the house and shut the door against a gust of chilly fall air.

"Then I'm sure she'll have Beasley saddled up before you know it."

Isaac let out a loud shriek and, still clinging to the dog's collar, raced up the stairs. "Giddy up, Beasley! Giddy up!"

Laughing, Paul made his way to the kitchen in search of Annie. Instead he found Rose languishing on a stool at the island. She had on a pair of distressed blue jeans that had more holes than denim and a Guns N' Roses T-shirt with a fringed hem. She was dumping spoonfuls of sugar into a cup of coffee, stirring after each addition. A large black knapsack sat on the floor next to the stool. It looked suspiciously bulky.

"Hey. How's it going?" she asked, her bored tone indicating she didn't actually care.

"Everything's going well. How are you?"

"Fine."

"Where's Annie?" he asked.

"Upstairs getting ready. You're early." She coughed into the crook of her arm.

He was five minutes ahead of schedule and

she made it sound as though he'd committed a crime. "How are you feeling these days?"

"Fine."

She didn't look fine. She was too thin, too pale, too jittery, her cough too deep and phlegmy for her to be fine.

"Not working at the restaurant today?"

She shook her head. "Babysitting."

"Ah, I see." Annie had asked her to come out here to look after Isaac? That was...unsettling.

"I've never babysat before. Sure hope the kid doesn't give me any trouble."

She was talking about Isaac as though he was just some...some kid, not her nephew. Isaac was one of the best and brightest little boys Paul had ever met. A real live wire, yes, but always polite, respectful, well-behaved. A testament to the way he was raised by two loving parents and a close-knit extended family. And yet Rose's first go-to was to anticipate a problem.

"I'm sure he won't be any trouble."

Rose arched her eyebrows. "We'll see."

Luckily, Annie walked into the kitchen, saving him from having to continue an awkward conversation with Rose. Annie looked amazing in slim-fitting black jeans and a sea-green pullover sweater with a green-and-gray print scarf looped around her neck.

"Paul, you're here," she said. "Would you like to have coffee before we leave?"

"No, thanks. We should get going." All week he had been looking forward to spending this day with her—no interruptions, no obligations, just the two of them.

"Okay." She turned to Rose. "I've left a list of everyone's phone numbers on the fridge door—mine, Dad's, Emily's and CJ's. There's leftover lasagna in the fridge for you and Isaac to have for lunch. You can warm it up in the microwave."

"Sure."

"CJ is down at the stable and then she's going into town right after her students leave. My dad has already left and won't be home until late this afternoon, and Paul and I will be back by dinnertime."

Rose drummed her fingers on the countertop.

If Annie noticed, she didn't let on.

Paul wished he could tell the young woman the seven-year-old child she was here to look after had better manners than she did, but that would have been out of line and it certainly wasn't the tone he wanted to set for his day in the city with Annie.

"Isaac is up in his room right now," Annie said. "He'll need to take Beasley out at some point, and I've told him they need to stay in the backyard. No wandering off, not even down to the stable."

"Sure."

"There's milk and fruit in the fridge and homemade chocolate chip cookies in the cookie jar if the two of you feel like having a snack."

"I can manage, okay? Now go. Have fun or whatever."

Annie gave her a quick hug. "Thanks, we will." When she looked up at Paul and smiled, any reservations he had about Rose vaporized. "I just need to get my coat."

He followed her down the hallway to the foyer and waited while she pulled on a pair of gray riding boots over her jeans and reached for a gray jacket.

"Let me help." He held the garment and settled it onto her shoulders after she slipped her arms into the sleeves.

"Thank you." She angled her face up to his and gave him a smile that lit up the room.

"All set?"

She picked up her handbag and a pair of gloves. "I'm ready."

He had been ready for this moment since

forever. He held the door for her and followed her out to his car.

"Brrrr," she said. "It feels cold enough to snow."

"It's not in the forecast," he said. "I checked."

She settled into the passenger seat and fastened her seat belt. "You thought of everything."

He slid behind the wheel and started the car. "I hope so," he said. But the truth was he had only been thinking about her, about how well things were between them, especially since the wedding and how spending this day together would cement their relationship. He hoped.

"You're taking me to an art gallery?" Annie asked. All week she had been trying to guess what he had planned for them today. Shopping at the Mall of America? She was not a fan of shopping and she intensely disliked a noisy, crowded mall. A Minnesota Twins game? She knew he liked baseball from hearing him and Jack talk about going to games when they lived in Chicago. Thankfully that's not what he had in mind. She couldn't see herself sitting in a ballpark on a day like this. She would not have guessed him to be an art aficionado, but visiting a gallery was by far the better option.

"Not just any gallery. This private gallery specializes in photography exhibits."

"Photography?"

"That's right. You've taken some amazing photographs, and your *Ask Annie* column on Emily's blog is a big hit. I thought you might like to see this show in particular. It's called *Snapshots of a Small Town*.

"Really? People come to a big-city gallery to see photographs of a small town?"

"They don't just come to look at them. They buy them, too."

Interesting. She gazed up at the sleek dark glass facade of the two-story gallery. Nothing about this building brought small towns to mind.

Paul was holding the door for her. "Should we take a look?"

"Yes, definitely. This is so thoughtful of you."

He held out his hand. She put hers into it, liking the way he gave hers a gentle squeeze before he laced his fingers with hers, then they went inside together.

The gallery's interior was as modern and chic as its exterior. The main floor was one huge space. A second-floor loft spanned the back half of the building. As soon as she stepped inside, Annie's eyes were drawn from the gleaming dark wood floors to the high ceiling and subdued industrial-style lighting. Throughout the main floor, free-standing walls divided the huge space into smaller areas.

Inside the entrance, the sales counter consisted of a clear acrylic desk. Its surface housed a small stack of catalogs, arranged with laser precision, a glass tray of business cards and a crystal vase of artfully arranged white freesia.

"Welcome." A tall woman dressed in a high-necked dress, opaque tights and stilettos—all black—seemed to appear out of nowhere. She selected the catalog on top of the stack without disturbing the ones beneath it and passed it across the desk.

"Thank you," Paul said.

The woman glanced down at their clasped hands and smiled. "Enjoy the exhibit," she said. "Be sure to let me know if you have any questions."

The images on the walls grabbed Annie's attention and she found herself immediately drawn into the exhibit. The color photographs were displayed in simple black frames with white mats. She walked from one image to the next to the next, taking in the subject of each photo, the composition, the light, the angles.

An old blue bicycle with chipped paint and a faded wicker basket leaned against the white clapboard of a shop with the word *Bakery* arching across the window. She could picture the cyclist stowing her purchases in the basket and riding home with the aromas of freshly baked bread wafting around her.

A battered wooden tool box and a newly constructed birdhouse on a workbench. She could smell the sawdust, feel the texture of the wood. What color would the builder paint it? What kind of birds would move in and raise a family?

"It's as though each picture tells a story."

She had forgotten Paul was still holding her hand until she felt him stroke her skin with his thumb.

"These are amazing," she said.

"They are. And so are yours."

"But I'm not a professional photographer."

He didn't agree or disagree. Instead he handed the catalog to her. "This will have a lot of information about the photographers and their work in this show. You can take it home with you."

"Thank you. And thank you for bringing

me here, Paul. This is so inspiring. When Emily gave me the camera, I never imagined taking pictures would be so—and I know this sounds silly—satisfying."

"I'm glad you discovered photography. Or maybe it discovered you."

"I don't know. Do you think maybe I can learn to take pictures like these? Pictures that tell a story?"

The intensity of his gaze took her by surprise. "Annie, you already do."

She felt her chest swell with an emotion she couldn't identify but was so overwhelming, she needed a minute to adjust to it before she could speak. He had planned this whole day for her. She would be too embarrassed to confess she had never been to an art gallery before. Riverton had been the center of life for all of her life—it was her home and she loved it and she never wanted to live anywhere else. She also loved how Paul had gone out of his way to open new doors for her, to show her that although she was a small-town girl at heart, there was still a big, wide world out here for her to explore.

And the way he was looking at her now… she could tell he was seeing her in a way no one else ever had. Suddenly she wasn't just a mom, a daughter, a sister, a whiz in the kitchen and everyone's go-to for organizing another bake-sale fund-raiser or the school's next fun fair. She was a real person with her own interests and possibly even some unique talent she had yet to explore. For a quick second, she thought about the unused reading chair in her bedroom.

"While we're in the city, do you think we'll have time to go into a bookstore?" She was going to put her chair to use, she decided, and she would start with a book on basic photography.

"Besides the gallery, and lunch, of course, I can't think of anywhere I'd rather go." He linked her arm with his and gently urged her along. "Still lots to see here."

He was right. She wanted to soak it all in, and she didn't want to miss a thing.

By the time they had toured the entire main floor, then climbed the wide staircase with its clear acrylic side panels—everything about this space was open, airy and fresh—to see the displays in the loft, Annie looked forward to checking out photography books and pouring over the show's catalog. Her reading chair would finally see some use. Most of all she was excited to pick up her camera. She wouldn't look for images, she would be searching for stories. Paul said she already did that without being conscious of it. She wanted to explore light and perspective and close-ups versus wide angles.

Back at the sales desk in the main reception area, the woman in black gave them another friendly smile. "What did you think?"

"I loved it," Annie said. "I've always considered art to be drawing and painting and I thought photographs were just a way to preserve memories or capture images for a news story. But these photographs are every bit as artistic."

"I'm glad you think so. The five photographers who contributed to this show have different styles, as I'm sure you noticed. What they have in common is their love for their small hometowns, both the history and the people who live there now."

Annie looked again at the cover of the *Snapshots of a Small Town* catalog. "It shows. I'm sure a lot of folks believe small towns are all the same, but they're not. It's the unique blend of history and current residents that sets each one apart." She was startled by her own observation and once again grateful to Paul for opening these doors for her.

"Did you have a particular favorite?" the saleswoman asked.

"I did. Upstairs there's a photograph of a

little round table in an apple orchard. It's set for tea for two, with a lacy tablecloth and cut flowers and mismatched vintage china. It looks so inviting." Annie had been completely captivated. Near the table was an old wooden wheelbarrow filled with rosy red apples. She had wondered who would be having afternoon tea in an orchard. The apple pickers?

"I know the one you mean. It does look inviting. And very romantic, don't you think?" the woman asked, glancing meaningfully from Annie to Paul and back again.

"Very." Annie felt her nose get warm, and the one-word response was all she could manage.

"Is that piece still for sale?" Paul asked.

She looked up at him, wondering where his question was going.

The saleswoman turned and retrieved a small laptop from the white credenza behind the main desk, tapped at a few keys and smiled. "I'm happy to say it is."

"We'll take it." Paul took out his wallet and handed a credit card to the woman, whose smile had suddenly become a little warmer.

"Thank you. I'll have my assistant wrap it up for you and I'll be right back to ring this through," she said before she disappeared into a back room.

"Are you sure?" Annie asked when they were alone.

"Judging by the amount of time you spent admiring this photograph, I figured it was your favorite. If the gallery owner hadn't asked, I would have."

"But…" Annie had noticed the prices and was aghast to think he would spend so much on it.

"No *but*s. I want you to have it. I hope you'll think of today every time you look at it. I'd also like it to be a reminder that your photographs are every bit as evocative."

"Thank you." She wrapped her arms around his neck and kissed him. They were still locked in the embrace when the woman returned with Paul's receipt and the framed photograph wrapped in brown paper.

Paul thanked her in return, tucked the package under his arm and led Annie outside into the crisp air. It felt even colder than it had earlier.

"So?" Paul asked. "What did you think?"

"I loved it. I can't believe we spent…" She checked her watch. "Two and a half hours? We've been here for two and a half hours?"

"We have. Where to next? Would you like

to go for lunch, or should we find a book-store first?"

It was already past lunchtime and she was starving, but she would enjoy the meal more after she found the book she was after. "Bookstore."

"Then your wish is my command, my lady."

And for the first time in her life, she felt a little like a character in a fairy tale. Cinderella? No, more like Eliza Doolittle.

CHAPTER TWENTY

THOMAS SAT AT a table near the back of the retirement home's social center. He had just finished a game of Yahtzee with a trio of octogenarians. Now he was watching the woman he loved drift around the room. He had worked as a volunteer here for the better part of ten years. He knew most of these men and women, some of them had become friends. Libby moved comfortably and confidently from one activity and conversation to another. Now she took a seat with an elderly widow with blue-gray hair whose husband had served in Korea more than six decades ago, admiring the photographs the woman kept in a small photo album she carried with her everywhere. Grandchildren and great-grandchildren. Thomas had looked at those pictures himself on more than one occasion.

Libby appeared to be much more at ease with that sort of thing. She leaned attentively close, pointing to pages as they were turned, asking questions. Pride radiated from the woman as she shared details about her family with Libby.

They had spent the morning here and it was now almost time for the residents to head to the dining room for lunch. While Thomas had played a few games of Ping-Pong with another resident who was also living life on wheels, Libby had read the morning newspaper to a small group of residents whose eyesight was failing. Then she had spent some time with a woman who tried to teach her how to knit until Libby declared she had been born with two left hands. After a physiotherapist showed up and wheeled Thomas's fellow Ping-Pong player away for a therapy session, he had joined a group who were having coffee and a game of Yahtzee at a round table in the corner. From time to time he would glance around to see what Libby was doing, sometimes catching her eye—exchanging a look and a smile—sometimes not. Either way, he loved having her here, appreciated her willingness to give back to people who had given a lot and risked so much more for this great country they called home.

Just before noon, several staff members came into the social center to help those residents who needed assistance to get to the dining room for lunch. Thomas waited for

Libby to cross the room to where he was, watching. True to what he now recognized as her style, she was wearing one of her colorful outfits—purple pants with a soft pink pullover that matched the large square-cut stones in her earrings.

"Hi," she said.

"Hi. You are amazing. Did you know that?"

"Funny thing," she said. "The last time I was out with a really handsome guy I know, I seem to recall he said the same thing."

"Handsome and wise. This guy sounds like the whole package."

She laughed. "Oh, he is. And he promised to take me out for lunch today." She put her hands on the arms of his chair and leaned in. "And after lunch," she whispered, "we could go back to my place."

He caught her wrists, holding her close. "Why, Ms. Potter. Are you propositioning me?"

"Mr. Finnegan!" she said playfully. "My only proposition is a cup of coffee and a slice of red velvet cake. Possibly a game of cribbage with my elderly mother."

"Sounds like a very decent proposal." He looped a finger in the chunky gold chain around her neck, gently tugged her closer for a quick kiss. "I accept, and I'll hope for something a little less...decent next time."

She gave him a saucy wink, unhooked his finger and straightened. "Should we go?"

"Definitely. I would suggest running out to the farm for lunch but Annie is out with Paul for the day. Cassie Jo's out, too, so Rose is there watching Isaac."

"Really?"

"You sound surprised." Frankly, so was he, but he'd be interested in her take on the situation.

"I am. I mean, I don't know your girls very well yet, but Annie seems very much in control and maybe a little overprotective of her son."

Bingo.

"Annie, Emily and CJ obviously have a very close bond."

Also true.

"I don't want to offend you, and I realize she isn't your daughter, but Rose seems to be the odd one out and, if you don't mind me speaking my mind, there may be good reason for that. She seems to have a few...issues."

They had arrived in the reception area, where they put their conversation on pause while they collected their jackets. When he had picked her up that morning, she'd been wearing a plaid cape that looked unexpect-edly perfect, in spite of being purple, gold and green and pale pink. The same shades of purple and pink in the outfit she was wear-ing. She had so much class and such a big-city style—a *vibe* as his daughters would call it—and yet she had seamlessly readjusted to small-town life.

"Whatever is on your mind, I want to hear it. And you're right about Rose. She has more than her share of issues. How about I fill you in over lunch?"

"I'd like that."

"Where would you like to eat?" he asked as they left the building and headed to the parking lot. "I was thinking we could drive over to Wabasha and check out that little Ital-ian place."

Libby pulled the front edges of her cape close to her body and looked up at the sky. "I don't know. Does it feel colder now than when we went out this morning?"

"Sure does. I'm thinking it might even snow."

"Me, too. Let's stay in town."

"Good plan," she said. Fifteen minutes later, they were settled at a table at the Ri-verton Bar & Grill.

"Good to see you, Mr. Finnegan. What can

I get you?" the waitress asked, pencil poised. Her name was Heather, Thomas recalled. She had been in school with Annie and had married the town troublemaker, Jesse Wilson.

"Do you know what you'd like to order?" Thomas asked Libby.

"I do. You?"

"I'll have the BLT," they said in unison, and then they both laughed.

"On sourdough," he said.

"Make that two."

"Toasted?"

They both nodded.

"Coffee?"

"Please," they both said.

Libby smiled at him after the waitress walked away. "Great minds," she said. "You were going to tell me about Rose, but I think you should wait until we're back at my place."

Never one to air dirty laundry in public, he completely agreed. "Good plan," he said. They could have talked at the restaurant over in Wabasha—no one would have known them there—but staying in town had been a wise idea. The sky was looking more ominous by the minute. So much so that he hoped Annie and Paul were considering cutting their day in the city short and heading home.

"Thank you for coming with me to the retirement home. You were a big hit."

"I had fun, believe it or not, and the residents really seemed to enjoy having us there."

"Some of them don't have any family nearby. Some don't have any family, period."

"Here you go." Heather set down two cups of coffee, cream and sugar.

"Thank you," Libby said to her. "That's so sad, isn't it?" she said to Thomas. "About those people not having family close by. I'm so glad I can be here for my mom. She couldn't have continued living by herself, and I know she'll eventually need more care than I'm able to provide for her at home. But for now and the foreseeable future we're okay with everything as it is."

Thomas had his own ideas about how he would like to see the "foreseeable future" unfold, though, and he'd be more than happy to accommodate Libby's mother in his vision. The importance of family was something he understood better than most.

"How does she like having the young Dr. Woodward taking care of her?"

Libby grinned. "I think she's halfway in love with him. Every time she sees him, she makes a joke about fifty years not being an insurmountable age difference."

"Good for her," Thomas said, laughing. "I think she might have some competition, though."

"Annie?"

"Yes. She might be coming around to seeing Paul as more than a friend, although I don't think she realizes it yet."

"These must be difficult times for her. It hasn't been long since her husband died, and there's her son to think about."

"All true, and I'm not saying she should rush into anything." Even the thought of his level-headed eldest daughter being impulsive made him smile. "I would like to see her happy, though, and Paul is a good man. What's more, it's as plain as day that he's head over heels for her, and for Isaac."

"Obvious to everyone but her?"

"So it seems."

"Annie strikes me as the type of woman who'll come around in her own time, and on her own terms. I like that about her."

There seemed to be some subtext to what Libby was saying. Thomas just wished he knew what it was.

"I married my husband because everyone thought we were a good match. In some ways, we were, at least in the beginning. Still, I should have waited, given it more time before agreeing to everything that everyone else thought was best for me."

Thomas reached across the table, took her hand in his. "I wonder what people think about us."

"I know this," she said. "If anyone tries to tell me what they think, I'm going to tell them to mind their own business."

"And what about taking your time this time?"

"At our age, time is a precious commodity."

Truer words were never spoken. Still, he had no intention of proposing to Libby in the Riverton Bar & Grill. He had a better idea. He planned to do it soon, but he also intended to do it right.

WHEN THOMAS PULLED into the driveway behind her mother's house, Libby was hoping her mother would be tired from her morning at the seniors' center and would want to rest. After their volunteer session at the veterans retirement home and lunch at the café, she was ready for some alone time with him. He had promised to tell her about Rose, which meant he would have to talk about Rose's mother, his ex-wife. And the honest truth— she was curious. She knew she could ask around. Plenty of people in Riverton loved nothing more than a good gossip session, but she wasn't interested in any of it. She wanted to hear his story, however he wanted to tell it to her.

She watched him transfer himself from the van seat to his wheelchair to the hydraulic lift, walked with him up the back sidewalk to the ramp she'd had built for her mother after she started using a walker, and followed him inside.

Her mother was sitting at the kitchen table with Thomas's daughter, drinking tea.

"Dad!" Emily jumped up and wrapped her arms around his neck. "I was hoping you would come in when you brought Libby home. Hi, Libby."

Libby placed a hand on her mother's shoulder. "Hi, Emily. Thank you for spending the morning with my mom."

"No need to thank me. It was fun, and I'm sure I gathered enough material for at least two new blog posts."

Libby laughed. "That's great. How was the whist tournament, Mom?"

"We played cards," her mother said, pouring herself another cup of tea. "I think we won. Right, Emily? Did we win?"

"We did." Emily winked at Libby and gave

an almost imperceptible shake of her head. "We were on fire, Mrs. Potter."

Thank you, Libby mouthed. "That's great, Mom. Congratulations."

"I need to get going." Emily hugged her dad one more time. "Jack should be home from the station by now. I'll see you at dinner tomorrow night. Hope to see you, too, Libby."

After she left, Libby started a pot of coffee. "How are you doing, Mom? Would you like to sit here with me and Thomas, or would you rather have a rest?"

"I think I should put my feet up."

"Okay, then. Come with me and I'll help you get settled in your room." She helped her mother to her feet and rolled her walker into position.

Thomas was watching the two of them, she noticed. "Nice to see you again, Mrs. Potter," he said.

"Good to see you, too, Thomas.

"That young man has good manners," her mother said on her way out of the kitchen. "Good-looking, too."

Feeling a little like the teenager she wished she had been, Libby glanced over her shoulder and laughed. There was no missing Thomas's grin.

After she settled her mother on the bed

and covered her with an afghan, she pulled the roller blind down and left the door ajar as she left the room.

"Be sure to give that handsome young man a slice of my red velvet cake."

"I will, Mom. Have a good rest." She was still chuckling when she returned to the kitchen. Thomas was clearing the table.

"I can do that," she said a little quickly.

He arched his eyebrows in a way that silently said, *Seriously? Do you* seriously *think I can't load a few dishes in the dishwasher?*

"No need to get on your high horse. You're a guest, which means there's no need to do dishes."

"Just hoping to get a slice of cake sooner rather than later."

"Coming right up." She set mugs and plates, forks and napkins on the table and took the cake saver out of the fridge.

"How's your mom doing?"

She filled their coffee mugs. "She's tired but I can tell she had a good day. I'm so grateful to Emily for spending time with her."

"Me, too, because it meant I got to spend time with you."

Libby felt herself blush. What she loved— yes, *loved*—about this man was his sincerity. Thomas was charming, of course, but it wasn't an act. She served two slices of cake, a generous one for him and a much smaller one for herself, sat and watched him savor his first bite.

"So, you were going to tell me about Rose."

"Right. Before I do, I should back up a little. Have I told you about my old army buddy, Nate Benson? We were in the same unit during the Gulf War."

"No, you haven't mentioned him. Does he live around here?"

"Unfortunately, no. He has a ranch in Texas. Three kids, like me, except his are boys."

"Have the two of you stayed in touch?"

"We have. At first it was Christmas cards and the occasional letter or phone call. Now it's easier to keep in touch with email."

"What about his family?"

"Interesting coincidence. His three sons are roughly the same age as my girls. When we were over there, swapping stories about our families and our kids kept us sane. Any time one of us would get a letter from home—notes from his kids, artwork, photos, that kind of thing—"

"That's so…" Libby dabbed the corners of her eyes with her napkin. "I'm sorry. It's very touching."

"Nate received a lot more of those packages than I did. My wife, Scarlett, wasn't much of a letter writer and the girls were too little to do it on their own. At the time my parents were still alive. My mother wrote as often as she could. She tried to get the girls involved and sent photos.

"Those mail deliveries were the highlight of our days, our weeks. News from home, getting to see how the kids were growing and changing, those things kept us going."

"Did you have any free time to write back?"

"I always made a point of it. So did Nate. Those letters gave us an opportunity to tell our families how much we missed them, how much we loved them."

Loved them. Which included the wife. That stung a little, but she put aside the envy.

"Did you tell them what it was like over there?" Everything she remembered about that war sounded terrible. Not exactly the sorts of things men wanted to share with their families, especially not their kids.

"Just day-to-day stuff. The weather, who was the best poker player. Nothing…real. It would have been too hard to write about."

"But they were probably watching on TV."

He was shaking his head. "Well, that's the

thing. None of the stuff on TV was really real. The insufferable heat, the never-ending sand, the gut-wrenching fear you feel after you've finally drifted off to sleep, only to be ripped out of it again when a shell lands less than ten yards away."

She couldn't begin to imagine how terrible it had been. But if he had been her husband, she would have wanted to know.

"The scariest part is how fast all of it becomes normal. Even the casualties."

She closed her eyes for a moment, found him watching her when she opened them, studying her intently.

"I'm sorry. I hadn't planned to go there."

"It's okay." Knowing about his past helped her to understand and appreciate the man he was now. "You were telling me about Nate and the letters."

"Right. So I mostly received mail from my mother, and she was careful to leave out a lot of the details about Scarlett—didn't want me worrying about the girls—so I didn't find out until I was airlifted stateside and eventually discharged from the convalescent hospital, and the army.

"I came home to Riverton and found a very different woman from the one I had married."

"I'm so sorry. Had she been...?" Unable

to bring herself to say the word out loud, she simply reached for his hand.

"Unfaithful? Not that I know of. It was worse. She'd become addicted to prescription drugs."

"Oh!" The possibility had never occurred to her.

"She couldn't stand Riverton, hated being on the farm even more, and then I rolled in. That was the deal breaker."

"And so...what? She left?"

Thomas nodded. Libby had felt betrayed and deeply angry when her husband told her he was leaving, and who he was leaving her for. But their marriage had been little more than a formality for years. There were no children, no extenuating circumstances.

"Did she go to rehab?"

"Not exactly. She went to Chicago."

As hard it was to believe, the woman had chosen drugs over this man, her husband. She had also done something right, though. She had left her daughters with him.

"Did you hear from her?"

"Not often."

"And the girls?"

"Never."

Her eyes went watery again and she swiped at them with her napkin. As difficult as those years must have been for Annie, Emily and CJ growing up, Libby believed their mother had done them a huge favor.

"Tell me about Rose."

"Scarlett never told me about her, but at some point she must have told Rose about us. Last summer, after Scarlett was…after she passed away…"

Libby had heard the news stories about the murder of three women in Chicago and had been shocked to learn one of them was Thomas's ex-wife. She waited for him to compose himself and continue.

"Rose came to Riverton and checked into the bed-and-breakfast."

"That must have been a shock."

"She didn't tell us who she was. I think she wanted to check us out, and by us I mean her sisters. Annie took the girl under her wing even before she knew who Rose was. Emily's the one who put two and two together and figured out Rose was Scarlett's daughter. Annie welcomed her into the fold right away, helped her find a job and an apartment, but Emily and CJ still haven't warmed up to her."

"And you?"

It took him a moment to respond. "I'm not sure. She had a tough life, in and out of foster homes. I see a lot of her mother in her, some of the good and, unfortunately, some of the not-so-good things."

"Drugs?"

He shrugged. "I'm not sure, but she definitely has issues with alcohol."

Libby felt a shiver pass through her. "And yet Annie left Isaac with her today?"

"When Annie looks at her, I'm not sure she sees what everyone else sees. She knows Rose has issues, but she believes if she gives her the benefit of the doubt, Rose will live up to her expectations."

"That is often true with children, but I'm not sure it works the same way with adults. Given everything Rose has been through, she might need to see a counselor. Maybe an addictions counselor."

"You're probably right. She is my daughters' sister but she isn't my daughter, so I've been trying to stay out of it."

Libby finished her coffee and sighed as she set the mug on the table. She felt as though she'd been dragged through an emotional ringer. Her slice of cake was untouched, but she noticed Thomas had polished his off while they'd talked.

"More coffee?" she asked.

"Love some."

After she refilled both mugs, Thomas reached for her hand before she sat.

"Is your mother likely to stay in her room for a bit?"

"I'm sure she's asleep."

"Good. I've been looking forward to some alone time with you." With that, he tugged on her hand until she was sitting on his lap.

"Oh!" she gasped. "What did you have in mind?"

"No more talking. I say we put the past behind us and explore the future. Our very…"

He kissed her.

"…immediate…"

Another kiss.

"…future."

With one hand on his shoulder and the other lost in his hair, she gave herself to the kiss. This was one of those moments when talking was highly overrated.

CHAPTER TWENTY-ONE

THE GALLERY TOUR had exceeded Paul's expectations tenfold. He had never seen Annie so animated, so intent on absorbing everything she saw. The impromptu trip to the bookstore had been another highlight. After asking for directions to the photography section, she had poured over books on basic photography, finally settling on two—a six-hundred-page encyclopedic volume and a beautifully illustrated book on basic digital photography.

The gallery and bookstore visits had taken longer than expected, which meant they had missed the reservation he'd made at a bistro near Lake Calhoun. Another time, he'd decided, and instead they had settled for deli sandwiches and bottled water at a place around the corner from the bookstore. The deli was crammed with tiny tables and abuzz with the conversations of patrons, and Paul couldn't think of any place he'd rather be. Annie—blue eyes lit with enthusiasm, looking happier than he had seen her in a long time—took his breath away.

"Thank you for convincing me to spend the day with you," she said. "I hadn't realized how much I needed time away. Thank you for taking me to the gallery and bookstore, for the photograph and the books. It feels like Christmas."

He didn't want to get too far ahead of himself, but he hoped by Christmastime their relationship would be solid enough for them to move from more than friends to something more like "maybe we'll get married someday." There was no rushing her, though. He knew that. He also knew she was sensitive to what other people thought, that it had been less than a year since Eric had passed away, that getting involved with another man so soon might be perceived by some as an impropriety.

So no, Paul did not intend to propose right away. It was far too soon. And if there was one thing he knew about Annie, she and the farmhouse were a package deal. Nonnegotiable. If he wanted to be with her, and if he dared to hope she would feel the same way some day, then he had to accept that.

For now he had his own obligations to fulfill. His father was still doing well at home, and while he had never expected to feel this way, this wasn't the time to consider moving him into long-term nursing care. So no, Paul wasn't about to propose anytime soon.

That said, he did want to finally be able to say "I love you" without scaring her off. And maybe even have her say it back. The thought made him smile, and then he felt himself grinning. A goofy grin, no doubt, but he couldn't help himself.

"What's so funny?" Annie asked, peeling back the paper wrapper around her turkey-bacon club. "Me, feeling like a kid on Christmas morning?"

Her knee bumped his and she didn't move it away. Paul sobered.

"Trust me. I'm not laughing at you. I like seeing you happy, and you look happy today."

He loved the way her self-consciousness made her nose turn pink. "I am happy," she said. "You have no idea how grateful I am that Emily gave me her old camera, and that you brought me into the city to see the exhibit at the gallery. I wish I had thought to bring the camera with me. I'd be taking pictures of everything right now."

He glanced around the busy deli. "What would you photograph in here?"

"See those jars of pickled vegetables on the

shelf by the window? The way the light filters through them? They remind me of stained glass windows. I would definitely take a picture of those."

He never would have drawn the parallel but now that she had, he could appreciate the likeness.

"And check out that huge old brass-and-copper espresso maker with the cagle orna-ment perched on its top."

The vintage machine was still in operation and held a place of honor on the counter. Paul had noticed it as soon as they'd walked into the restaurant.

"It sort of reminds me of an altar."

Huh. She was right.

"So we're eating in a place with an altar and a stained glass window. What does that say about us?"

She shrugged. "We have an appreciation for good food." He could practically see the wheels turning. "Do you know what I'm thinking?" she asked.

"You think this would make an interesting post for Emily's blog," he suggested.

Her eyes flashed. "Exactly. Now I'm re-ally disappointed I didn't bring my camera."

"Can't you take photos with your phone?"

"Oh. Of course I can. I always forget about my phone."

She pulled it out of her bag and checked for messages before she clicked on the camera app. She took a few seconds to frame the shot of the jars of pickled vegetables and then turned slightly in her chair to capture the massive espresso machine. She took several other shots before she turned back to him with a smile.

"That's it?" he asked.

"One more."

Before he understood what was happening, she snapped one of him.

"There. Now I'm done."

Okay. Interesting. "Is that for the blog?" He hated to ask but he had to know.

"No. Emily blogs about people. My posts are about other things, mostly food and stuff around the house."

"Except the one about the wedding."

"You read it?"

"Wouldn't have missed it."

"I hope you don't mind. I don't know who took the photograph of us dancing, but I decided to use it since neither of us was completely recognizable in it."

"I didn't mind at all." Quite the opposite. He had been flattered. Who wouldn't be?

They looked incredibly good together. He was encouraged by her willingness to use a picture, publicly, that so clearly depicted them as a couple. And to the people who mattered, they were *completely* recognizable.

Annie was checking messages again.

"Anything from Rose?" he asked.

Without looking up from the screen, Annie shook her head.

That should be a relief. It *was* a relief. From the time they had left the house, Annie hadn't said anything about the girl and he hadn't dared broach the subject. Yes, he was concerned about Annie's blind trust in her half sister. However, there was a fine line between that and breach of privacy, and it was a line he would never—*could* never—let himself cross.

"There's a text from Emily, though." She smiled and angled her phone so he could read it.

Just left Mrs. Potter's place. Dad's there with Libby. Soooo cute together. ♥

The message made him smile, too. All three Finnegan sisters were devoted to their father and wanted to see him happy. He loved that about this family. He was also secretly grateful to the two younger sisters and their dad for not only championing him, but also providing opportunities for him to be alone with Annie. Today had been the exception— not that he could fault them for having lives of their own.

She slipped her phone into her bag, ate the last bite of her sandwich and dropped the crumpled paper wrapper into the plastic basket.

"I've had a wonderful time, Paul. Thank you again."

"I hope we can do it again." Soon.

"Me, too."

He stood and eased himself through the narrow space between their table and the one next to them, then helped her with her jacket. She smiled up at him and he was on the verge of kissing her when it seemed something over his shoulder caught her attention.

"Is it snowing?"

He half turned and glanced through the window behind him. Sure enough. Huge, thick flakes floated to the ground. It would have been a pretty scene—a photo-worthy one—if they didn't have a two-hour drive ahead of them.

"It sure is."

Worry lines appeared on Annie's forehead. She hastily pulled on her gloves and picked up her purse. "I hate driving in the snow. Maybe we shouldn't have come all the way into the city, or maybe we shouldn't have stayed for lunch."

Not wanting the day ruined by unnecessary concern, he steered her between the tables to the door. "We'll be fine. My car has good snow tires, and the roads won't be too bad yet."

He had plenty of experience driving in winter conditions far worse than this. In Chicago, he'd had his fair share of late night calls when he'd had to get to the hospital, regardless of the weather and road conditions. A patient had taken a turn for the worse, another doctor was ill and Paul needed to cover. And then there'd been the time when a loaded school bus had been hit by a semi on the interstate. What had started as a light snowfall had unexpectedly turned into a full-on blizzard by midafternoon, and although he'd been having a rare day off, he'd had to drive to the hospital as soon as the call came through.

Telling Annie these things now would not alleviate her concerns so he kept them to himself. Even for his own peace of mind, he wished he hadn't remembered the school-bus incident.

Outside the restaurant, afternoon shoppers were scurrying to their cars. He was glad he'd found parking nearby and as he opened the door for Annie, he briefly held her gloved hand in his.

"Don't worry, okay?" This was like telling a mother bear not to protect her cubs. "I'll get us home in one piece."

By the time he started the car, she had her phone out. "I'm calling Rose to let her know we're on our way."

"Good idea."

"Hmm. No one's answering at the house." She paused, then left a message. "Dad. CJ. It's Annie. Paul and I are leaving the city now and it's snowing. We'll be home as soon as we can."

Paul eased into traffic. The snow was melting the instant it hit the ground, so the streets were wet but not slippery.

"I'll try Rose's cell phone." There was a touch of panic in her voice, reminding him of the morning she'd brought Isaac to the clinic after he had fallen off his horse. And given the way Eric had died, Paul completely understood her overprotectiveness.

"She isn't answering her phone, either. What if—"

"Annie. They're probably outside, taking the dog for a walk, maybe."

But the message she left in Rose's voice mail was a little more agitated. "Rose. Why aren't you picking up? It's snowing really heavily here."

Actually, no, it isn't.

"Give me a call as soon as you get this. By then I should be able to give you an idea of when we'll be home." She ended the call and lowered her hands to her lap with the phone clasped between them.

Paul could tell her exactly when they'd be home—the roads were clear and traffic was moving along nicely—but he knew they'd both be better off if he could keep her distracted.

"Do you have more ideas about the church and food article you're thinking about writing for the blog?"

"Well…"

Her response was hesitant at first but he listened and asked the occasional question as he maneuvered onto the freeway and out of the city. To his dismay, the snow was falling heavier as they drove east and traffic was starting to slow. If Annie noticed—and of course she did—she didn't say anything. Instead she kept talking about her next story, which then segued into another subject.

About twenty minutes outside of Riverton, they encountered a bad stretch of highway and he had to slow down because the car ahead of them fishtailed on an icy patch. Although Paul slowed and kept a safe distance before it was safe to pass, Annie stopped talking and focused on the road ahead while periodically sneaking peeks at her phone to see if she had missed a call or text message. Every time she looked up again, he could tell she hadn't and he knew it was killing her.

THIS WAS IT, Libby thought. This thing with Thomas was the real deal. *This* was love. After more decades than she cared to acknowledge, she was ridiculously, crazily, madly in love with her high-school crush. The surreal part was this time her feelings were reciprocated. He was a thoughtful man in the broadest sense, with ideas and views about society and politics and world events, and yet he wasn't opinionated. What's more, he valued and respected her thoughts on those topics. And he made her feel young again, the way he'd pulled her onto his lap and kissed her.

After their brief make-out session, she had

poured more coffee and they had settled in the living room to watch a documentary on Iceland—a place that, oddly enough, interested both of them.

The phone rang as the credits rolled, and as she got up to answer it, the scene outside the living room window caught her attention.

"Oh, my goodness. Look, Thomas. It's snowing."

"So it is," he said. "I should probably get home."

In the kitchen, Libby picked up the phone. "Hello?"

"Libby. Hi, it's Emily. Is my dad still there?" There was no mistaking the concern in his daughter's voice.

"He is. We just realized it's snowing so he'll be on his way home right away. Would you like to talk to him?"

"Sure…no… I mean…could you please tell him to meet me at the hospital? There's been an accident."

CHAPTER TWENTY-TWO

THE WHOLE FAMILY was assembled in the waiting room when Annie burst through the entrance doors with Paul a step behind her. "What happened?" she asked. "Where is he?"

CJ was the first to jump up and meet her with an embrace. "He'll be okay, Annie. The doctor is checking him out now."

Emily appeared on her other side, hugging her as close as her expanding belly allowed. "Isaac's going to be all right. Dad's in there with him."

"What about Rose?"

"They have her in another room," CJ said.

"She's a little more banged up but she's going to be okay, too," Emily said. "Isaac was wearing a seat belt but Rose wasn't."

Not wearing a seat belt? What on earth had she been thinking? "My poor little boy. He must be terrified. Where is he? I need to see him."

Stacey McGregor, dressed in crisp green scrubs, came into the waiting room from the small ER at the back of the health center. Relieved to see someone she knew and trusted was here to look after her son, Annie rushed up to her. "How is he? Can you take me to him?"

"Of course." Stacey put her arm around Annie's shoulders, led her away. "He's been asking for you. You, too, Dr. Woodward."

Annie turned back, extended a hand. "Please come with us?" She knew his colleague, Alyssa Cameron, was an excellent physician, but right now she needed someone she would trust with her life, and Paul was that someone.

"Do you know what happened?" Annie asked. None of this made any sense. "Did my sister say why she took Isaac out in her car?"

Stacey shook her head. "I haven't spoken to her. All I know is that they were on River Road on their way back to the farm. I guess they hit an icy patch and her car slid off the road."

Annie's breath caught in her chest and it took some effort for her to exhale. Paul squeezed her hand. Stacey led them into an examining room.

"Mom! Look! I got a new stuffy." Isaac lay in a hospital bed clutching a fuzzy brown teddy bear that had its arm in a gauzy white sling. Annie's father sat next to him. "An' I'm getting a cast on my arm."

"A cast?" Annie rushed to him.

"He's a brave little boy," Thomas said.

His arm was broken? Rose had taken her son out in that broken-down car of hers, driven off the road and *broken* Isaac's arm? "Oh, baby. I'm so sorry. I shouldn't have left you. I should have stayed home today. Does your arm hurt?"

Isaac shook his head against the pillow. "Melissa's mom gave me some medicine to make the hurting go away, an' Dr. Cameron says my cast can be whatever color I want so I'm going to have a blue one."

Thomas wheeled himself out of the way to give Annie more room. "I'll head on back to the waiting room."

"Thanks, Dad."

Annie gently ran her hand over her son's curls, noticed the bandage on his forehead as she did. "What happened here? Did you bump your head?|

"It's just a scrape," Stacey said. "Isn't that right, Isaac?"

"Yup. I'm going to call this bear Henry."

Stacey patted his curls. "That's a good name."

Paul joined Alyssa Cameron in front of a

light panel on the wall, quietly discussing the X-ray clipped there.

Annie swayed a little, her panic almost getting the best of her. Her son had been in a car accident and brought here to the hospital. Had he come in an ambulance? He had been X-rayed and who knew what else, and she hadn't been here for him. No, she had been in the city, flattering herself into believing she might actually be a photographer, daring to imagine having another man in her life, fantasizing about a life beyond her family. What was she thinking? Her family *was* her life. Isaac was the most important person in her world, the one person who fully depended on her…and she had let him down.

"I'm so sorry, honey. I shouldn't have left you on your own."

"I wasn't by myself. Auntie Rose was there. She's funny. This morning she put the music on real loud and we danced in the living room and then we ate lunch and then she broke one of your dishes—" He clamped the hand of his good arm over his mouth. "Oops. I promised I wouldn't tell."

"It's okay. I don't care about the dish." She wanted to mean what she said, but she knew herself well enough to know that when she went home she would check the trash can and inspect the cupboards to figure out what was missing. "I only care about you."

Paul and Dr. Cameron crossed the small space and stood together on the opposite side of Isaac's bed. Annie looked up at them, fearing the worst.

"Isaac, you are one lucky little boy," Alyssa said. "Paul, Dr. Woodward, has looked at the picture we took of your arm and he agrees you have a tiny, and I mean the tiniest, hairline fracture in your radius."

"What's a radius?"

"It's one of the two long bones in your arm that extend between your wrist and your elbow," she said.

Paul stroked Isaac's head, and Annie thought he leaned a little closer as he detected the bandage on his forehead. "The good thing about a kid's bones..."

Annie was pretty sure this last bit was aimed at her.

Paul moved his hand to Annie's shoulder, gave it a squeeze. "Kids' bones are soft, so they fracture easily, but it also means they heal very quickly and with few to no complications."

Dr. Cameron nodded in agreement. "So we're going to get Nurse Stacey to take you to the cast room."

Isaac held up his teddy bear. "Can Henry come, too?"

"He sure can. Henry knows all about casts."

While sitting in the cast room, Annie fretted with the strap of her handbag while a technician distracted Isaac with idle chitchat about teddy bears and digging up dinosaurs and building snow forts now that winter appeared to be here. Half an hour later, she led her son into the waiting room, his bear securely tucked under his good arm, his newly blue-casted arm supported by a matching sling and his pain medication tucked in Annie's purse.

Everyone rushed to gather around him—her father and Libby, Emily and CJ, and Paul. For the first time since she'd arrived at the clinic, Annie realized she hadn't seen her half sister.

"What about Rose?" she asked. "How is she doing?"

Everyone looked at everyone else while they avoided looking at Annie.

"She's going to be fine, but there's a chance she'll need surgery we're not equipped to perform here," Paul said. "We had an ambulance take her to the hospital in Rochester."

"Surgery? So this accident…" It must have been bad. She glanced at her precious boy, smoothed his hair. She needed more details, but she didn't want him to have to relive the nightmare. The details would have to wait. "I think it's time we went home, don't you? I'll fix some dinner."

"I'm going to stay here and give Alyssa a hand," Paul said. "Then I need to get home and check on my father. I'll call you later to see how Isaac's doing. Call me if you need anything, okay?"

"I will." She watched him walk away and wished she could ask him to stay.

"I'll run Libby home and meet you all at the house."

"You and Isaac can ride home with me," CJ said. "Emily's coming with us. Jack had to swing by the police station and then he'll come and pick her up."

"Sounds good." Annie let her sisters shepherd her to the parking lot. The snow had stopped and as dusk dimmed the sky, the blanket of white made everything seem a little brighter.

Settled in the backseat with Isaac, Annie was suddenly overcome with bone-deep exhaustion. "I don't know if I'll have enough energy to make dinner."

Emily glanced into the backseat. "CJ and

I will fix something while you get Isaac settled in."

Annie yawned. Her sisters' idea of fixing something ran along the lines of canned soup, maybe hot dogs. Tonight she was too tired to care.

ANNIE WAS STARTLED awake when CJ stuck her head into Isaac's room and quietly called her name. She had lain down next to her son, thinking she would close her eyes for a few minutes until he fell asleep.

"I'm sorry, I must have dozed off." She blinked and rubbed her eyes. "What time is it?"

"Dinnertime."

She looked at Isaac, saw his eyes were closed, his long lashes fanned adorably across his cheekbones, the rise and fall of his chest slow and even.

Her sweet little man. She decided not to wake him.

"How long was I asleep?"

"Forty-five minutes, maybe?"

She stood, stretched and followed CJ downstairs to the kitchen.

Her father, Emily and Jack were already seated at the table. To her surprise, they had made a salad, defrosted a container of meatballs in tomato sauce, cooked pasta, set out a basket with thick slabs of the sourdough bread she'd baked yesterday, along with tall glasses of water with ice and sliced lemon.

"We made one of Isaac's favorites in case he decided to get up for dinner," Emily said.

"He's worn out and the meds made him sleepy. I think it's best he get some rest." She and CJ joined the others and everyone dug in. Annie filled her plate, surprised to find herself famished.

For a few minutes they ate in companionable silence. She had questions, plenty of them, but it was easier to eat and pretend this was like any other dinner. Normal.

"How was your date with Libby, Dad?"

Thomas grinned. "We had a fine time. The folks at the retirement home loved her. How was yours?"

"It wasn't a…" Who was she kidding? The outing with Paul had most definitely been a date. "He took me to an art gallery in the city. And a bookstore, and then we had lunch." She realized the photograph he'd bought for her and the books she'd chosen were still in his car.

"What did you think of the exhibit?" Emily asked.

"I loved it. But I wish I had stayed home."

CJ slathered herbed garlic butter onto a slice of bread. "The accident wasn't your fault."

"Of course it was. If I had stayed home, Isaac wouldn't have been in Rose's car and none of this would have happened." But it had. "I need to know the details," she said. "And I need to know how Rose is doing."

Her sisters both looked to Jack. "The call came in just before two o'clock," he said. "Isaac used Rose's phone to call 911."

"He...what?"

"As close as we can tell, they went into town right after lunch. Rose did a little... shopping. It started snowing around one, and by the time they were headed home, the conditions were already getting bad. The snow was freezing as soon as it hit the pavement and Rose was driving on bald tires."

Anger roiled in Annie's gut. "What was she thinking? And what was so important she needed to risk my son's life by driving into town in a blizzard in that old junker?"

"In all fairness, it wasn't snowing when they left."

"My point is, she had no business leaving. What was she shopping for?"

Everyone at the table exchanged looks. Jack answered her question.

"Rose had been drinking. We think she ran out of booze around lunchtime and decided to risk the drive into town to get more. She had an unopened bottle of vodka in her trunk with a receipt showing she had just purchased it."

Annie covered her face with her hands. Rose had been drinking, in the morning, while she was supposed to be looking after Isaac. She didn't have a drinking problem. She was an alcoholic. Everyone had tried to tell Annie, and she had refused to listen. She had felt sorry for Rose, had even convinced herself that as soon as the girl realized someone believed in her, she would turn her life around. Instead she had turned Annie's upside down. She lowered her hands and immediately picked up on everyone's concern.

"I'm okay."

"No, you're not." Emily squeezed her hand.

"And no one expects you to be," CJ said.

Annie looked to her father, who so far was keeping quiet.

"The important thing is to keep everything in perspective," he said. "Isaac is okay."

Annie wished she could be sure. Eric had broken his leg on a ski trip and seemed to be doing fine. But then he had developed a blood clot as a result, and six weeks after the accident he was gone. What if...?

"Don't go there," her father said. "You heard what the doctors said. It's a hairline fracture and they don't anticipate any complications."

"What about Rose?" Annie still didn't know the full extent of her injuries.

"If she'd been wearing her seat belt, her injuries would have been minimal," Emily said. "Apparently, she hit the steering wheel pretty hard, and then hit her head on the side window when the car veered into the ditch."

Annie closed her eyes, trying not to picture it, trying not to think about how terrified Isaac must have been.

Emily helped herself to another slice of bread. "She has a couple of fractured ribs and Dr. Cameron was worried about the possibility of a collapsed lung. That's why the decision was made to send her to a bigger hospital."

Just as well, Annie decided. If Rose had been kept at the health center in Riverton, Annie might have felt obliged to see her. Now was not a good time. Like her dad said, she needed some perspective. For that to happen, she needed some distance, too.

She sipped her water, sighing as she set the glass on the table. "Here's what I don't understand. I *trusted* her. I tried to *help* her. And *this* is the thanks I get? There are stretches of River Road where her car could have ended up *in* the river. They could both be—" Her voice broke but it wouldn't have mattered. She couldn't have said the unthinkable out loud.

There was no missing the looks exchanged around the table.

"What?" she asked. "This could have been a lot worse."

Jack pushed his plate away and rested his forearms on the table. "Annie, I wish I could say cops seldom see this sort of thing but the truth is, it happens far too often."

"And we've tried to tell you what's been going on with Rose," CJ said. "I guess you weren't ready to hear it."

Emily shot their younger sister a look and reached for Annie's hand again. "But we understand why you wanted to help her."

"It takes a professional to treat alcoholism," Jack said. "It's a disease and like any disease, it requires professional treatment. Counseling, detox, maybe even a stint in residential rehab. But unlike a lot of other diseases, treatment is rarely successful if the patient isn't cooperative. Rose has been to the clinic a few times and I'm sure Paul has encouraged her to get professional help. Rose probably hasn't been willing to listen."

"Wait...what?" A sick feeling pooled in her gut. "You're saying Paul knew about this? He's her doctor and he's known about this problem all along? He let me leave her here to look after Isaac?"

Jack ran a hand through his hair, blew out a breath. "Okay, I was out of line. Paul didn't tell me this in so many words. He couldn't."

Emily was quick to defend her husband and his friend. "There's a little thing called doctor-patient confidentiality, Annie. Paul could lose his license to practice if he ran around town talking about his patients. We're just speculating."

"But we're not just anyone. We're family." Even as she said it, she knew she was being unreasonable. But seriously, how could he have let this happen?

CJ chimed in. "Annie, you're not being reasonable. Would you want your doctor to discuss your medical appointments with one of us?"

"Of course not." She pushed away from the table and carried her dishes to the counter, started loading the dishwasher. "But Paul was here this morning. He knew Rose would be on her own with Isaac. He could have done something. He could have changed our plans, made up an excuse to stay in town, or better yet stay at home. He had no right to risk my son's well-being."

Emily and CJ looked at each other, shrugged and started to clear the table. Their father backed his chair away.

"Dad?" Annie always valued his opinion, and he'd been awfully quiet through this. "What do you think?"

"I still say you need some perspective, and I can see you're not going to get any tonight. For now I think we should count our blessings our little boy is okay and Rose is going to make a full recovery. We can save the rest of this discussion for tomorrow, when calmer, cooler heads will prevail."

He rolled out of the room without giving her a chance to say there was nothing wrong with her perspective. Nothing. Nothing at all.

CHAPTER TWENTY-THREE

IN SPITE OF being up and down at least a half dozen times to check on Isaac during the night, Annie was up long before the sun. With anger and resentment all tangled up with lack of sleep, she knew that lying here awake replaying the previous day's events would only make her angrier and more resentful. Better to keep busy, she decided, so she slid out of bed, put on a sweatshirt, her favorite old jeans and a pair of thick wool socks.

She checked on Isaac again—still sleeping—before she went downstairs to put on coffee. She let the dogs out, half smiled as Chester gingerly padded out into the white blanket of snow. Beasley let out a yip and leaped across the yard, paws barely touching the ground until he flipped onto his side, then his back, making the equivalent of doggy angels in the snow. In spite of her mood, watching his pure enjoyment had her full-on grinning. Silly pup.

In the utility room, she started a load of

laundry, and then in the kitchen she poured herself a mug of coffee, inhaled the scent as she sipped it. She pulled on a jacket and boots and let herself out into the crisp early-morning air. The eastern sky was light enough for her to see the clouds had cleared overnight and they were in for a glorious sunrise. She would have to come out with her camera, she thought. And then she felt guilty for thinking about herself when she should be thinking about Isaac.

She flipped on the yard light, grabbed a broom and swept snow off the steps. Later, she would go in search of the snow shovel. For now, she made her way through the ankle-deep white to the chicken coop. The inside was warm and the chickens were happy. Even happier after she fed them. She had forgotten to grab a basket on her way out so she tucked eggs in her jacket pocket.

When she returned to the kitchen, she emptied her pockets into the egg basket on the counter, then ran upstairs to check on Isaac. His eyelids fluttered open as she entered his room.

"How are you feeling?" she asked. "Did you sleep well?"

He nodded groggily. "My arm feels heavy." He lifted it and let it drop onto the comforter.

"Does it hurt?"

"Nope. Can I watch TV?"

"Do you want to come downstairs?"

He shook his head. "Can I watch it in your room?"

"Sure you can." She seldom used the television tucked away in the armoire, but anytime Isaac was sick, this was where he wanted to be. This morning she was happy to tuck him into her bed, cozy beneath her down duvet, his arm supported on a plump pillow, the remote in his good hand. "I'll be right back with some juice and fruit. That should keep you going till breakfast."

"And the walkie-talkies?" he asked.

"And I'll bring the walkie-talkies." Those were part of the tradition. Annie could work downstairs or even out in the yard. Isaac could recuperate upstairs and call her if he needed anything.

After she had him settled, she went to her kitchen, took out ingredients and went to work. An hour later she had made a dozen each of her family's favorite muffins— lemon-cranberry and carrot-pineapple—and started on an apple strudel. Throughout the process, she had radioed Isaac twice to make sure he was okay and made two more trips up and down the stairs to check on him and cart his dishes down. On the second trip she'd found Beasley on the bed with him and hadn't had the heart to admonish either of them for breaking the no-dogs-on-the-furniture rule.

In the midst of it all, she had also caught a glimpse of the early morning sky and slipped outside to take a few shots as deep purple-blue faded to mauve and then warmed to coral and rose as the sun inched toward the horizon.

After everything that had happened yesterday, making the time now to take the photographs seemed unnecessarily self-indulgent, and yet she hadn't been able to stop herself. Yesterday Paul had flattered her into thinking she was someone she wasn't, and she had been vain enough to believe him. And after the second batch of muffins went into the oven, she took out her phone, and while she sipped a second cup of coffee, looked through the pictures she had taken at the restaurant yesterday. She was not an artist. She was a mother who enjoyed taking pictures. There was a difference, she reminded herself.

Still...she scanned the images on her phone one more time. From a technical standpoint, they were probably amateurish. She had no idea and no way of judging for herself. The composition was interesting, even she could see that. But that wasn't the point.

She was the mother of a young boy who needed her to look after him. Yesterday she had let them both down. As for his father, she didn't even want to go there.

PAUL SETTLED HIS father at the kitchen table with his tea, toast and soft-boiled egg.

"I need to make a call, Dad. Check in with the clinic. I'll be right back."

He took the phone into the living room and sat at his mother's old writing desk by the stairs, but instead of calling the clinic, he dialed the number of the hospital in Rochester. He introduced himself and asked to be connected to the nursing station in the ward Rose had been admitted to.

Relieved to learn her vitals were good and she had come through the night without the need for surgery, he asked that she not be discharged until he came by to see her later in the morning. Before he made the drive there, he wanted to run out to the farm, see how Isaac was doing, drop off the print and Annie's books and make sure she was okay, too. If he played his cards right, he would find a way to get her alone and pick up where they'd left off yesterday, before Jack had called to tell her about the accident.

Next, he made a call to a colleague from medical school who was now in Madison, practicing psychiatry with a specialty in addictions and substance abuse. Encouraged by the outcome of that call, he returned to the kitchen to check on his father.

The old man was staring out the window into the neighbor's backyard, watching two young children tumbling in the fresh snow, shrieking as they tossed handfuls of the white stuff at one another, laughing with their dad as he showed them how to roll snowballs and stack them to build a snowman.

"Do you still play with that Evans boy?" his dad asked.

Momentarily taken aback until he realized his father had slipped fully into the past, Paul poured himself a cup of tea from the pot on the table and took a seat.

"Sure I do," he said. "Jack and I see each other all the time."

"Good kid, that Evans boy."

Right. He had grown up hearing his father talk about what "good kids" other parents had and how Paul would be so much better off he would emulate them.

"Never as smart as you, though."

Startled, Paul waited to see if his father would elaborate.

"Remember your first bicycle? The one with the training wheels?"

"I sure do." He'd loved that bike. It was too big for him when his parents bought it, but it was bright, shiny blue, tricked out with training wheels and the seat lowered as far as it would go so hc could reach the pedals.

"You were the first kid on the block to learn to ride a two-wheeler. I was proud of you."

Paul was stunned. There were no other words. Just stunned. Somehow he felt as though the disjointed pieces of his life had suddenly, miraculously slid into place. The one woman he had always loved was finally within his reach. That, he had hoped for. This? Never. His father might be living in the past, but he was also making up for it.

"Thanks, Dad. I had a good teacher." At this point, what was the harm in one little lie?

Or was it a lie? He had a vague memory of learning to ride the two-wheeler. It was a milestone in every kid's life, and at thc timc it had felt like a monumental achievement. Every time he had wavered, he remembered his father's words.

"Don't look down. Keep your eye on the sidewalk ahead of you, at least two houses ahead. If you want to succeed, you need to keep your eye on where you're going, not on where you are right now."

That kind of advice had been all but lost on an almost five-year-old, but it must have resonated because it had become the force that had guided him through high school to college, from college to medical school, and from there to a fast-tracked career at one of the top hospitals in the country. Coming home had always been his father's expectation but never part of Paul's plan. Now that he was in Riverton, he knew he'd made the right decision at exactly the right time.

His father had already forgotten about the bike. His breakfast now had his undivided attention as he scooped soft egg out of the shell by carefully coordinating his spoon in one hand, with toast in the other.

I was proud of you.

As Paul watched his father and heard the echo of those words, he experienced something akin to affection. And he promised himself if he was fortunate enough to become a father, he wouldn't make his child wait thirty years to hear those words from him.

PAUL STOMPED THE snow off his boots before he climbed the freshly swept front steps of the farmhouse. In town, the snow on the streets was already turning to brown slush, but out here, the blanket of white was largely untouched, except for the occasional tracks left by birds in search of a meal.

He knocked on the door and noticed he wasn't greeted by barking. Maybe the new puppy was out in the backyard. The house seemed unusually quiet but finally he heard footsteps. The door swung open and there was Annie, dressed in dark jeans, an off-white turtleneck sweater and a salmon-colored zip-front hoodie that made her skin glow.

Her eyes told a different story. These were angry eyes, which were bewildering enough, and then even more so when he realized her anger was directed at him. The anticipation of seeing her that had filled him since waking that morning now left in a rush, leaving him deflated. Something was not right.

"Good morning." He held out the wrapped photographic print and the package of books she had left in his car yesterday.

Silently, she took them, held them close to her chest, like a shield, and wrapped her arms around them.

"Annie? Is everything okay?"

She shook her head, blinked back the tears

that suddenly filled her eyes. He reached for her but she retreated.

"What is it?"

"You knew."

"I knew…?" What he could he have possibly known that would cause her to be this angry?

"You knew Rose had a serious drinking problem."

This was true. It was also true that Rose's problem was no secret. He assumed everyone knew, including Annie. "Are you saying you didn't?" he asked, choosing his words carefully.

"How could I?" she asked. "I mean, it's obvious the poor kid has problems, and I know she had too much to drink at Emily and Jack's wedding." She shrugged. "I figured her behavior that night was just one of those things. A one-off. I never dreamed she would drink and drive, and I *never* would have left Isaac with her if I thought, if I knew, if you'd told me…" The rest of her words seemed to catch in her throat.

What was she saying? That the accident was *his* fault?

"I'm not sure what I could have told you that you couldn't already see for yourself. I can tell you that Rose is a patient of mine, although to be honest, I'm not sure I should even be telling you that. I definitely can't tell you anything about her medical history. I could lose my license."

"What about me? What about Isaac? Are you saying you care more about Rose than you do about us?"

Proceed with caution, he warned himself. Annie, usually the voice of reason, wasn't herself. She was worried about her son, especially in light of the way her husband had died. She was scared. She was likely even a little angry with herself for leaving Isaac with her irresponsible half sister.

"My feelings for Rose are strictly professional. My feelings for you and Isaac..." Sensing it was now or never, he took the plunge. "I love you, Annie. I love Isaac, too. I would never do anything to hurt either of you."

Eyes wide, a little fearful even, she moved farther into the house, one hand on the door as though she was about to close it. Not the reaction he had hoped for. In fact, pretty much the exact opposite. She slowly shook her head and he felt his world implode. This was it. This thing between them had hardly had a chance to get started, and now it was over.

"I can't do this," she said. "I shouldn't have

let myself get involved with a friend of Eric's. I shouldn't have let you think this—" She waved her hand back and forth. "This thing between us was going someplace. I'm sorry."

"Annie, wait. Let's talk about this."

But she was still shaking her head as the door clicked shut. He lifted his hand, considered knocking again, but he knew it was futile. It was just a door but it might as well have been a ten-foot-thick wall of brick.

He went to his car, sat and stared at the house for several minutes while he considered his options. He was certain of one thing. Annie had feelings for him. He'd known from the way she looked at him, laughed with him and responded to his touch that she felt the same way he did. She could deny it six ways from Sunday, but those feelings of hers were as real as his. He would give her some time, some space. She would come around, he was sure of it. Good thing he was a patient man. Speaking of patients, he needed to check on Rose.

He started his car and set off down the driveway to River Road. Rose needed to get some help, and he wasn't taking no for an answer.

ANNIE HAD BEEN clearing away the breakfast dishes when Paul had shown up. She wished he had called first. She could have ignored that because she hadn't wanted to talk to him, much less see him. As soon as she'd heard the knock, she had known it was him. She'd been tempted to ignore it but he would see the cars parked out front and would know they were home. Luckily, the rest of the family had been occupied when he arrived.

CJ had headed to the stable right after breakfast. If she had been in the house, she would have insisted Paul come in for coffee. Isaac had balked at the idea of spending the rest of the morning resting in bed upstairs, so his grandfather had volunteered to keep him entertained. The two of them were now in her dad's room, playing a card game. Beasley was in there with them, otherwise his barking would have alerted everyone in the house that someone was at the door. Her father would have invited Paul to stay, and Isaac would have wanted him to come in and talk about dinosaurs.

Now he was gone and she was alone in the kitchen, except for Chester, who was sleeping peacefully on his bed.

So yes, she'd been lucky. She finished loading the dishwasher, wiped the counters, dried her hands on a towel. She leaned on the edge of the sink and stared through the window at the winter wonderland outside.

She didn't feel lucky. She felt fear, anger, guilt. And she had never felt so alone, not even after Eric died.

The view went blurry. She swiped her eyes with the towel.

This was stupid. She was being stupid, crying for something she couldn't have. She needed to focus on the anger. This was Paul's fault. It *was*. He shouldn't have stood by and allowed her to leave her son with an alcoholic. She tried to focus on the anger, but her own guilt and fear were already gnawing at the edges of it.

She hated this feeling of being out of control. Why couldn't she be just plain angry? Why did all these other emotions have to get involved and make her feel like a crazy person? Crazier still…why did she already miss him so much?

CHAPTER TWENTY-FOUR

BY THE FOLLOWING Friday, almost a week after the accident, Thomas had made a decision. Life was short—a life that currently had an incredible woman in it, he reminded himself—and it was time he started living it. Libby was, well…she was amazing. She had strong family values. She was community-oriented and she had a generous spirit. She was elegant and easy on the eyes, and he was completely in love with her. It was time to pop the question. He had already picked the place, now he just needed to find the right time.

Libby was still at school but he would send her an email, let her know he was thinking about her, extend an invitation to Sunday dinner. He would ask her to come early, invite her to go to the gazebo with him. He had the perfect place, the perfect time, the perfect woman. And then he could share the happy news with the family while they were gathered around the dinner table.

He rolled to his desk, turned on the computer and opened his email. Before he could compose one to Libby, he spotted a message from his friend Nate Benson. The header grabbed his attention.

Subject: Our worst fears

"No. No, no, no. Not Nate's youngest son. Please, God. No."

Thomas steeled himself and opened the email.

My dear friend,

I have feared writing this email since our boy enlisted. Matt's unit ran into some trouble last night. There is good news with the bad. He's still alive, which can't be said for everyone in that convoy. We were told he was okay, helped get a few of his comrades to safety. He was going back to help one more when they triggered a land mine. Sound familiar, my friend? There's always one more, isn't there?

He's been airlifted to a hospital ship. He's going to make it, so we're told. But one of his legs is bad, real bad. They're doing what they can to save it.

This has hit us hard, especially Angie. He's her baby, you know? She wants to head over there but that's not going to happen. It's hard, but all we can do now is wait for him to come home.

I apologize for putting this in an email but we're not up to making phones calls right now. I know you understand.

Nate

Thomas covered his face with both hands. He hated these stories. Nate's son had a long struggle ahead. His body could be nursed back to health. By the sound of things there would be scars, visible physical ones. The emotional scars ran deeper, took longer to heal. Sometimes they never did. Thomas felt like he'd been one of the lucky ones. Most of his emotional scars had been inflicted closer to home when he had been left to raise three little girls on his own. In spite of losing the use of his legs, he'd been lucky in a lot of ways. In fact, when it came to his daughters, he often considered himself three times lucky.

He wanted to call Nate, hear his voice and know he was okay, but he also had to respect his friend's need for privacy. Instead, he clicked on Reply and started to type.

Nate,
    There are no words. You know I'm here for

whatever you and your family might need. If your boy needs a quiet place to recuperate, you be sure to send him our way.

The farm was quiet, relatively speaking. It wasn't Texas, but there were horses and, maybe more importantly, solitude.

We've got plenty of space in the house, or he can bunk in the room in the stable, where the stable hand stayed back in the day when we had one. Whatever you and Matt need, don't hesitate to ask.
Give my love to Angie.
Thomas

After sending the email, he opened a new message and selected Libby's address from his contacts and typed "Sunday dinner" into the subject line.

Libby,
I hope you'll join us and bring your mother with you. Come early. I have a proposition for you.
Thomas

ON SUNDAY AFTERNOON, Libby helped her mother out of the car and walked slowly beside her as she pushed her walker up the ramp to the door of the Finnegan farmhouse.

"I've been here before," Mable said.

"I'm sure you have." Her mother would have known Thomas's parents and had no doubt been here on several occasions.

"Whose place did you say this is?"

"The Finnegans. Emily's father, Thomas, lives here with his two other daughters."

"Emily is a good girl." Mable's breathing had turned to a wheeze by the time they reached the top of the ramp. "She's having a baby. Did you know that?"

"Yes, I did. Are you feeling okay, Mom?"

"I'm fine, dear. All I'm feeling is old."

CJ greeted them at the door, took their coats, led them inside. The kitchen was abuzz with pre-Sunday dinner activities, and the whole place was filled with the scents of herbs and spices, roasting meat and the two apple pies sitting on cooling racks on the counter. Annie stood at the island with a mountain of potatoes in front of her and a paring knife in her hand. Emily and her husband, Jack, sat at the table with Thomas.

Through the French doors she could see Isaac in his bright blue parka, romping with his border collie. He was a bright, engaging child and the broken arm had hardly fazed him. If anything, it had made him something of a hero among his classmates.

Emily rose as quickly as she could, given the ever-increasing size of her belly. She gave Mable a warm hug and settled her at the table. "I'll get you some tea, Mrs. Potter. I know just how you like it."

"Thank you." Libby squeezed the young mother-to-be's hand. She smiled at Thomas. "Hi."

As much as Libby adored his family, she still felt a little shy around them. He broke the ice by taking her hand and pulled her down to his level for a quick kiss.

"We have that thing, remember?" he asked. "While it's still daylight, Libby and I are going to take a stroll to the gazebo," he said to everyone else.

His daughters exchanged "the look" she had come to recognize as their secret, silent communication. They were a close-knit family, as tight as three sisters could be, and they deeply loved and respected their father. If it was possible to miss something she'd never had, she missed this sisterhood.

Knowing her mother would be happy here with Emily and Jack and the rest of the family, Libby followed Thomas to the front door. "A stroll?" she asked.

He gave her the quirky smile she had come to love and reached for his jacket. "Hey, you're looking at the guy who put the roll in stroll."

She loved the way he made her laugh and feel so at ease. She handed his gloves to him, pulled on her own. "You said in your email you have a proposition for me. I'm curious to know what it's about." If she had to guess, she would say it had something to do with volunteering at the veterans' retirement home.

"All in good time. I'll explain when we get to the gazebo."

"Why the gazebo?" Although last week's snowfall had melted, the temperature still hovered around the freezing mark.

"It's kind of a Finnegan family tradition. You'll see." And that's all he would say.

They strolled down the driveway in companionable silence, save for the crunch of gravel beneath his wheels and her boots, and then crossed River Road to the gazebo on the riverbank. The river was still open, its gunmetal surface reflecting the gray, late-afternoon sky. It wouldn't be long before the river froze over and winter would come to stay and stick.

Thomas took the ramp and joined her as

she climbed the steps and sat, facing the river, on the bench.

Libby could see her breath as she looked out over the Mississippi. "It's always so beautiful here, no matter what season we're in. Even wintertime."

"I loved winter as a kid," Thomas said.

"I've always been more of a spring-and-summer gal."

"No winter sports for you?" he asked. "Sledding, ice skating, cross-country skiing—I did it all."

Back in high school he had always been athletic. Losing the use of his legs must've been unimaginably difficult. "I have no idea how you coped."

"My daughters depended on me. I had to cope. Besides, the qualities that make a man a good man…those things are up here." He tapped his temple with an index finger, and then placed his hand over his heart. "And in here. Not here." He patted his thigh.

If she'd had any doubts about being with Thomas—and truthfully, she had—they were swept away by what he had just said. She had never loved anyone as much as she loved him. She held out her gloved hands and he took them in his.

"Thank you," she said. "I needed to hear that, to be reminded it's true."

"I had an email the other day from my old army buddy, Nate Benson."

"He's the one with a son who is currently on a tour of duty overseas?"

"Yes, in the Middle East. His unit was hit hard this week."

"Is he okay?"

"Badly injured but he's alive."

"Oh, Thomas. Your friend's family must be devastated."

He nodded. "It's just about gutted Nate. The medics are fighting to save Matt's leg and it looks like he'll have a long recovery ahead of him."

"I'm so sorry."

"I've invited him to come here when he gets back to the States. He's been around horses all his life and I think Cassie Jo's therapeutic riding program might be good for him." Thomas grinned. "Cassie Jo might be good for him, too."

Libby narrowed her eyes at Thomas. "You're not trying to be a matchmaker, are you?"

"Never. CJ would never let me get away with it. But she does have a way with horses and people."

"So, is that the proposition you mentioned in your email? I'll be happy to help if you think there's anything I can do."

"No, I have something else in mind for you."

His slow, lazy smile made her wish he would kiss her. Instead he glanced outside the gazebo, checked the sky.

"Gets dark early this time of year."

He removed his gloves and pulled a small, flat-black wafer out of his jacket pocket, angled it so she could see a row of little buttons on one side of it. He pushed one of them, and the gazebo glowed with dozens of tiny white lights.

"Thomas, this is beautiful. Did you do this for me?"

"I did, with a little help from my friends. Jack and Paul gave me a hand."

"It's stunning. It's…wait. Is that music?"

He nodded.

"The Beatles?"

He nodded again.

She listened to the lyrics and laughed. "This isn't really a proposition, is it?"

"More of a proposal." He slipped the remote back into his pocket and brought out a velvet ring box.

Libby felt her eyes go wide.

"Libby Potter, like the song says, when I'm sixty-four—"

"I will still need you." The words came out in a rush. "I'll still feed you, too."

They laughed in perfect unison.

Thomas reached for her left hand and pulled off her glove. Still feeling wide-eyed, Libby watched as he opened the ring box and took her breath away.

"Oh, Thomas." Nestled in the box was the most beautiful ring she had ever seen.

"The stone is called a golden topaz," he said.

"I love it." He slid it onto her finger. It was a perfect fit. The smoky-gold stone set in a circle of small diamonds sparkled with the reflection of the twinkly lights decorating the gazebo.

"I hope you like it. You wear color so well," he said. "A diamond on its own seemed too plain."

She gazed at it, misty-eyed. "Thomas Finnegan, that is the nicest thing anyone has ever said to me."

He held her hands. "Just to make it official... Libby Potter, I love you. Will you marry me?"

"Yes. Yes! Of course I will."

He pulled her to him and she went readily,

sliding onto his lap, slipping her arms around his neck, settling her lips on his.

When she raised her head, finally, and met his gaze, she saw the love in his eyes matched the love in her heart.

"Let's go back to the house and share our news."

The idea momentarily jangled her nerves. "How will your family feel about this? About me?"

"They already love you as much as I do. They'll welcome you with open arms. And I have an idea that young Isaac will be pretty happy about his grandma being his second-grade teacher."

Grandma. She was going to be a grandmother, a stepmother. She was going to be Thomas's wife. "Where are we going to live? You have your home, your family. I have my mother and her place." She hadn't thought about any of this until now and the logistics looked insurmountable.

"Hey, slow down. We'll take it one step at a time, work things out. I'm guessing a 'spring-and-summer gal' is going to want a spring or summer wedding, so there's no rush."

She stood and took Thomas's hand. "I love you."

He took out the remote and turned off the lights and music as they left the gazebo. "Come on. Let's go home."

CHAPTER TWENTY-FIVE

As THE WEEKS after the accident trudged by, Annie did her best to hold her emotions at bay while plodding through the motions of preparing for the holidays. Thanksgiving came and she busied herself by decorating the house and planning meals for their traditional family dinner. The next day she did it all over again for the guests who had checked in to spend the weekend kicking off the holiday season with trail rides followed by hot cocoa by the fire. This was Annie's favorite time of year, but this year her heart wasn't in it.

Her only real distraction was helping Emily prepare the nursery for the baby, who was due at Christmastime. For the baby's sake, Annie hoped it wouldn't be born on Christmas Day. Every child deserved to have its own special day. Annie also wished Emily and Jack had been willing to find out if the baby was a boy or a girl, but both parents had wanted to wait. This meant the nursery had to be gender-neutral, although in the end that had worked out fine.

Isaac's crib was given a fresh coat of ivory paint. They hauled a vintage dresser out of the farmhouse attic, painted it to match the crib and topped it with a changing pad so it could serve double duty. Emily had decided she wanted the walls done in a soft shade of gray, which had horrified Annie until the room was complete and then she loved it. They painted an old wicker rocker to match the walls and sewed ivory cotton covers for the seat cushions. The crib's bedding and other accessories were in soft shades of robin's egg-blue, with a few splashes of orange interspersed for contrast. The overall effect was calm and soothing, and Annie loved it.

Working on the nursery had also been good because it took her away from the farm and gave her something to think about besides how Isaac's arm was healing, where Rose had disappeared to and how none of this would have happened if Paul had been honest with her. And of course, she had snapped photos every step of the way, knowing she could easily get a month's worth of *Ask Annie* columns out of decorating the nursery.

They finished the room on an afternoon in mid-December. Annie arrived at the farm before the school bus dropped off Isaac and with plenty of time to start dinner. She glanced through the mail CJ had left on the kitchen table and found an envelope addressed to her. She didn't recognize the handwriting and the return address in Madison wasn't one she recognized. The sender wasn't identified. Interesting. She sat at her desk at the end of the counter, slit the envelope and pulled out a sheaf of lined pages. She unfolded them, gave them a quick scan.

A letter from Rose.

No one had heard from her in weeks. Almost six weeks, Annie realized. In typical Rose fashion, she had abruptly left her job and high-tailed it out of town as soon as something bad happened. Rose had literally disappeared, but according to the return address she hadn't gone far.

Annie quickly folded the letter and stuffed it into her back pocket. She couldn't read this here and risk someone walking in on her. This was the first time she had heard from her half sister since the accident and she had no idea what to expect.

Upstairs, she closed her bedroom door, pulled out the letter and smoothed out the folds.

Dear Annie,

Rose here. I know you totally hate me right now and I don't blame you one bit. What I did was irresponsible and dangerous and I am so, so, so very sorry that Isaac got hurt. He's such a cool kid and he's very, very lucky to have you for a mom.

So here's the thing. I screwed up, big-time, and I am so sorry. Did I already say that? I did. Well, that's okay. I'll probably say it again.

The thing is, I'm in rehab. At first I didn't want to be here but now I've been here for a whole month and I'm doing okay. Really good actually. I'm not allowed to have visitors or use the phone to talk to people because I'm supposed to be working on my own issues. And I have been, and I still am. God knows I've got a lot of issues.

Dr. Woodward is the only person I see that I knew before I got here. After I got out of the hospital, he arranged for me to come to this place in Madison. He comes to see me twice a week, mostly because he's my doctor but he's kind of a friend now, too. He found this place and talked me into coming here and it's been good.

Anyway, I'm sure you already know this because he must have told you by now.

Emily had speculated that Rose may have agreed to go into a treatment center. Annie assumed that if she had, the decision would have stemmed from being charged with DUI after the accident. She never would have guessed that Paul had set this up for her. And now he was making the trip to Madison twice a week to see her? Contrary to Rose's assumption that Paul had provided her with any of these details, he hadn't said a word. Annie hadn't let him. And since he was Rose's doctor, he probably couldn't.

I'm in a twelve-step program now. Some steps are easier than others. Writing this letter is one of the hard ones because I have to tell you I'm sorry for everything I've done to hurt you. If you can't forgive me—and I won't blame you if you don't— I will accept that. But the thing is, I should not have been drinking while I was looking after Isaac, and I should not have driven into town with him while I was drinking. When Paul told me he had a broken arm and a cast, I broke down and bawled my eyes out.

Reading the confession brought tears to Annie's eyes, too. Rose had been gone for weeks now. During that time, Annie had been clinging to her resentment around her half sister's betrayal of her trust. She had also been nursing a grudge over what she perceived to be Paul's deception. She had tried talking to her father about the way she was feeling but he had been uncharacteristically disinclined to listen to what she was trying to say. Instead he had reiterated his earlier suggestion that what she really needed was a little perspective.

Her father was also preoccupied with Libby, and who could blame him? She was a remarkable woman, she clearly loved their father, and Annie, Emily and CJ adored her for it. Isaac was crazy about her, too, both as a teacher and as a future grandmother.

As for perspective, Annie wasn't sure what that meant, and her sisters were no help at all. Emily said she needed to sit down with Paul and give him a chance to explain himself. CJ told her that since she was busy blaming everyone else for what had happened to Isaac, she ought to take a good, long look in the mirror while she was at it. When Annie had indignantly asked what that was supposed to mean, CJ said she needed to figure that out for herself.

Annie turned her attention to the letter.

I'll be here for two more weeks. For now it feels like the right place for me to be, but I'm not sure what I'll do or where I'll go after I'm discharged. Don't worry, though. I won't be coming back to Riverton. I've caused enough trouble for you and your family. I was hoping you all might be my family, too, but I don't belong there. I thought about going to Chicago, but Paul doesn't think that's a good idea. I don't have any support systems there, but there would be a lot of negative influences.

If you want to keep in touch—and I hope you will but totally understand if you don't—I can send you my new address as soon as I'm settled. Like I said, visitors and phone calls aren't allowed but if you write to me at this address, I'll get it.

Your sister (sort of),

Rose

Annie reached for a tissue and dried her eyes. Her *sort of* sister was in rehab. Thanks to Paul. Rose would be released in two weeks, only days before Christmas, but if she wasn't returning to Riverton, where would she go? Was she strong enough to be on her own, alone for the holidays? Paul was probably the only person who could answer that question. But she had been irrationally avoiding him since the morning he had dropped off her books and photograph.

She let the pages fall to her lap and looked to where she had hung the framed photo of the afternoon-tea table for two in an apple orchard. She'd had doubts about hanging the photograph in her bedroom, afraid it might serve as a reminder of that wonderful, horrible day, but she felt oddly at peace every time she looked at it. The trees laden with bright red apples, the baskets brimming with more fruit, the table set with pretty china, succulent pastries and savory sandwiches. The scene represented a life filled with love and abundance. In many ways, it represented her life.

Perspective.

Her father's word came to mind. She had been given every opportunity for a full life. Yes, there had been tragedy—her mother's abandonment, her husband's untimely death, Isaac's injuries—but mostly there had been happiness and abundance.

Rose's life had been nothing like hers. After she had come to Riverton and revealed her true identity, Emily and CJ had been wary about her motivations. Annie had felt sorry for her and had arrogantly set out to fix things. But all she had really done was overlook Rose's problems and make excuses for them. None of that had helped Rose, though, and Annie had most likely enabled her high-risk behavior.

What Rose needed...

Get over yourself. Annie had no idea what the young woman needed, but she knew someone who did. Paul had looked past the grunge clothing, dark makeup and broody attitude to see Rose's real issues, and he had addressed them. Even after Annie had pushed him away, and he had reached out to help Rose anyway.

Perspective.

Annie folded the letter and slipped it into the drawer of the side table. Her father was a wise man. Had she finally found a glimmer of the perspective he'd been talking about? If she talked to him now, admitted that she had made mistakes with Rose, would he be forthcoming with some more advice? She sure didn't have all the answers, very few, actually, but she was sure of one thing. Letting

Rose check out of rehab and spend Christmas alone was not the right thing to do. Continuing to make Paul the fall guy wasn't right, either. She just hoped it wasn't too late to fix her mistakes.

THE "AFTER ANNIE" days—which was how Paul had come to think of them—had settled into a predictable monotony. Up early, breakfast with his father, work at the clinic, home in time to make dinner. Driven to keep busy, he worked every extra shift he could. Once or twice a week he and Jack met for lunch, and those get-togethers had become his only connection to Annie and the Finnegan family.

What he learned was that life for Annie was business as usual. She had decided to reopen the bed-and-breakfast for the holidays. She baked and cooked and hosted family dinners. She volunteered at the school. She was helping her father and Libby plan a summer wedding. And she continued to write her weekly *Ask Annie* column on Emily's blog. She had posted the photographs she had taken at the dcli on that fateful day in the city. He had looked at them at least a dozen times. Did that make him a stalker? He hoped not.

Twice a week he drove to Madison to see Rose, and with every trip he was blown away by the transformation. The girl had put on weight, abandoned the excessively dark makeup and acquired what was best described as a healthy glow. On his most recent visit, she told him about the letter she had written to Annie. She hadn't said she was anxiously awaiting a reply. She hadn't had to. The anticipation in her eyes said it all. And when she had asked about Annie and Isaac, he had done his best to paint an evasively rosy picture. From his colleague, Alyssa, he knew Isaac's arm was healing nicely so he told Rose that the little boy was looking forward to having the cast off. That was a no-brainer that didn't require firsthand knowledge.

On his last visit, he had had a lengthy consult with Rose's counselor. In several weeks, Rose would be discharged and they needed to work out a reintegration plan for her. Unfortunately, Rose insisted there was no way she was returning to Riverton. In his opinion, going back was her only option for a successful transition from the sheltered environment of the rehab center to a normal day-to-day life that would be rife with temptation and countless opportunities to relapse. Rose needed a safety net. As Paul saw it, the Finnegans were the only people who could provide one. And he didn't know who would be harder to convince—Rose or her family.

THE MORNING AFTER receiving Rose's letter, Annie waited until Isaac had left on the school bus and CJ had set off for the stable to teach a riding lesson. Then, with the house quiet, she whipped up a batch of her father's favorite muffins and invited him to join her in the kitchen for coffee.

"Chocolate chips," her father said as he sliced into the still-warm muffin. "This must be important."

It was long past time to keep beating around the bush.

"I've heard from Rose." She pulled the now well-read letter out of her back pocket and slid it across the table. She sat, sipping coffee and nervously nibbling the crispy bits from the edges of a muffin while he read it.

He refolded the letter and set it on the table. "So."

So? She knew her father well enough to know that wasn't all he had to say, but it was all he was going to say right now.

"So," she said. "Rose is in rehab. Emily thought she might have had to go to avoid serious penalties because she'd been drinking and driving, but I thought that kind of treatment was voluntary."

Her father took a generous bite of his muffin and drank some coffee. He tapped the letter with his forefinger. "Doesn't say anywhere in here that she was forced into it."

True, but it didn't say she hadn't been. Unless…

"Do you know something I don't know?"

"Probably." Her father picked up his cup, smiled at her over the rim before he took another sip. "Not about Rose, though."

"Dad, I'm being serious."

"I did not know she'd gone into rehab. Good to hear, though. None of us could have given that kid the help she needed."

Annie sighed. "Not even me. I was arrogant enough to think that being her big sister was all the help she needed, and too naive to realize that her problems were bigger than I thought they were. And way too big for me to manage."

"Don't be so hard on yourself. You did a whole lot more than anyone else. Emily and Cassie Jo and I…we all knew she had a drinking problem and none of us tried to intervene."

"Thank you for trying to make me feel better."

"Only you can do that," he reminded her. "What I'm saying is that you were a sister to Rose. She appreciated what you did for it, looked up to you, that much was obvious. I'd say it's because of the things you did for her that she agreed to go into this rehab place when Paul made those arrangements for her. You gave her hope, and she didn't want to let you down."

Tears stung Annie's eyes. She swiped them away. "I truly wanted to help her, but I stupidly didn't pick up on the drinking. That was her biggest problem and I didn't see it."

"Like I said, you shouldn't be so hard on yourself. For one thing, you don't have any experience with that sort of thing."

"What if I overlooked it because I knew it was something I couldn't fix? What if I only paid attention to the things I believed I *could* fix?"

Her father covered her hand with his big, strong one and gave a gentle squeeze. "Then I guess that would make you human."

"I really did want to help her."

"And what about now? Do you want to help her get back on her feet again or do you still think she's a write-off?"

"I never thought that, and yes, of course I want to help her."

"Have you replied to the letter?"

Annie shook her head. "No yet. It only came yesterday."

Her father slid the letter close to her cup. "I know you, Annie. You like to think things through, sometimes more than once."

"Are you saying I overthink things?"

He laughed. "Do you think you do?"

Truthfully, yes. "I tend to."

"So, this situation with Rose. Have you thought about it enough?"

"I have." She picked up the letter. "I'll write to her tonight, invite her to come here when she's discharged, spend Christmas with us."

"That's my girl."

"What do you think Emily and CJ will say?"

"They're good people, just like you. Rose is their sister, too. They'll want to do the right thing."

He was right. She knew he was.

"Have you shown the letter to them?"

"No. I—I wanted to talk to you first."

"And now that you have my stamp of approval, it's time to have a sit-down with them." Her father polished off his muffin and reached for another. "I figured something was up the minute I saw the muffins. You usually try to make them…healthier."

"You say that like it's a bad thing."

He laughed. "Libby says chocolate is always a good idea."

"I love Libby. She's so…" Annie sighed. "She's perfect. For you and for our family. We all love her."

"So do I." Thomas leaned back, crossed his arms, even looked a little smug. "And I'll be honest. When you suggested coffee and I saw the chocolate chip muffins, I got my hopes up."

"Hope for what?"

"I thought maybe you were finally ready to talk about Paul."

Paul. Of course. "I've already tried. You told me I needed perspective, remember?"

"I remember." He watched her closely as he slid his empty cup toward her. "Any more coffee in that pot?"

Asking for more coffee was her father's way of saying *let's talk*. Finally. She wasn't sure she would like everything he had to say, but after reading and rereading Rose's letter, she was ready to listen. She refilled their cups and sat.

"So." He stirred milk into his coffee. "About that perspective. Do you still believe this whole mess was Paul's fault?"

One of the many things she most loved

about her father was his directness. Except when it was her least favorite thing. Either way called for complete honesty on her part.

"I never truly believed he was to blame." There. She admitted it.

"Have you told Paul?"

She shook her head.

"Interesting. If it wasn't his fault, then whose was it?"

"It was Rose's fault for drinking and driving. It was my fault for giving her more responsibility than she was able to handle. I realize now that I was angry and afraid and... and I felt guilty for moving on after Eric."

Her father said nothing, waited for her to continue.

"That's the thing about perspective," she said. "Right after the accident, I was afraid for Isaac. What if...?" She couldn't bring herself to say it out loud, so she pressed on. "I was furious with Rose, and I mean really, *really* angry. What she did was reckless and irresponsible."

"And Paul?" her father asked.

Annie stared at her hands folded in her lap. "I'm not sure how I feel about Paul. All he did was invite me to spend the day with him in the city. We went to an amazing art gallery. He bought me a beautiful photograph.

We went to a bookstore, we had lunch. We were having a great time. He made me feel…"

That was the thing. He made her feel things she believed she had no right to be feeling.

"I feel guilty."

"Ah ha." He smiled. "Now we're getting somewhere."

"I don't know what to do," she admitted. "I like Paul. A lot. He's wonderful with Isaac, he's been a good friend to me, he's fun to be with."

He kisses like a dream.

"Nothing to feel guilty about, if you ask me. Unless…maybe there's more to this than wanting to be his friend?"

She felt her nose turn pink and hoped her father didn't notice.

"I…he… I think he might be in love with me."

His father tipped his head back and laughed. "You think he *might* be? Annie, that man is head over heels for you. If I wasn't crazy mad in love with Libby, I'd have said I've never seen a man so smitten."

"But he's…he was… Eric's friend, too."

Her father reached for her hand. "They were the best of friends, no question about that. Did Paul ever say or do anything inappropriate while Eric was alive?"

The question shocked her. "No, never! Paul would never—no, he's always been a perfect gentleman." Which was true even after they had taken their friendship to a somewhat more-than-friendly level.

"So then what's the problem?"

"He's Eric's friend," she repeated. "It isn't right."

"Says who?"

She shrugged. "No one, at least not to my face. But even if it was okay, it's too soon. It's been less than a year since Eric's been gone. He was my husband, my son's father, I loved him. I'll always love him."

"Of course you will. Eric was a good man. A good husband, a good father. Everyone expected the two of you to have a long, happy life together. He was too young to die, no question about that. But he *did* die and you're on your own now. No one expects you to stay that way."

Everything he said made sense. It would make even more sense if they were talking about someone else. "It's too soon."

"Too soon for…friendship? For someone to fall in love with you? To find yourself falling for him?"

"Yes. No, not too soon for friendship. But everything else? Yes."

"I see. So what would be a respectable amount of time? A year? Two years? Ten?"

"I don't know. And I'm not falling for him. He's a good friend who happens to be in love with me."

"Oh, honey." Thomas's laugh was soft and filled with affection. "You have already fallen for him."

Annie stared at him. She opened her mouth to speak, closed it again when she realized she had nothing to say.

Her father, ever patient, simply waited.

"I have not," she said after she finally collected herself.

"Oh, yes you have. If you hadn't, then you'd have nothing to feel guilty about and we wouldn't be having this conversation."

"Seriously, Dad? I think…" *What did she think?* She didn't know what to say.

She sipped her coffee while she considered the implications of what he'd said. Had she fallen for Paul? She had enjoyed their chats over morning coffee, had looked forward to them, even, and had been disappointed on the days he couldn't make it. Those few lunch dates at the café in town had been easy and fun. The night of Emily and Jack's wedding had been magical—dancing with him in the gazebo, kissing him. She loved how he was so thoughtful, praising her photography, taking her to the show at the gallery. She covered her face with her hands.

Her father was right. She was in love.

She lowered her hands, found him watching her. "I am such an idiot."

"No, Annie. Nothing could be further from the truth. You're a beautiful person, inside and out, and I'd say you're a lucky one, too."

"Lucky?" Surely he didn't truly believe that.

"Finding someone you love, someone who'll love you back...that's not something that comes along every day. I guess that makes us both lucky."

"Listen to you, all philosophical and romantic. I'm so happy for you and Libby, we all are. I just don't think I'm ready to make that kind of commitment."

"No one, not even Paul, expects you to be. All I'm suggesting is that you give love a chance."

Thomas held out his coffee cup. She picked hers up and clinked it against his.

Give love a chance. She could do that. She wasn't rushing into anything, but she could give love a chance.

CHAPTER TWENTY-SIX

ANNIE SPENT THE rest of the day baking and
thinking and baking some more. Christmas
was coming, so she had a good reason to
fill the freezer with shortbread and lemon
squares and her famous pumpkin-cranberry
loaf. Baking was second nature and she liked
to keep busy, and her sisters were right. It
freed her mind to ponder Rose's letter and
the conversation she'd had with her father and
her newly acknowledged feelings about Paul.

That evening, once dinner was over and
Isaac was settled for the night, she would sit
down and compose a reply to Rose. Emily
and CJ agreed with her and their father that
inviting Rose to spend the holidays with them
was the right thing to do. Once the New Year
rolled around, there would be plenty of time
for their half sister to make decisions about
her future and whether or not Riverton was
the right place for her.

Dealing with Rose would be easy. The
challenge was figuring out what to say to

Paul. She needed to be honest with him, explain how she felt about him. He deserved that. Her father was right, though. She was in love with Paul, but the circumstances were far from straightforward. She needed him to understand that moving on to a new relationship so soon after losing her husband didn't feel right. Not yet. Her father believed Paul would be happy to wait. Annie wasn't so sure, but there was only one way to find out.

After she cleared away the baking dishes and stowed the fruits of her labor in the pantry freezer, she made herself a cup of tea, took it upstairs and settled into the reading chair in her bedroom. On her cell phone, she opened a message to Paul.

Can you come out for coffee tomorrow morning? I owe you an apology.

His reply was immediate.

I'll be there. No apology needed.

He was wrong about that. Putting her faith in Rose had been a huge mistake. Instead of owning up to it, she had blamed the accident on Paul, and then she had pushed him away.

Now that she was ready to *give love a chance*, she hoped he'd be able to forgive her.

THE NEXT MORNING, as Paul carefully maneuvered around a farm truck hauling a load of hay down River Road, he realized how much he had missed the leisurely drive to the Finnegan place. The day had started out crisp and cool, and the sun, now angled low in the sky, sparkled off the iced-over river. His heart rate sped up as the gazebo came into view, reminding him of the dance with Annie, the kiss.

He honestly had no idea what to expect today. Her text message had been brief and, to his mind, a little cryptic. She said she wanted to apologize. Fair enough, but what did that mean? Did she intend to say she was sorry and then tell him to leave her alone? Or maybe she would say she was sorry and hoped they could still be friends. That would be harder than the first option. What he hoped to hear was not an apology at all. He hadn't liked her reaction to the accident, but her anger was understandable. He was afraid to hope she was ready to put the past behind them and go back to being friends, and he didn't dare hope for anything more.

At the top of the driveway, he parked,

gratified to see that Thomas's van and CJ's truck were gone. Isaac, he knew, would be at school, and this meant Annie was home alone.

He knocked at the door and she opened it right away. She was dressed for comfort and yet she made blue jeans and a red-white-and-gray plaid flannel shirt look fit for the runway.

"Hi." She sounded almost shy. "I'm glad you came."

Nothing could have kept him away. "I'm glad you invited me."

"Come in. Coffee's ready."

He followed her into the kitchen, as he had on many other visits. This time was different. The difference was as tangible as the scent of fresh coffee and warm apple strudel. Instead of sitting at the kitchen island, as they often did, she had set everything on the round table near the double doors that led to the veranda. She poured coffee and served them each a slice of her legendary pastry.

"Thank you."

"You're welcome."

"Cream?"

"No, thanks."

Although he hated the awkward formality,

he knew it was best to keep quiet and let her do the talking.

Annie picked up her fork. "I had a letter from Rose."

"She mentioned that she had written to you."

"She said you've been going to see her a couple times a week."

"I have." Annie had said she wanted to apologize but this conversation had him wondering if she planned to dole out some more blame along with it. Her response caught him off guard.

"Thank you for doing that, for everything you've done for her. It's good to know she didn't have to go through this on her own."

With that, his tension eased. "I was happy to be there for her, happy she was ready to accept help. She's the one who's done all the work, though."

"It couldn't have been easy for her."

"I'd say it's been the polar opposite of easy."

Annie stabbed a piece of strudel with her fork and held it above her plate. "I've written to her and invited her to come here and spend Christmas with us when she's finished the program. I hope she says yes."

"Under the circumstances, that's very generous of you."

"We're the only family she has. I don't know much about this sort of thing—her being an alcoholic—but I hope that being around people who care about her will help her stay sober."

"I hope so, too."

Annie set the fork and uneaten pastry on her plate. "I shouldn't have turned a blind eye to her problems. I know now that by defending her, I was also enabling her."

"It happens with a lot of families."

She sighed. "I also realize I shouldn't have left her here to look after Isaac. Everyone else was busy and…" She paused and he watched the tip of her nose turn that adorable shade of pink. "I really wanted to spend the day with you."

Paul resisted the urge to reach for her hand, sensing he'd be further ahead to follow through with the conversation. "I wanted that, too. I have to say, though, I was surprised to see Rose here that morning."

Annie looked humbled. "You weren't alone. CJ and my dad were shocked as well. They both warned me, but I didn't take them seriously. I also understand why you couldn't say anything."

Paul took a deep breath, allowing the relief to flow through him.

"Now this is the part where I apologize," she said. "I should have listened to you and believed you. I should have accepted that you're a professional with a job to do. I was wrong, and I'm sorry. I hope you can forgive me."

"Done," he said without hesitation. This time he followed his instincts, reached for her hand and felt a rush of gratitude when she didn't pull away. "I knew exactly where you were coming from, Annie. The anger, the fear…especially after what happened to Eric. I've been waiting and hoping we would find a way to resolve this because I've missed… this. I've missed us."

"About us…"

He stroked the palm of her hand with his thumb, waited for her to continue.

"We have feelings for each other," she said. "*I* have feelings for *you*. But I was married to your best friend and it hasn't been that long since he passed away and this feels too soon and so unexpected and I just want to slow down and…and not go so fast."

Of all the directions Paul had hoped this morning's conversation might take, he hadn't dared anticipate this. "Annie, I have a confession to make. I've been in love with you since we were in high school."

She looked genuinely stunned.

"But you and Eric were the power couple. You were perfect together." That's what he'd always told himself, even though he never fully believed it. "So I stepped back, went away to college, stayed away. You were my best friend's wife and I had no right to have those feelings for you. Even now, if it hadn't been for my father's health, I would have stayed away. But once I was here, I couldn't stay away from you. I loved you then and I love you now. I have waited a long time for this and I will wait some more. So you take all the time you need. I'm not going anywhere."

And with that, she was on her feet and in his arms. After she kissed him, she tipped her head back and smiled. "I'm not sure I deserve this, but I hope I'm worth the wait."

"You do, and you will be." Undoubtedly.

And when she kissed him again, he sensed the wait just might be shorter than expected.

EPILOGUE

Christmas Eve...

THE WAITING ROOM of the Riverton Health Center had been decorated like a TV holiday movie. The reception desk was strung with glittery garland, paper snowflakes were suspended in the windows and a huge tree filled one corner. An artificial tree, no doubt to abide by health and safety codes, instead of the giant pine that now dominated the living room of the Finnegan farmhouse and filled the air with the promise of Christmas. But every inch of this one had been covered with decorations, just like the one at home.

For the first time in a long time, Annie felt as though she was in a good place. Even being here, in a place for which she had an intense and long-standing dislike, felt right because tonight she was about to become an aunt. She had hoped Emily and Jack's baby wouldn't be born on Christmas Day...every child deserved his or her own special birthday...and it looked as though her wish was about to come true. Not that Christmas Eve wasn't hectic, but at least it meant Annie's niece or nephew could celebrate on a day when everyone else wasn't getting presents, too.

Now, as she looked around at the expectant faces in the waiting room, her heart swelled. Her father and Libby, heads bent in quiet conversation, were holding hands.

CJ paced the room, periodically stopping to check her watch and then stare at the clock on the wall. "How much longer is this going to take?"

"It'll take as long as it takes," their father said.

Isaac sprawled in the seat next to Annie, looking through the newest dinosaur book Paul had given him. "What are they going to name the baby?"

"I don't know," Annie said. Emily and Jack had decided not to reveal their choices to anyone.

"If it's a boy, they should call him Rex."

He laughed along with everyone else.

"It's a good name," he said.

CJ scruffed his curls. "Sorry, sport. They're not going to name him, or her, after a dinosaur."

"Maybe they'll call him Fred," Fred said.

That earned him a round of guffaws.

He shrugged. "It's a good name is all I'm saying."

He'd been Emily's best friend for as long as everyone could remember and had insisted on being called when she went into labor. Even on Christmas Eve, he claimed there was no place he'd rather be. And Rose's being here likely had something to do with that.

As for Rose, she sat quietly, knitting a red-and-white-striped scarf. She said one of her counsellors had suggested the activity, and she claimed it calmed her nerves and kept her hands busy. Annie knew she still smoked— Paul said it would be too hard for her to beat more than one addiction at a time—but the uncharacteristic knitting did keep her from heading to the parking lot every fifteen minutes to light up. She had returned to Riverton three days ago, a completely different person from the one who had left, and it wasn't just the knitting.

Rose was more subdued, but in a good way, and with a newfound confidence. She looked healthier, her appetite had improved and she even asked Annie to help her choose some new clothes that were, in her words, "a little less out there." Annie had been happy to oblige. Her half sister now wore dark blue jeans that didn't have a single rip in them and a hot-pink long-sleeved pullover covered with white hearts. She had added a matching pink streak to the bangs she kept tossing out of her eyes. Annie wasn't sure the look qualified as less "out there," but it worked for Rose.

All of this, Annie acknowledged, was thanks to Paul. She looked up at him now, feeling his love in the curve of his arm around her shoulders, seeing it in his eyes, hearing it in his whisper.

"I love you, too," she whispered back. The words, once so impossibly hard to say, came easily now.

He had kept his promise and was being incredibly patient with her. But as the frequency of his visits to the farm increased and he pitched in by shovelling snow and putting up holiday decorations and even folding laundry for her, she was feeling less and less inclined to slow things down.

The double doors burst open at the end of the waiting room, bringing the family to their feet as Stacey McGregor emerged. "Dr. Woodward? Dr. Cameron would like to see you for a brief consult."

"What's happening?" CJ asked. "Is something wrong?"

"Dr. Cameron says Emily and the baby are both doing fine. Shouldn't be much longer."

Paul gave Annie a quick kiss. "I'll be back with an update as soon as I can," he said to everyone.

Annie watched them rush back through the double doors, and then she sat.

CJ was at her side immediately, arms around her. "There's no point in worrying. Stacey wouldn't say everything was okay if it wasn't."

Annie hugged her back. "Telling me not to worry is like telling me not to breathe."

"I know, but I had to say it anyway."

Annie could see her father and Libby were trying to keep their concern hidden, but Rose was now clinging to Fred's hand, and Fred didn't seem to mind one bit.

The seconds ticked by into minutes. At the ten-minute mark, CJ stood up and resumed pacing. Ten minutes later, the doors opened again and the wait was mercifully over.

Jack appeared, beaming with pride and carrying a white-swathed bundle. "Everyone, I would like to introduce the newest member of the family... Amelia Grace."

With misty eyes, Annie looked past this proud new father to Paul, just steps behind him.

And she knew.

She rushed to him, threw her arms around him. "Thank you for bringing her safely into the world."

"She was in good hands all along. Just a minor complication."

After everyone admired Amelia and declared her to be the most beautiful baby to have ever been born, Jack whisked her back to her mother.

"Is Santa still coming?" Isaac asked, bringing everyone back to earth and making them laugh.

"He will," Thomas assured him. "But first we have to get you home to bed, maybe put out some milk and cookies for him."

They all drifted out to the parking lot. Thomas was driving Libby home, Isaac and Rose were returning to the farm with CJ, and Fred was making his own way home. Annie asked Paul if he would drive her home before returning to his father's place, and he quickly agreed.

After the others drove away, Annie took Paul's face in her hands and kissed him.

"What was that for?" he asked, sliding his arms around her waist.

"That was for being so patient and understanding all these weeks and months."

"Annie, I love you. I'll wait forever if that's what it takes."

She shook her head. "Forever is too long. How about we shorten that up a little?"

Even in the dark, she detected his surprise. "Annie Finnegan, are you proposing to me in the middle of a hospital parking lot?"

She loved that he could always make her laugh. "Wouldn't dream of it. Besides, I'd rather be proposed to. I'm just saying…" Her breath caught before she could finish.

"What are you saying?"

"I'm saying that when I saw you following Jack and the baby out of the delivery room, you looked as though you would like that to be you someday."

She heard him suck in a breath, saw his slow exhale in the cold night air.

"More than anything."

She gazed up at his beautiful handsome face framed by the starry night sky. "Me, too. I didn't even realize it until I saw Amelia's precious face and those tiny, perfect fingers, but I want that, too. I want another baby. I want a baby with you."

"Annie, I don't know what to say."

"How about Merry Christmas?"

He kissed her instead, lifting her off the ground and spinning them both across the snowy parking lot. She was laughing and breathless when he set her down.

"You have just made me the happiest man alive. Merry Christmas, Annie Finnegan."

As they stood shoulder to shoulder, gazing up at the stars and the thin crescent moon, Annie was already looking ahead to what next Christmas had in store for them.

* * * * *

LARGER-PRINT BOOKS!

GET 2 FREE
LARGER-PRINT NOVELS
PLUS 2 FREE
MYSTERY GIFTS

Love Inspired®

Larger-print novels are now available...

LILP15

WESTERN WP PROMISES

YES! Please send me **The Western Promises Collection** in Larger Print. This collection begins with 3 FREE books and 2 FREE gifts (gifts valued at approx. $14.00 retail) in the first shipment, along with the other first 4 books from the collection! If I do not cancel, I will receive 8 monthly shipments until I have the entire 51-book Western Promises collection. I will receive 2 or 3 FREE books in each shipment and I will pay just $4.99 US/ $5.89 CDN for each of the other four books in each shipment, plus $2.99 for shipping and handling per shipment. *If I decide to keep the entire collection, I'll have paid for only 32 books, because 19 books are FREE! I understand that accepting the 3 free books and gifts places me under no obligation to buy anything. I can always return a shipment and cancel at any time. My free books and gifts are mine to keep no matter what I decide.

272 HCN 3070 472 HCN 3070

Name _____ (PLEASE PRINT)

Address _____ Apt. #

City _____ State/Prov. _____ Zip/Postal Code

Signature (if under 18, a parent or guardian must sign)

Mail to the **Reader Service**:
IN U.S.A.: P.O. Box 1867, Buffalo, NY 14240-1867
IN CANADA: P.O. Box 609, Fort Erie, Ontario L2A 5X3

* Terms and prices subject to change without notice. Prices do not include applicable taxes. Sales tax applicable in N.Y. Canadian residents will be charged applicable taxes. This offer is limited to one order per household. All orders subject to approval. Credit or debit balances in a customer's account(s) may be offset by any other outstanding balance owed by or to the customer. Please allow 4 to 6 weeks for delivery. Offer available while quantities last. Offer not available to Quebec residents.

WPBPA16R

LARGER-PRINT BOOKS!
GET 2 FREE LARGER-PRINT NOVELS PLUS
2 FREE GIFTS!

HARLEQUIN

super romance

More Story...More Romance

HSRLP15